THE WORLD

—— OF ——

NICHOLAS LORD

NOVELS BY
HARRIS L. KLIGMAN

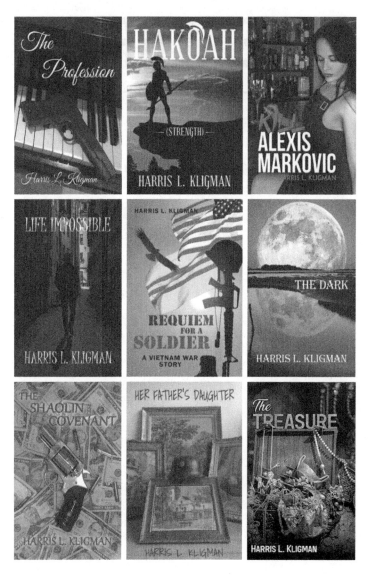

Pick Up Or Download Your Copies Today

THE WORLD
— OF —
NICHOLAS LORD

HARRIS L. KLIGMAN

ISBN: 9798373684576

Any references to historical events, real people, or real places are used fictitiously. Names, characters, and places are products of the author's imagination. Printed in the United States of America

10 9 8 7 6 5 4 3 2 1

(Paperback) First Edition: April 2023

https://www.HarrisLKligman.com

Follow Harris L. Kligman

Find Harris L. Kligman on AUDIO

*Dedicated to my son **Rob**, whose relentless urging motivated me to start writing.*

And

*To my wife **Nancy**, whose strength and fortitude kept our family intact over the many lengthy absences.*

— 1 —

CHAPTER

NICHOLAS LORD SLOWLY TURNED HIS HEAD. WHEN HE MADE EYE CONtact with the bartender, he pointed to his drink and then turned away.

He glanced casually at the dance floor and then at the table where a man and woman had just finished dinner. At an adjacent table were two men whose eyes moved constantly, the bodyguards.

The bartender leaned forward as he placed the bourbon down and whispered, "He just ordered two cognacs."

"Okay, Mr. Shin, do it," and Lord moved the palm of his hand across the bartop and toward the bartender. When he lifted his hand, the bartender quickly covered the glassine packet, and then moved toward the glasses and bottle of Remy Martin.

With his fingers still curled around the glassine packet, the bartender used his thumbnail to cut a small opening. After emptying the dense white powder into both glasses, the bartender poured in the cognac.

He called out a waiter's name, and then pointed at the drinks. Seconds later, the waiter placed both glasses on a tray and walked to the table where the man and woman were seated.

Nicholas Lord watched the man say something to the woman and then lift his glass. The woman smiled, picked up her glass and then sipped the cognac. The man laughed, and then moved the glass to his lips.

Lord again turned toward the bar and waited until the bartender approached. "Okay, you know the drill. I'm out of here. We'll meet later," and then he placed two ten dollar bills on the bar. "This should cover the bourbon."

Nicholas Lord moved off the barstool, walked slowly in between the tables and glanced at the laughing couple enjoying their drinks and each other.

Lord nodded at the maitre d' as he made his way through the main entrance. Then he turned left and began walking along 57th Street toward the Avenue of the Americas.

As he walked his mind formulated the sequences of events that would happen to both the man and woman. The white powder was thallium sulfate, a soluble poison that was odorless, colorless and tasteless. It is a slow acting poison, whose symptoms of abdominal pain, cramping, vomiting and diarrhea wouldn't appear for several days. Then respiratory paralysis would occur, followed by death. The delayed time frame would enlarge the number of possibilities regarding the cause of death.

Yes, he thought, Santiago Perez would journey to a better place. One must never forget that there are always those who correct a perceived wrong and a critical misstep can be a life altering experience. The woman's death, while unfortunate, simply was the way it would be. He laughed as he thought, now she could accompany her boyfriend to another world. What the Lord giveth, the Lord taketh.

Lord walked into the parking garage and took the elevator to the third floor landing. After he exited the elevator, he stood motionless as he surveyed his surroundings. Satisfied that there was nothing that posed an imminent threat, he walked slowly toward the white Bentley Continental GT Coupe, and in minutes was heading toward Riverside Drive.

2

CHAPTER

NICHOLAS LORD STOOD AT THE EDGE OF THE PENTHOUSE ROOF GAR-den situated atop the ultra-luxury skyscraper on Fifth Avenue, Manhattan. He moved his head in one direction and then back as he took in the panoramic view of the city below.

"It never ceases to amaze me."

"I feel the same way," replied the elegantly attired man standing near an ornate iron table with a cracked glass top.

The woman seated in one of the wrought iron chairs nodded and then said, "I concur. Nothing like it on the continent or anywhere else outside New York."

Then she locked eyes with Nicholas and asked, "Do you care for more champagne?"

"Yes, thank you. It's delicious."

"Yes it is. A 2003 vintage which was a difficult year for champagne, but this is excellent."

She lifted the champagne bottle from the silver ice bucket, and filled Nicholas Lord's flute.

"What shall we drink to? We've covered wealth, health and happiness. What else?"

The elegantly attired man said, "Let us drink to longevity, to a long life and all those previous things we toasted to."

Then the woman said, "To longevity," and both men responded in kind.

The woman moved out of her seat and walked toward Nicholas and the other man. "If you gentlemen will excuse me for a moment, I need to freshen up."

As the woman disappeared into the apartment, the man moved to where Nicholas was standing. "I assume that everything went as expected."

Nicholas nodded. "A walk in the park, Mr. Dixx. It should be a day or two, three at the most, then it's over. There is no tracing anything back to the organization although assumptions will be made. The message should be clear to those who need to understand that certain actions have consequences."

"Of course they do, and you, Nicholas, were the instrument to set those consequences in motion.

Someone hacked into what was supposedly a secure wallet. Two hundred and fifty thousand dollars in cryptocurrency was stolen from me. Perez is just the beginning. We've started with the Mexicans since they sold us the drugs, then we move onto the others, those boys in Harlem. We apply pressure where we have to. No one, and I repeat, Nicholas, no one steals from me."

After a long pause, Dixx continued. "But I'm not naive, Nicholas. The Mexicans may speculate that what happened to their man Perez, wasn't a chance happening. There's an outside chance they may accept what will happen to Perez as a one in a million medical occurrence, a coincidence, bad timing and may not connect anything to us. Or they will assume that we were involved somehow, but how, will remain unexplainable. Either way, they will react or they will not. It's that simple, Nicholas, and it always is, isn't it?"

"I'm a what if guy, Mr. Dixx. I tend to lean on the negative side that all things will happen and I, we, need to prepare for the storm. We can't be sure that the Mexicans were responsible for the stolen crypto, but if they were, and I concur with you, they might connect Perez's death to it."

Dixx stared at Nicholas for several seconds before speaking. "That's what I like about you, Nicholas. An understanding that while certain situations remain static to a degree, everything else is in constant motion. It's that motion we have to prepare for and anticipate."

"You both seem to be engrossed in a deep conversation of sorts. I hated to interrupt, but standing here for several minutes and being ignored isn't my idea of fun," then she smiled.

"Sorry, Madison, I'm the culprit, taking too much of Mr. Dixx's time with matters that could wait and should wait until the sun shines tomorrow. In fact I need to leave. I have an appointment with someone that needs to be kept," and he laughed and added, "No, not that kind of appointment."

"Thank you for the champagne and the view. I enjoyed both and it was nice to see you again, Madison. I'll see myself out."

Nicholas waved and then turned. As he started to walk away, Dixx called out, "Wait," and then handed him an oversized white envelope. "See you on Wednesday, say about ten. Does that work for you, Nicholas?"

"The day after tomorrow. Yes, that works Mr. Dixx. See you then."

Lord exited the building's elevator at the parking level, then drove to West 32nd Street and parked in front of Grace Park's Bar & BBQ. Before he left the vehicle, Nicholas took out the envelope from his jacket pocket and counted out fifteen one-hundred dollar bills.

He walked through the revolving door and then paused until he saw the man seated at a corner table.

Stopping a step away, Lord nodded and then said, "Long time no see, Mr. Shin."

The man smiled, looked at his watch then pointed to a chair.

Once Lord was seated, he said, "I'll have what you're drinking."

"It's an OB, the locally brewed popular beer like we enjoyed during our days together in Korea."

"That works. A little something to jar the memory."

The man called Shin motioned toward a waiter, pointed to his beer and held up two fingers.

"It worked out smoothly, didn't it Nicholas?"

"Yes, he'll journey to another place shortly. Time will tell if the message has been received in the way we intended."

Lord stopped speaking as the waiter approached the table. Once the beer and glasses were placed on the table, the waiter asked if there would be anything else. Lord shook his head no.

Nicholas waited until the waiter was out of sight, then moved his hand toward the Korean. He turned his hand slightly to his right revealing the roll of green bills. "Take it, you've earned it."

The Korean took the money, looked at it for a moment and then placed it in his shirt pocket. "It looks like a lot of money, Nicholas."

"It is, and you earned it."

"I keep thinking, Nicholas, that you are still very smart man, and that we make good combination since early days in Korea."

"Yes, we do, Mr. Shin, and it will always be that way."

"I am planning to stay on as bartender for few weeks more. Then give notice. I assuming nothing further will take place there. Is that correct, Nicholas?"

"Yes. Perez was a surprisingly easy mark. He never varied his routine. The place he went to drink and entertain always remained the same. He thought the two strong armed boys that shadowed him would be enough to guarantee his safety, but he was mistaken, wasn't he, Mr. Shin? He didn't realize that you would be there."

Shin smiled, then chuckled. Your idea, Nicholas, that I should get job as bartender. Nice touch indeed and well paying job too." Shin pointed to his shirt pocket and laughed.

"It'll take a few days for the powder to work. We won't meet until after you give notice. No contact until then."

Shin shook his head yes as he poured some beer into Lord's glass. Then he lifted his own glass and said "Geonbae." (Cheers in Korean)

3

CHAPTER

NICHOLAS LORD LEFT MANHATTAN AND FORTY-FIVE MINUTES LATER
arrived at his home located on a cul-de-sac in Stamford, Connecticut. Parked
in his circular drive was a Mercedes convertible.

He held the smile as he walked through the unlocked front door. She
was standing off to one side of the foyer as she said, "What took you so long?"

"I had to meet someone. Friendship and business sometimes come together and this meeting required a little more than a few minutes. I left as
soon as I could."

"I assume he," and she enunciated the word he, "didn't mind you leaving?" and then she smiled. "Do you want a drink?"

"I think I've had enough, Madison."

"Okay, Nicholas, then let's sit a while."

Lord nodded and started walking toward the sofa where the woman
was now sitting.

Madison held up her hand. "Not here, try the piano bench over there."

Lord turned slightly and looked at the black, Kranich and Bach piano in
the corner of the room. "It's a little late for that, isn't it?"

"It's never too late or too early, Nicholas. Play something, then we'll talk."

"Talk is what you had in mind?" and Nicholas feigned a hurt look.

"Talk soothes the soul, but music stimulates it."

"Do you need to be stimulated, Madison?"

"Answer your own question, Mr. Lord, and now let's have some music."

"Do you think the neighbors will care? It's a bit late."

"Since when did you start to care about your neighbors?"

"So right, Madison. What do you want me to play?"

"Play 'Over the Rainbow.' I always believed that at the end of that rainbow there would be the happiness I've always wanted."

Nicholas Lord smiled as he walked to the piano. Once he was seated he rippled the keys, then began playing a slow rendition of the song. Madison began to sway to the music, and then started to sing, "Somewhere over the rainbow, skies are blue, and the dreams that you dare to dream, really do come true…ooh ooh ooh," and then she began to laugh.

Nicholas continued playing the song in a slow melodic way, then he started over again in an upbeat tempo. Madison started clapping, then gyrating back and forth until she was dancing around the room. Between bouts of laughter and singing, she was alone in some magical place.

When Nicholas finished, she rushed over and kissed him. "That was absolutely beautiful, Nicholas. I didn't know you could play the piano," then she laughed.

"Neither did I. Beginner's luck I guess."

"Ya know what, Madison, I think I'll have that drink, then we'll talk."

They sat close to each other. Nicholas turned slightly and said, "You start."

"Okay. Our situation is becoming complicated. That's nothing new, I know that. I'm where I belong now, here, not where I was earlier this evening."

Nicholas was about to say something but held back, knowing she wasn't finished.

"Maybe long ago, whatever that means, I needed something and I found it, or thought I did, with Xavier Dixx. He was good to me and I felt I owed him something. Despite the age difference and everything else, I was determined to make it work.

Then you came along, you appeared, and don't give that look, Nicholas. I know it takes two to tango. Sooner or later Dixx will know if he doesn't already. He seems to know everything and when he makes the connection or the anger of my betrayal consumes him, he won't hesitate to repay me for my infidelity. And I guarantee you, Mr. Lord, he will have something special for you."

Lord interrupted, "How did you manage to get away tonight?"

"I told him I wasn't feeling well, That time of the month. In a pinch, it always works with the male species."

"Won't he check, to see if you're at your condo?"

"Maybe, so what? Isn't a woman allowed to go out shopping or whatever with or without her period?"

Lord looked at the woman for several moments and then burst out laughing. "How the hell should I know?"

Madison couldn't help herself and laughed. "Okay, Nicholas Lord, let's table this conversation for another time. Why not follow me to a more comfortable place," and then Madison stood up and walked toward the bedroom.

✦✦✦✦✦✦

The next morning they both sat at the kitchen table. Madison, holding her coffee cup slightly away from her mouth asked, "How are we going to rectify this situation Nicholas? I'm privy to most of what's going on in your world as Dixx is okay discussing some things openly when I'm around.

I can't shake the feeling that he knows more about me, and us, than he lets on. I have this premonition that he's waiting for the right time to settle with me and you. And that time could be when this situation with the Mexicans is over or when the mood strikes him."

Madison looked down at the table and then brought her head up quickly again. "You know his man, Colby, those tattooed arms and that shit on his neck tells me all I need to know about him. He's scum! The kind that Dixx likes for his dirty work."

Lord smiled. "You mean work other than I do?"

"You know what I mean, damn it! With you, there's professionalism. You're educated, a college boy and army vet. How and why you got into this life is none of my business, but I'm glad you came along and so is Dixx. The heavy lifting couldn't be handled by someone like Colby. He doesn't have enough brain matter between his ears. You're a valuable asset for Dixx, but not an indispensable one."

"You're right, Madison. You usually are. Women have that intuitive thing. Knowing that something is true without conscious reasoning. To be totally honest, I like the benefits that are derived from what I do. And what I do, can't be done by just anybody, despite what the fiction writers and movie producers project. And yes, I know that the material things don't mean very much when you're always looking over your shoulder and thinking about a life altering situation that can happen at any time."

Before Lord could continue, Madison started speaking.

"What do we really need, Nicholas? As I see it, we only need each other. I'm assuming you want me as much as I want you and this thing between us, isn't not just a stop along the way. I didn't come from much back in that small town in Nebraska, and I don't need much now. Sure Xavier opened up a world I never knew, and yes, I liked it, but I don't need it. There is a very big difference between like and need. Everything he's given me has cost me in one way or another. Now I'm in a predicament that may well cost me more than I could have ever imagined, my life."

"I will never let that happen to you."

"I know what you just said, you mean, Nicholas, but you cannot guarantee me that. Dixx has multiple means to correct what he believes is a challenge, a threat, against his authority and him personally. He hasn't survived this long by being stupid."

"It has nothing to do with being stupid. You can become too self-assured and more importantly he has never encountered someone like me. Remember, Madison, what the Lord giveth, the Lord taketh."

Ramon Delgado turned his head to the right and gazed at the hills that surrounded his luxurious home. Then he turned back and stared at the man seated at the table.

"It's peaceful here. Do you feel the same way, Alejandro?"

"Sí, Jefe yes impresionante." (Yes boss and it's awesome)

"You can never experience anything like this in the rural villages that make up most of Sinaloa's capital. Why would anyone want to live anywhere else?"

Delgado laughed and added, "They couldn't afford this, could they, Alejandro?"

Before the man could answer, Ramon Delgado slammed his fist into the man's jaw, driving both him and his chair backward. As the man struggled to move into a kneeling position, Delgado hit him again.

Turning toward the three men standing at the deck's doorway, Delgado pointed to the now unconscious form of Alejandro Sanchez.

"Tirar el hijo de puta (Throw the son of a bitch) over the railing, and then check to make sure he's dead. Get rid of the body and then come back here. We have business to discuss and what happened to him is just the beginning if I don't get some answers."

The tall Mexican known as Mateo nodded at Delgado then said to the other two, "I'll take care of it." When he reached the unconscious body, he bent slightly, lifted Alejandro Sanchez in one fluid motion, and then tossed him over the railing.

4

CHAPTER

NICHOLAS LORD DROVE INTO THE GARAGE ON FIFTH AVENUE AND TOOK
the elevator to the penthouse level. Lord was mildly surprised to find Xavier
Dixx waiting steps away from the elevator as the door opened. It triggered a
feeling that shouted caution.

"Good morning, Mr. Dixx."

Xavier Dixx nodded once, then moved his arm in a way that conveyed
follow me. As they walked, Dixx pressed a button on his phone pad and the
glass doors to the penthouse deck opened.

"Please take a seat, Nicholas. I assume you can handle another cup
of coffee?"

"I can always handle another cup, Mr. Dixx," and he was about to add,
and a few more things, but he managed to hold himself in check.

At that moment he heard Madison say, "Good morning," as she moved
onto the deck holding several cups of coffee on a tray, together with some
assorted pastries.

"Hello, Madison. Nice to see you again," and then he turned away and
faced a smiling Dixx.

Once the woman left, Dixx motioned toward the pastries.

Lord politely declined and waited for the inevitable to begin. When it did, the tone in which Dixx spoke didn't surprise him. It was guttural and challenging.

"While I expect setbacks from time to time, this is a classic fuck up if there ever was one. Why the hell I ever agreed to accept payment in some fucked up digital shit called cryptocurrency…" and then he stopped speaking. When Dixx continued, he said simply, "I must have been in a mind-fog."

Lord watched as Dixx moved his hand to his mouth and then became quiet.

When he spoke again he seemed more relaxed. "The way it was explained to me by that spook we sold the drugs to…" and then Dixx stopped again.

After several moments of silence he asked, "What was the Black's name? I can't think of it."

"Deontay Johnson. He runs the crew known as the Harlem Originals."

Dixx nodded, then said, "I'm not blaming anyone, Nicholas, except myself. I didn't get where I am by being stupid or taking unnecessary risks. I went against my initial instinct and the results were predictable. The colored boy was persuasive as he related the so-called safety of that shit called crypto.

That digital form of cash can easily be stolen or even lost. Hackers, most likely the Mexicans, can and did penetrate the wallet my money was stored in. I know that much, and I know a personal hard drive isn't safe. The results are as I expected, despite assurances from that spook.

We've sent a message to the Mexicans and I think it's time we sent one to the Harlem Originals. We own a detective in the Midtown Precinct South. I'll make contact and get some information on Mr. Deontay Johnson and the Harlem Originals. Let's meet here tomorrow, same time. Does that work for you, Nicholas?"

"I'll be here tomorrow at ten, Mr. Dixx."

◆◆◆◆◆

They sat, again, on the deck overlooking the New York City skyline. Colby, and several others of Dixx's crew, stood nearby.

Lord thought about asking where Madison was, but as quickly as the thought materialized, it evaporated. It wasn't any of his business where she was, so why was he concerned? Then his thought process answered the question just as Dixx began speaking.

"Our police contact says Johnson has a rap sheet a mile or so long. Picked up for numbers running and a series of petty thefts at fourteen, Johnson was sent to the Crossroads Juvenile Center in Brownsville. When he was back on the streets, he graduated to pushing drugs and then running a crew that specialized in strong arm stuff.

After a five year stint in Attica Correctional Facility, he returned to the place he calls home, and now runs the Harlem Originals. These collections of misfits specialize in drugs, prostitution and sex trafficking. Johnson has a legit setup which he uses for a front for his activities. It's the Rainbow Bar on Frederick Douglass Boulevard in Harlem. He calls home a townhouse on 124th Street.

This is a picture of him," and Dixx handed Nicholas his cell phone.

Lord studied the picture, then handed the phone back to Dixx.

"Can you send me this?"

Dixx nodded then said, "It's done."

Dixx then looked at Colby and then back at Nicholas Lord. "I guess that sums up who Deontay Johnson is, or is the proper terminology, was?"

Lord smiled and started to get up.

"Just one more thing, Nicholas. If you need any help, Colby here is available, aren't you Colby?"

"I'm always available, Mr. Dixx. I live a forty-eight hour day every day," and then Colby turned toward the two men standing near him and smiled.

"I'll remember that," and he nodded at Colby.

Then Lord turned and faced Dixx again. "Do we have a…a black available that I can partner up with if need be?"

Dixx looked at Colby who nodded and then answered, "I have several. One man, and a woman who is not bad in the looks department. Probably has some white blood in the mix."

Dixx thought Colby's comment was worth a smile, while Lord just shook his head slightly.

"Can the woman be trusted?"

Colby smiled and held it. "Of course she can, Mr. Lord. She's property so to speak, and when you own property you can do pretty much as you please. She knows what's good for her and what's bad.

She's experienced both. You have my number. Just contact me if and when she's needed. She'll do what she has to do. Just take it a bit slow. They ain't the smartest books in the library," then Colby laughed.

"We may be in touch," then Lord moved his eyes from Colby to Dixx. "If there's nothing else, I have some business to take care of."

I'll be expecting to hear something positive from you shortly Nicholas."

"You can count on it, Mr. Dixx."

+ + + + + + +

Serenity Allen and Nicholas Lord sat at a small table in the Rainbow Bar on Frederick Douglass Boulevard in Harlem. The night was just beginning for the crowd that considered themselves regulars. The house DJ kept the crowd on its feet with one rap tune after another.

The occasional stares they got from the dominantly black crowd didn't impact Nicholas, although the woman was experiencing some difficulty.

"Ignore them. This is twenty, twenty-two and racial separation is a thing of the past. Just ask any of the screwed up politicians that play race for all it's worth."

The woman nodded yes. "You're right. I...you...we, have the right to be together, and if they don't like it, well fuck them!"

Lord smiled. "Couldn't have phrased it better myself."

"You said this is strictly a drink and dance evening. No after involvement, right?"

"Yeah, That's pretty much it. I'm just here to observe, nothing more. The problem is I'm lily white and despite what I said a moment ago about this being twenty, twenty-two and the racial thing, this is still Harlem and there

— 15 —

are certain people here that have a real dislike for us white boys. Probably more so when that white boy is with a black sister.

However, be that as it may, we're not here to make new friends or a statement to advance the civil rights cause. We're just here for a look-see, then when I've seen what I need to see, we're gone and you're a little richer for being my faithful companion."

Serenity laughed. "That was quite a speech. Are you planning to run for political office?"

"No. You have to fake friendship with too many people. I like to take sides."

"Very astute of you, Mr. Lord. And by the way that's a very unusual last name. Did your parents believe you were some heavenly being?"

"No, not at first, but as I grew, they definitely decided I was something unusual so they felt I had the appropriate last name."

"Am I missing something?"

"I don't think so. Just consider me as someone who gives and takes, like the Lord."

Serenity couldn't help but laugh. "You are very crazy, Mr. Lord."

"Indeed I am."

"Do you care for another drink?"

"I'm okay, still nursing this one," and she pointed to her half filled glass.

Nicholas turned toward the clapping off to his right. Three men and a woman walked slowly to a table at the center of the room. As they walked, greetings and high-fives were exchanged. Two of the men waited until a six foot two or three inch man and the woman were seated, before they sat down.

Serenity followed Nicholas' head moment and they both watched as several waiters brought a bottle of Remy Martin cognac and Dom Perignon champagne to the table.

Serenity said just above a whisper, "must be some kind of fat cat."

"I like the way you put that. Most definitely. The greeting he got and the service, speaks volumes."

As he held his drink in his hand, Nicholas Lord compared the man sitting at the center table with the cell phone photo Dixx had shown him. His mind fused them together in one composite photograph, a photograph of the Harlem Originals gang lord, Deontay Johnson.

"Time for another drink, but before we get to that, would you care to dance?"

Somewhat surprised, Serenity hesitated, then nodded her head yes. As they walked, several sets of eyes followed them as they made their way onto the dance floor.

The dance floor was crowded as men and women gyrated to the up tempo rhythm that blared through the speakers at the rooms' four corners.

"Do you know what this song is called, Serenity?"

"I haven't the slightest idea. Rap isn't my thing. I like jazz."

"Well, it just so happens I know this song. It's called, 'Don't Stop Now' and it's by Hakeem and the Lover Boys."

"How in the world did you know that? I would have thought that you'd be the last person on earth who would."

"Surprises are part of life. It just happened that I heard it played on a radio station this afternoon and I locked onto the group's name, 'Hakeem and the Lover Boys.' One crazy fucking name," and then Lord laughed as he continued moving back and forth to the blaring beat.

When the song finished and another started playing, Lord motioned with his head toward the table area. "Ready?"

"Yeah, too many bodies out here and that rap stuff is for the crazies that think it's music."

"Yes, I concur with that one hundred percent."

As they made their way back to their table, the same sets of eyes that followed them initially, followed them again. One in particular was Deontay Johnson.

5

CHAPTER

ONCE THEY WERE ON THE STREET, LORD STOPPED AND DISCREETLY handed Serenity Allen an envelope. "That's for the companionship tonight. Thank you."

Serenity placed the envelope in her purse, then looked up at Nicholas. "Will I see you again, Mr. Lord?"

"There's always a possibility."

"I'd like that," and then she smiled.

Nicholas pointed to several taxis waiting by the curb. Once Serenity was seated, Lord leaned into the cab. "Driver, I know your badge number and name," pointing to the certificate fastened to the dashboard. "Make sure the lady gets home safely."

Lord waited until the taxi disappeared, then started walking until he reached a gray sedan parked a block away. He tapped lighty, then opened the front passenger door.

"Everything okay?"

"Yes. She was everything you said and a bit more."

Colby smiled.

"Drive to 124th Street. Park at the corner on the east side of his block. We'll wait there until Johnson gets home."

After Colby parked the car between two other vehicles, Lord asked, "Do you have my envelope?"

"Yes, Mr. Lord," and Colby handed Nicholas a medium sized manila envelope.

Lord ran his fingers over the tape seal. Satisfied that it wasn't tampered with, he tore the envelope open and removed the cell phone.

As he sat there, Lord's mind focused on the cell phone he was holding, specifically the RXD cyclonite, a sand-like powder, white in color and highly explosive. Lord pictured the cyclonite packed into the cell phone along with a small blasting cap and wired so that when the ringer is activated, the electric current jolts the blasting cap which then sets off the primary explosive. All he needed now was the target, and that would come at some point.

Lord was brought back to the moment by the ringing. His mind pictured the cell phone he was holding and the ensuing explosion before he realized it was his personal phone ringing.

He looked at the screen then turned toward Colby and said, "I've gotta take this."

Lord opened the car door, then stepped away after closing it.

"Hello, Madison. Is anything wrong?"

"No. I just needed to talk to you."

"Well, I'm here but time is somewhat limited. I'm handling a matter for Dixx."

"In a way, that's why I'm calling. I haven't seen him since you and I were together. He's left messages on my phone, but I can't get myself in the right frame of mind to call him back."

"I was with Dixx several times over the past few days and didn't see you. I was wondering why?"

"Well, now you know. I'm okay otherwise, but I'm…" and then Madison stopped speaking.

After moments of silence, Lord said, "It might be a good idea to reconnect. I know that's not what you want to do and honestly, I would rather you break the connection with him. But for all the reasons we discussed, it might be better to call him back until I can figure out something for us."

"And how long will that be?"

"I want to give you a time-frame, Madison, but in all honesty, I don't know. Several matters need handling for Dixx and until I can finish, I'm between a rock and a hard place. I know that's not what you want to hear, but you matter to me and I can't, and won't tell you anything but the truth. And the truth right now, is I'm up to my neck in alligators."

Madison laughed. "Can you arrange for one of those alligators to devour Mr. Xavier Dixx?"

Lord laughed despite himself. "Yeah, maybe. We'll see. Meantime, play it cool. Do what you have to and stay focused."

"Okay, Mr. Lord. Words of wisdom perhaps. But please, Nicholas, let's get out of this web as quickly as we can before the spider eats us both. Ciao."

As Lord started moving back toward the car, a black Cadillac Escalade turned the corner at a high rate of speed. The SUV careened to a stop in front of a three-story townhouse near the end of the block. The doors opened quickly and Johnson, a woman, and two men got out. The four laughed and jostled with each other as they staggered their way to the front door.

Lord waited until they were inside before he moved toward the car again. After he closed the passenger side door, he said, "We wait until whatever it is they're going to do is finished. No telling how long, but I'm assuming, not long."

When the lights went off inside the townhouse, Lord looked at his watch, then he turned to Colby and said, "We wait another fifteen minutes, then I'll do it."

They sat in silence as Lord applied several strips of metallic adhesive tape to the back of the cell phone. When he was finished, he looked at his watch then moved his hand to the door handle and pushed the door open with the sole of his shoe.

After closing the door, he walked quickly toward the SUV. He dropped to his knees, rolled over on his back and maneuvered his way under the SUV. After attaching the cell phone to the Escalade's gas reservoir, Lord made his way out, then ran back to the car.

Once inside, he smiled. "Just one more thing to do, Colby, and that will happen when Johnson starts his day, whenever that is. Meanwhile we wait. If you want to grab a few z's go ahead. I'll wake you when the fourth of July is about to start," and then Lord laughed.

"I'm okay, Mr. Lord. I don't get a lot of downtime with Mr. Dixx, so sitting here with nothing to do is just fine by me."

"Okay then. I'll grab a few. Wake me when there's movement."

Lord closed his eyes, but sleep was evasive. After about twenty or so minutes he straightened up in his seat, and looked over at Colby. His eyes were closed. Lord smiled, then looked at the townhouse. The interior lights were out and from all appearances, Johnson and his crew were doing whatever it was that they do. Lord let a half smile form on his face as he thought about the way he phrased the thought.

It was quarter to seven in the morning when the front door of the townhouse opened, and Johnson and two men came out. They walked slowly to the parked SUV and got in.

Lord nudged Colby with his elbow.

"I'm up, Mr. Lord, and I see them. Just give me the word when you're going to do your thing, and I'll get the car moving."

"Get the car moving now, and get us the hell out of here."

Colby started the ignition and placed the gear shift in reverse as Lord dialed a number on his cell phone.

Colby twisted the wheel hard left, spinning the car in a half circle, then pressed the accelerator to the floorboard as the car shot forward.

Several seconds after dialing the number, the connection was made and the sequence started. Through a short burst of electrical current, a signal was sent from the ringer to the detonator cap. Once this signal was received, it activated the detonator charge, which then ignited the explosive cyclonite material.

The explosion lifted the Escalade several feet off the ground while simultaneously engulfing it in a red-orange fireball.

"Keep it moving, Colby. Make miles between them and us."

"Okay, Mr. Lord. You're reading my mind."

6

CHAPTER

AFTER COLBY PULLED TO THE CURB IN FRONT OF THE FIFTH AVENUE
skyscraper, he looked over at Lord.

"Take the car to Hudson Salvage and make sure they chop it up good,
so nothing's left to connect us."

Colby nodded a yes.

"Everything went well tonight, Colby. It was a pleasure working with
you again, and I'll make sure Mr. Dixx knows. He'll probably want to get
your version of what went down, and that's fine with me. See ya around,"
and then Nicholas opened the car door and began walking toward the entrance
to Dixx's building.

Lord looked at his watch as he stepped out from the elevator. The door
to the penthouse was open and Dixx was standing there when he looked up.

"Hello, Nicholas. You seem a bit worn. A difficult night perhaps?" Then
Dixx smiled.

"That's one way of putting it. The matter with Deontay Johnson is over,
but as you know, Mr. Dixx, there's always another to replace him."

"Yes, of course, there is." Then Dixx paused a moment before asking, "Why are we standing here? Come in, please."

Dixx pointed toward the deck. "I'll join you in a minute or so. Would you care for coffee or a drink, Nicholas?"

"How about both, Mr. Dixx. It must be five p.m. somewhere," and then he smiled.

"Yes indeed. What's your persuasion in the drink department?"

"A Stoli vodka over ice with a twist of lemon, if that isn't too much trouble."

"Not in the least," and then Dixx turned and walked toward the kitchen area.

Lord seated himself in one of the chairs and glanced at the New York City skyline. The images that floated across his mind wasn't the skyscrapers, but the red-orange fireball that consumed the Cadillac Escalade.

His concentration was broken by the female voice. He turned and locked eyes with Madison as she placed the coffee and vodka down.

"Hi, Madison. Nice to see you again," and Lord smiled.

She smiled back, and then turned as Dixx approached.

"You don't have to leave us, Madison. Stay a while."

"Thanks for the invitation, Xavier, but I need to freshen up a bit and you boys have some boy-talk to do."

Then she waved and walked toward one of the bedrooms.

"Just like a woman, right, Nicholas?"

"They're a complicated species, Mr. Dixx," then Lord laughed.

"Not a bad choice of words. Now to business. You look a little worse for wear Nicholas. That once elegant suit isn't so elegant anymore."

"I was doing a little auto repair earlier this evening and neglected to change my clothes."

Nicholas paused for a moment, and then laughed. Dixx joined in.

"And was the repair satisfactorily completed?"

"Yes, Mr. Dixx, and noteworthy as well. You'll probably be hearing about an explosion that happened early this morning."

Dixx nodded then motioned toward the coffee and drinks on the table.

Lord reached for the vodka and waited to see what Dixx would do. Once Dixx lifted his glass of vodka, Lord said, "A una larga vida y salud." (To a long life and health-Spanish)

"Ah, I seem to have forgotten one of your many attributes, your ability with languages. You'll have to translate for me please."

"What I said, Mr. Dixx was, "To a long life and health.""

"Very appropriate, Nicholas. At least for some of us that's more or less going to happen. For others, perhaps not."

Lord let the words roll around his mind as he tried to figure out if what Dixx said was some type of threat. Recalling his conversation with Madison, during which she mentioned that Dixx probably knew of their liaisons, Lord deduced that it was very much a veiled threat.

He sipped the vodka, then placed his glass on the table.

"I hope the drink is okay, Nicholas."

"Perfect."

"Would you please summarize what took place with the former Mr. Deontay Johnson."

"A pleasure, Mr. Dixx. Once Johnson and his crew left the bar, we were waiting for them at his townhouse. It was about two or so in the morning. They went inside and reappeared about six forty-five a.m. During that four plus hour period, I attached a cell phone bomb to his vehicle's gas tank.

When their vehicle started to move, I set the cell phone bomb in motion. Colby meantime was moving us away from the area so that when the bomb ignited, we were a safe distance away. The bomb detonated and if the explosion didn't kill the three occupants, the ensuing fireball did. And by the way, Mr. Dixx, Colby was an asset."

"Something I expected, but I'm always glad to hear that."

"What did you do with the car?"

"Colby said he'd take it to Hudson Salvage and have them chop it up into little pieces."

Dixx smiled, then pointed to the drinks and coffee. "That vodka seems to be getting warm and the coffee cold."

After they both took several minutes to drink a little of both, Dixx continued.

"Okay Nicholas, a message has been sent to the Mexicans who supply us with the fentanyl and heroin, and the group that buys it. Whether we're implicated in either of the two events, remains to be seen. Maybe someone with half a brain might try to connect us, or maybe not. They both have plenty of enemies who want what they have.

We, on the other hand, are projected as the neutrals who buy and distribute. Be that as it may, I am still out two hundred and fifty thousand dollars. Maybe neither the Mexicans or the Blacks are responsible, or maybe one of them is.

I've been thinking, Nicholas, it might be worthwhile to meet with the Mexicans and set their minds at ease with regard to anything linking us with Perez's death. You previously explained that the poison would take several days to kick in and that when death did occur, it would appear that the cause was respiratory paralysis."

Dixx looked at Lord in a way that made him think that a confirmation was required, so he answered, "Yes, that's correct, Mr. Dixx. That would be the obvious conclusion the medical examiner would make."

"Okay, then we arrange a meeting with the Mexicans. Are you okay with that, Nicholas?"

"It might be too soon after Perez's death. They're not totally stupid, and Delgado or one of his lieutenants might wonder why we want to meet when we rarely do. I'd wait a bit, and concentrate first on the Blacks. Let's see who replaces Johnson as head OG. (Original Gangster) The underbosses will do what they have to in order to find out who sent their leader on a trip to another world. Could be they'll look in our direction."

"Why would they do that?"

"For the same reason you just outlined with the Mexicans."

Dixx slowly nodded his head in agreement then asked, "You're thinking we should wait until a new King Shorty (Name for a gang leader) is installed?"

"Yes Mr. Dixx. We then know who and what we're dealing with. The

Mexicans, Delgado, can wait a bit, but I agree not too long. We need to cement some relations and project our unwavering loyalty to our arrangement with them."

"Okay, Nicholas, we wait."

Lord reached for his glass, swallowed the contents and then stood up. "If there's nothing else, Mr. Dixx, I think I'll arrange an appointment with my tailor and get a new suit made," then he laughed.

"There is nothing else, Nicholas, and to help you pay part of that extravagant price your tailor charges, here's a little something," and Dixx handed Lord an envelope. "I'll contact the Blacks and arrange a meeting, then I'll be in touch."

Nicholas waved the envelope. "My tailor and I both thank you for your generosity. I know the way out so don't get up. I'll be waiting to hear from you."

When Nicholas reached the foyer, Madison was coming out of one of the bedrooms. "Leaving so soon, Mr. Lord?"

"Yes, have a pleasant day, Madison."

"I definitely will, and it's so nice to see you again, Mr. Lord."

7

CHAPTER

JAMAL LOMAX ACKNOWLEDGED THE PLEDGES OF LOYALTY FROM THE assembled members of the Harlem Originals. He was now King Shorty, aka the Crowned King of a well organized and sophisticated street gang. A gang that didn't hesitate to use violence to control their neighborhood and boost their illegal money-making activities, which included drugs, robbery, gun and human trafficking, and prostitution.

When the meeting concluded, Lomax and two of his lieutenants moved slowly through the crowded clubhouse and toward the door. When they reached the door, Jamal Lomax stopped and turned back. The noise level was at its peak when he raised his fist in the air and shouted, "Harlem Originals forever."

Thirty plus pairs of feet stomped the wooden floor and a crescendo of voice shouted, "Originals, Originals," over and over again.

⸻ ✦✦✦✦✦✦ ⸻

After the four-door sedan pulled curbside, Lomax and his lieutenants walked slowly past a number of people standing behind a roped off area and toward the main entrance of the Rainbow Bar.

Once inside, Lomax stopped and slowly looked around.

Satisfied with whatever it was he was trying to determine, he started walking through the throng of people toward the vacant table at the room's center. As he walked, heads moved in his direction and eyes followed him until he was seated.

Almost immediately a bottle of Dom Perignon champagne and Remy Martin cognac were placed in front of him. The waiter then moved several steps away and waited. When Lomax pointed to the champagne, all three flutes were quickly filled.

Lomax looked at the waiter and when eye contact was made, he nodded and said, "Stay close. We're celebrating tonight."

"Of course, Mr. Lomax, and congratulations."

Lomax smiled, lifted his glass and toasted, "Harlem Originals forever."

His two lieutenants repeated the toast.

After he set his flute down, Lomax looked casually around the room. Something at the bar caught his attention and he leaned toward one of his lieutenants and asked, "Do you see those three sisters at the bar?"

"Yes, Boss, noticed them as soon as we walked in."

"Well, I must be slipping or I need my eyes examined, or both."

The two lieutenants chuckled.

"Trey, why don't you approach those lovely ladies and ask them if they'd care to join us. Tell them we're celebrating and hate to celebrate with boys only."

Trey Mims smiled and then nodded. "Ain't gonna be easy, Jamal, but I'll use a wee bit of extra charm."

"You do that now, and don't disappoint me."

As Mims walked toward the bar, Darius Baxter, Lomax's other lieutenant leaned toward his boss, "Wanna bet whether he does it or not?"

"Sure, a c-note, one hundred green, says we will soon have three lovelies sitting here."

"You're on boss. I'm gonna hate to take your money," and then Baxter laughed.

They both watched Mims as he approached the bar. After several minutes the women were laughing and then he pointed back at where Lomax and Baxter were seated. Several minutes later, Mims, the three women and a waiter carrying the women's drinks approached the table.

Mims smiled, "Gentlemen, may I introduce these lovely ladies?" Pointing to the one standing at his left, Mims said, "This is Miss Jada Robinson and next to her is Zuri Harris, and finally, Miss Serenity Allen."

After the women took their seats, Lomax asked if they wanted to stay with their drinks or enjoy either the champagne or cognac. All three opted for the champagne.

"I think we need some food to go along with the champagne. Everyone okay with that?"

The women replied yes, along with Mims and Baxter. "Okay, that's settled."

A large plate of hickory smoked BBQ ribs was placed at the center of the table along with a bundle of linen napkins.

Lomax saw the three women alternating looks between the plate of ribs and the napkins, and quickly said, "You all look beautiful tonight and I know you don't want to get your dresses soiled, so I've ordered plenty of napkins so that won't happen."

They nodded and smiled.

"Okay ladies, shall we begin?"

The three men keep the women laughing during the meal and when they finished they moved on and off the dance floor where the rap rhythms like Eminem's "Berzerk," Drake's "Worst Behavior," and Clipse's "Grindin," kept the night festive for the party crowd that filled the Rainbow Bar.

When they were all seated again, Jada Robinson looked first at the two women and then at the men, and said, "I hate to be a party pooper, but I need to get up early tomorrow. I'm still a working girl and this is a weeknight."

Serenity quickly added, "Jada right, gentlemen. We three need some beauty sleep or we can't be the gorgeous women we are."

That brought some laughter and a few pleas from Mims and Baxter to stay, but the women were persistent.

Serenity stood up, leaned toward Lomax and kissed his cheek.

Then Lomax asked, "Will I see you again? In fact, will we see all of you again?"

"There's a good possibility you will," Zuri Harris answered.

Jada Robinson shook her head in a definite yes, and Serenity said, "You can count on it. We like the club, the music, the company, the ribs and the bundle of napkins. We'll be back"

The three men laughed and clapped their hands.

Lomax looking at Serenity Allen said, "If we don't, I can guarantee we will send someone looking for you all."

"Well it may be hard to find us. Three beautiful women like us are never easy to find." With that said, Serenity turned and walked toward the main entrance followed by the other two women.

Lomax watched the women leave, then turned his head back to Mims and Baxter. "I didn't think it was going to end like that. I thought we'd score for sure. Just show ya, ya never can tell."

Baxter reached into his pocket, took out his wallet and handed Lomax a one hundred dollar bill.

Mims asked, "Where's mine?"

Baxter laughed. "It was a bet between Jamal and yours truly whether you'd get the ladies to the table."

"Obviously my dear, Baxter, you've underestimated my charm and per-suasive powers."

Lomax laughed. "That's so true since I'm one hundred dollars richer. And by the way, there's nothing to worry about. We'll be seeing them again and the wait, trust me, will be worthwhile."

At that moment the club's main door opened and Serenity Allen walked in and continued until she was again at the center table.

Three sets of eyes were staring at the woman.

"Back so soon? Did you forget something?"

"A matter of fact I did. I forgot to give you this," and Serenity handed

Jamal Lomax a folded piece of paper. He glanced briefly at the paper then placed it in his shirt pocket.

"Good night boys and sweet dreams."

After Serenity left and several 'high fives' were exchanged, Lomax said, "She's one good lookin' piece of all right. I've never seen them here before. Did either of you?"

Baxter lifted his left hand, rubbed his chin, then said, "I think I've seen that one, the one named Serenity before."

Lomax locked eyes with Baxter and asked, "How so?"

"I can't be one hundred percent sure, boss, but I think it was the night Deontay was bopped." (Killed)

"Okay, give me more."

"She's a good looking dolly bird. Not easy to forget. I remember her or someone that looks damn like her, 'cause she was with a cracka. (White guy) There ain't too many honkies that come in here, especially with sisters."

Lomax moved his head slightly and then sat quietly. Baxter and Mims did the same.

"Okay! A cracker with a sister. Happens, not often but it happens. Don't see no connection to Deontay, but you never know. I think it's a stretch but, like I say, you never know. I was going to hold off on the matter of Deontay, but since we're talkin' about it, let's talk. I want the word out on the street that there's some large bread (Money) we're willing to fork over for the right information regarding the who did it. You got that? No one fucks with us and no one gets away with bumpin' (Killing) a Harlem Original. Not never!"

Lomax became quiet again. After a number of minutes he said, "Okay, enough thinking. It's another day already and we've got work to do. Let's do this thing."

8

CHAPTER

LORD LOOKED AT HIS WATCH AS HE SAT AT THE ROUND GLASS KITCHEN table in his Stamford, Connecticut home. It was a few minutes later than the last time he looked. Sleep had been evasive, and he couldn't remember if he had managed more than a couple of hours of real sleep.

He brought the coffee cup up and tasted the cold brew. He thought, I'm letting my mind wander and the coffee gets cold. A bad combination.

Lord walked to the sink, poured out the coffee, then refilled the cup. He stood with his back against the sink wondering what he would have to contend with over the next twenty-four hours, and then said out loud, "Screw it. I'm a survivor and I'll continue to be one. Let 'em come."

As he lifted the coffee cup, his cell phone rang. Momentarily unsure where he left it, he looked around the sink area, then shifted his gaze toward the kitchen table. He saw the black phone and moved toward it.

"Hello Y K, how are you this fine morning?"

"I'm okay, Nicholas. Wanted to tell you about my happenings."

"I'm all ears. Go ahead."

"I'm still working as bartender. When I told Mr. Hobbs that I'm leaving, he gave me raise to stay and said I'm number one bartender. So I'm here for while longer. I think it's okay to stay since no one knows anything, Nicholas."

"Yes Y K, It's okay to stay. You make excellent drinks as one of our past acquaintances knows."

Shin laughed then said, "You very funny man, Nicholas. So I stay as bartender. You know how to reach me if you need anything. Until then I say goodbye to you, Nicholas."

"Okay Y K. Thanks for bringing me up to date. We'll be in touch. Be well and josimhaeyo." (Be careful-Korean)

Lord placed the cell phone back on the table and lifted the cup to his lips. "Damn it's cold again." He repeated the previous sequence when he reached the sink and then brought the refilled cup back to the table and sat down. Then he said just above a whisper, "Drink the coffee, boy, and relax."

Just as he reached for the cup the cell phone rang again. He looked at the dial then answered. "Good morning, Mr. Dixx."

"Hello, Nicholas. We have a meeting with the Harlem boys at three this afternoon. Let's meet here at my place at one p.m. and go over a few things."

"That works." Anything else, Mr. Dixx?"

"No. See you at one," and then the connection ended.

Lord reached for the coffee and took a slip. "Damn, cold again. Okay, the hell with it. I'm not spending any more time wrestling with a coffee cup." Then he laughed at the absurdity of it all.

⋅ ⋆✦✦✦⋆ ⋅

"Let's go over it one more time. The new OG of the HO's," and then Dixx smiled, "is a dude named Jamal Lomax. He has the typical rap sheet, juvenile detention center, then graduated to Louisiana State prison and took some advanced degrees at Rikers Island."

Colby and Lord smiled at the way Dixx phrased it.

"He's earned his rep, and the HO's won't miss a beat pushing drugs and everything else they do. We just play it cool regarding the late Mr. Johnson and make sure the new crowned king understands nothing has changed. We'll still be their principal supplier of heroin and fentanyl. Any questions?"

"Okay gentlemen, let's go."

<hr>

Twenty minutes later Colby parked the Maserati Quattroporte sedan in front of a storefront on 116th Street.

From the time they left the vehicle and walked toward the store's entrance, eyes followed them. On either side of the doorway were two large black guys with four others standing in a loose semi-circle a few steps away.

"We're here to see, Lomax."

The Black standing at the right side of the doorway answered "Yeah, we know. They're waiting," and motioned then in.

As Colby walked past, the Black said, "Nice wheels man."

"Yeah, they are, aren't they? Save your pennies," and he held the smile.

Once inside the room, Dixx and Lord took seats at a large rectangular table. Colby remained standing and braced himself against one of the walls near the door. Sitting on the opposite side were Lomax, Mims and Baxter, and standing behind them were five gangbangers.

"Would you all like something? Some champagne perhaps?"

Dixx asked, "What are we celebrating?"

"Nothing in particular. Do we need a reason to drink champagne?"

Dixx smiled. "Point well made, Mr. Lomax. Let's drink champagne."

Lomax looked toward the nearest man and nodded.

The gangbanger nodded back, walked toward a rear door and disappeared. Moments later he reentered the room carrying several bottles of Dom Perignon, and followed by a woman carrying champagne flutes on a tray.

After the champagne and flutes were placed on the table, the woman locked eyes with Nicholas.

Lord was about to say something when an inner voice screamed, no.

He watched as Serenity Allen turned away and left the room.

Lomax noted the brief eye contact between the two and asked Lord, "Do you by chance know that young lady?"

"No, I just like beautiful things."

"Is that what she is, Mr. Lord? A beautiful thing?"

"Indeed, and much more."

Lomax shook his head. "Yeah, maybe they are things, but what would we do without them?" and then he laughed. "Gentlemen, if you'll allow me," and then Lomax uncorked one of the bottles and poured the champagne.

"Let's drink to longevity and the money that will allow us to enjoy it."

As the five men lifted their glass, Dixx said, "To longevity."

"Okay, now that our vocal cords are lubricated, why this meeting, Mr. Dixx?"

"For one thing, I wanted to congratulate you in person on your new leadership role and secondly, I wanted to make sure you knew that nothing would change. The same arrangement we had with Deontay will continue with you."

"Very reassuring, Mr. Dixx. We appreciate you coming all the way from Fifth Avenue to visit us brothers in this run down section of Harlem."

Then Lomax laughed as he lifted his glass.

"Appearances can be deceiving, can't they, Mr. Lomax? What is projected by one person, sometimes proves a detriment for another. A low profile is always best in some circumstances."

Lomax shook his head, but Dixx felt sure he didn't understand a thing he said. In fact he wasn't sure what he said made any sense.

"Any update on why, regarding, Deontay?"

"Nothing yet, but it definitely was a professional hit. We got our feelers out and sooner or later we'll know what we need to know, and then…" Lomax didn't finish, he didn't have to.

"When will we receive the next shipment?"

"I'll confirm it to you over the next several days, but it looks like the end of the month, eight days from today."

Lomax nodded his head. "You have my cell number. Just use the same code, the same as you used with Deontay. I acknowledge the same way."

"Okay, and by the way payment is now going to be in cash, like the old days. No more crypto. Is that understood?"

"What's wrong with…" and then Lomax stopped. "Okay, cash it is. If we're finished with the business, can we get back to the champagne?"

Dixx smiled, "By all means."

After Dixx, Lord and Colby said their goodbyes and left, Lomax sat alone with Mims and Baxter.

"What do you make of what just happened, Mims?"

"Could be like he said boss. Just a friendly kiss up to cement relations. Then again maybe he was trying to feel us out re Deontay or get a fix on whether you were going to continue buying from him."

Lomax shook his head more or less in agreement. "I think there's more to the meeting, but I can't finger it. By the way, did you lock on to the way Lord looked at Serenity? I'm bettin' he knows her or vice versa."

"I was watching that cracker all during the time he was here. I know I saw him before. Remember boss, when I mentioned that some white boy with a good lookin' sister was at the club the night Deontay was bumped. (Killed) Well, while I can't be one hundred percent, I'm sure that cracker was with your new lady."

"Well then, Mr. Baxter, I guess I need to have a talk with Serenity. Please ask her to join us."

When Serenity entered the room, she moved hesitantly, knowing that something wasn't quite right.

"Please sit-down, Serenity. I need to ask you some simple questions and I need some simple answers. Understand?"

The tone of Lomax's voice told the woman all she needed to know, and inwardly she felt the fear and apprehension rise in intensity.

"Three men were here moments ago. One you know, don't you?"

Lomax purposely left out who he was referring to, allowing the woman to lead him to where he wanted to go.

Serenity's mind churned with options, but she knew she had only one.

"Yes, I do know two of them."

"Which two?"

"The one called Nicholas Lord and the other one, Colby."

"How do you know them Serenity, and please, make long sentences."

"I know Colby from the streets. He helped me out of several serious situations, paid off some people I owed money to, and we became friends."

When she saw the half smile form on Lomax's face, she quickly said, "Not that kind of friend. I owe him big time, but he was always a decent guy and never took advantage of me. Seems the man named Lord needed a companion for an evening and Colby asked me if I wanted to accompany him.

He said it was strictly dinner and a few drinks and nothing else was required. I figured, why not. I like the nightlife, and anybody Colby would recommend, would be first class and he was. That's it...all of it. There's nothing more."

Lomax simply sat quietly staring at the woman. Then he leaned forward and asked, "Are you sure there's nothing more, Serenity? Maybe you can recall what night it was and where you went."

"Sure, it was about ten days ago, a Wednesday, and we went to a place called the Rainbow Bar."

"Okay, thank you, Serenity. That clears up a few things. Tonight we party, so pretty up. We'll start early, say nine p.m. and we'll pick you up at your apartment. Darius and Trey Mims will join us and hopefully Miss Robinson and Miss Harris will as well. See you then, and take that worried look off your face. Sometimes I come on too strong. Nothin' to be concerned about."

"Okay, sounds like fun. I'll see you all at nine," then she waved her hand as she walked out of the room.

Lomax waited until the woman disappeared. "Okay we know something more now. Maybe it's just a coincidence that Lord was there and maybe not. My instinct tells me it was no coincidence he was at the Rainbow."

Mims spoke up. "But boss, how did the cracker, assuming it was him, manage to rig Deontay's SUV. Ain't something you can do in a few seconds. No one could have gotten close to that vehicle."

"Well someone did, and I bettin' it was Lord or someone associated with him and Dixx. By the way, anything back from the streets?"

"No, nothing despite the large (Money) we're offerin' for directory assistance. (Information) No one seems to know nothing and that's surprising. They know who Deontay was, and who we are. Something is gonna come."

Lomax slowly shook his head yes, "But not soon enough. I want the score evened and then some."

9

CHAPTER

COLBY PULLED INTO THE UNDERGROUND GARAGE OF DIXX'S APART-
ment building and parked in his reserved spot. After leaving the vehicle,
Dixx said, "One moment gentlemen. Take the rest of the day off. I'm sure
you have things to do," then he looked at Lord. "Did you visit your tailor
yet, Nicholas?"

"Not yet, Mr. Dixx. Too many other things are taking priority."

"I need to go over a few things, the Mexicans included. Shall we meet
here tomorrow say, ten a.m. Does it work for both of you?"

"Works for me," replied Colby, and Lord shook his head yes when Dixx
and his eyes locked.

"Okay see you both then."

They both watched Dixx enter the elevator and after the door closed,
Lord asked Colby. "Did you make sure that car we used the other day is
untraceable?"

"Yep. Now pieces of this and that, care of Hudson Salvage."

"Okay, one less problem to be concerned with. The major one right now
seems to be the woman, Serenity. Seems she's hooked up with Lomax."

"Yeah, noticed that too. Gonna have a lil' talk with her sooner rather than later. I got the feeling from our little pow-wow that something isn't right. Despite the half-brain those black boys have, they use it every once in a while, and I left there feeling they think we had something to do with their main man getting killed."

"I get that feeling too, and I always trust my instinct. Serenity is going to open up a door for them."

Colby brought his hand up and rubbed his eyes. "Could be. I'll find out and let you know before we meet Dixx tomorrow."

"Okay, I'll be waiting to hear from you. Do you need a ride?"

"No, I'll take a taxi. I'm okay."

Lord waved as he walked toward his car.

⁘ ✦✦✦ ✦ ⁘

Colby, still standing next to Dixx's car, waved as Lord drove off. Then he took out his cell phone and dialed Serenity Allen's telephone number.

She picked up on the first ring.

"Hi Colby, nice surprise hearing from you. How have you been?"

"Well, since I last saw you about forty-five minutes ago. I'm coping."

"I thought you'd be doing better than just coping," and then she laughed.

"Well, Serenity, that depends on what I have to cope with and right now, at this very moment, I'm coping with why you're hanging out with one, Mr. Jamal Lomax and friends?"

"It's not a complicated story. Do you wanna hear it?"

"I'm all ears."

"Me and two of my girlfriends were at the Rainbow Bar a few nights back. Your friend, Nicholas, took me there. It was a fun place so when the girls and I got together for a night out, I suggested that place.

When we were sitting at the bar, one of Jamal's boys came over and asked us to join them. We did, and at the end of the night I gave Jamal my telephone number. We had a few dates and I just happened to be there when you and the others came in. That's pretty much it."

— 40 —

"Now listen carefully, Serenity, and think before you answer. Did Lomax or anyone else ask if you knew Dixx, Lord or me?"

Colby waited several seconds and then asked, "You still there?"

"Yes, I'm still here. I'm thinking so I get it right the first time."

"Okay, I'm ready when you are."

"It was like this, Colby. Jamal asked me if I knew any of you. He's not stupid and I guess he saw my eyes connect with Lord for an instant. I told him you saved me big time. He didn't ask any specifics about how, and I didn't tell him any.

I told him you are a stand-up guy and when you asked me if I would like to accompany a friend for dinner and drinks at some fancy club, I said yes. Why wouldn't I? It sounded like a fun evening and I told him that there was nothing else involved, no afterwards anything. He asked me if I remember what night it was and I told him it was about ten days ago on a Wednesday.

He seemed okay with what I said and the way I said it. In fact, when I finished he invited me to a party at the Rainbow tonight. He's picking me up at nine, so I gotta get all pretty, and that takes some time. Is there anything else Colby?"

"No, nothing else at the moment. Get yourself all pretty and have fun. You know how to reach me if you need me, and I know how to reach you."

⁂

Dixx asked, "Anything anyone wants to say before I start?"

Colby answered yes. "I spoke with the woman, Serenity Allen, and without going into the specifics, she did tell Lomax that she was with Mr. Lord at the Rainbow on the night Johnson met his maker."

Dixx moved slightly forward and placed his forearms at the edge of the table. "I think you should enlighten us a bit more. For example, why did she tell Lomax anything?"

"Seems Lomax or one of his two underbosses caught some eye contact between the woman and Mr. Lord."

"I still don't understand, Colby, what does eye contact have to do with anything? If she's not bad looking, why not make some eye contact?"

"It's not the way they read it, and a little something in our world is a much bigger something in theirs, so she was questioned. Lomax and his crew are intimidating, especially for a woman who is a new hanger-on. Anyway, I believe that they assume there's a connection with what happened to Johnson and us, specifically with Mr. Lord."

"Okay, so what?"

"The so what, is even if they don't have any hard evidence that we're involved, they don't need any. All they need is the belief, a feeling, that we're responsible, and that's enough for them to blow one of us down. (Kill one of us-gang slang) And the most likely one to go down, is Mr. Lord here."

Nicholas smiled as he looked away from Colby and at Dixx.

"Could be, and I'm siding with Colby that they're leaning toward a connection, us, and the demise of their, Mr. Deontay Johnson. If they put out a contract, a hit on me for example, or Colby here, it will appear random, not something planned in retaliation. Just a happening, and I'm not about to let that become a reality."

"How would you stop it, Nicholas?"

"I have an associate, Mr. Dixx. He has some," and Lord paused for several moments before he continued, "some friends that do heavy lifting. I'd like to arrange another incident where we take out one or more of Lomax's crew and send him a message he won't forget. There will be nothing that traces anything back to us, just as there isn't with Deontay Johnson. The only thing the Harlem Originals will have is another dead body or two, and a major problem with who is sending their bros to another world."

Dixx shook his head from side to side. "I'm thinking Nicholas, that if another dead body or two turns up, they'll have to retaliate, proof or no proof. Lomax will have to do something or he loses his kingship, so he'll take one of us out, and worry about whether it was the right move later on."

Lord held up his hand, and Dixx stopped speaking. "Agree, he's going to do something. He's obligated to, and it'll be us. Before he does, we hit him again. Then we have another sit-down and we tell him we'll settle the score for him. We know who it is."

"I'm not following this, Nicholas. Why does one or two more dead bodies help with Lomax?"

"It shows him, whoever it is, can take out his people whenever they want, and there's nothing he can do about it."

Dixx moved his head from side to side, then sat quietly for several minutes. After making eye contact with Lord and Colby, Dixx said, "I'm still out two hundred and fifty thousand dollars and those dead bodies aren't getting me any closer to recovering any of it."

"Can you be sure of that, Mr. Dixx? Nothing like a few dead fellow gang members to jar the memory a bit.

Nothing is happening now to get us any closer to the missing money, so why not rattle the cage a bit more?"

Dixx looked over at Colby. "What do you think?"

"I don't like it, but Mr. Lord may be right. Nothing has happened to move us closer to the lost money. Doing nothing isn't going to change that. Maybe, Mr. Lord is right. Let's keep making waves until something happens."

Dixx smiled at the jumbled way Colby expressed himself, but it made some sense.

"Okay then. Let's rattle the cage again and see what flies out. I'll leave it to you to work out the details. One of you will let me know when it's over, and I'll arrange another sit-down with Mr. Jama Lomax, assuming he's still around."

"Okay, Colby, now that you and Mr. Lord are here, in my little piece of heaven called an apartment, what do you want from me?"

"We need your help, Serenity. If it goes according to plan, it will be a good payday for you, and we, both Mr. Lord and myself, will be indebted to you. You will have two guardian angels for the rest of your life."

"You're not making sense, Colby. Get to the point."

"Lomax is a bad dude. Getting involved with him is not something you want to do. Nothing, and I mean nothing, good can come from the relationship. Trust me, we know.

What we want you to do is simple. There's a club, a bar whose name and address will be provided. We want you to invite Lomax to go with you this Saturday night."

Serenity interrupted. "He won't go alone. He'll take Baxter and Mims with him, plus several bodyguards."

"That's okay. The more the merrier as the saying goes. Once you get there, enjoy yourself. That's all you have to do. Tell him you like the music there, the atmosphere and you think he would enjoy a new place. Just get him there this Saturday, the 6th, and let him do his thing. We'll take care of everything else. It's that simple."

—10—

CHAPTER

NICHOLAS LORD, SEATED AT A CORNER TABLE, WAVED AS THE MAN entered Grace Park's Bar & BBQ. When he reached the table, Lord pointed to the seat across from where he was sitting.

Y K Shin sat down, then lifted the bottle of OB beer. "Nice touch Nicholas. You already have beer waiting."

"I always try to anticipate, Y K," and then Lord smiled.

"You looking well, Nicholas. Things going good for you?"

"They're manageable, Y K, and thanks for meeting me here. I know it's late and you've worked a full shift."

"In fact a shift and a half this night. Boss thinks I number one bartender and thinks with more pay, I do the job of two."

Nicholas laughed. "Your boss knows a good bartender when he sees one, right Y K?"

"Absolutely so, Nicholas. Now, what we do next?"

"There's going to be six people this Saturday at your place. Three black men and three women. We're going to send one of the heug-in namjadeul (Black men-Korean) to a better place."

"How will I know which one, Nicholas?"

"You can pick any one of them and surprise me."

Shin smiled. "You funny man, Nicholas. I never really know your thinking, but you always know how to make things interesting."

"Ah, Y K, aren't surprises the most interesting part of life?"

The Korean wasn't sure what Lord was saying, but nodded in agreement anyway.

"The boss is a tall guy, and will probably be the one ordering. The usual is champagne, Dom Perignon, and maybe a bottle of Remy Martin. Money isn't a problem with them. Do what you have to do and we'll meet here after you close."

Then Lord pushed a white glassine envelope across the table and watched as Shin placed it quickly into one of his pockets.

"I see you here again, Nicholas, on this Saturday night after working," then Shin smiled, stood up and started walking toward the door. He stopped after several steps and said, "Thanks for the beer."

"Hangsang hwan-yeong-ieyo." (Always a pleasure-Korean)

<hr />

Xavier Dixx sat on the deck of his penthouse, looking across the table at Madison.

"You've been staring at me, Xavier, for the last few minutes. Is there something wrong with my make-up?"

"Definitely not. You're always beautiful, make-up or not."

"My, my, such compliments, and the day is only beginning."

Dixx looked at his watch and then back at Madison. "It's almost ten thirty in the morning, and while I was admiring you, Madison, I was thinking about doing something, and this little diversion of ours helped me come to a decision."

"What you just said, Xavier, didn't make much sense to me, but if staring at me helped you decide something, good for me, and good for you. Now if you'll excuse me, I have to do some girl things which will give you some time to do your boy thing."

Dixx couldn't help himself and laughed.

After Madison left the deck, Dixx reached into one of his pockets and took out his cell phone.

When Lomax answered, Dixx said, "This is the Uptown Man. I think we need to have another sit-down tonight. I've developed some information that may be of some value to you."

"Do you know what day it is today, Mr. Uptown Man? It's Saturday, and Saturday night is party night and a bit more. You and your information gonna have to wait until Sunday. Will it hold till then?"

"Yeah, it'll hold. We'll be at the store, say two in the afternoon. You'll be functioning by then, won't you?"

"Don't try to be a smart ass. You can't pull it off."

Dixx smiled as he said, "See you at two Sunday," and then hung up and dialed Colby's number.

"Yes, Mr. Dixx."

"I wanted to bring you up to date on something. I spoke with Lomax moments ago and requested another sit-down tonight. I knew what he was going to say about being obligated and wouldn't be able to, so we fixed the sit-down for tomorrow, Sunday, at two in the afternoon.

I told him we had some information that could be of help to him. This is where I need you and a trusted member of your team. I need to meet both of you here. Telephone me when you're on your way."

+ + ◆ ◆ + + +

When the two men entered, Dixx pointed toward the deck. After they were seated, Colby asked," You remember Jadyn Brason, don't you, Mr. Dixx?"

"Indeed I do. I remember you, Jadyn, as a smart and intelligent young man. Colby, here, made a good choice in selecting you."

Brason looked at Colby, then back at Dixx and smiled.

"Appreciate the compliment, Mr. Dixx. Happy to help you in any way I can."

"What we need, Jadyn, is a little role playing. We're going to meet up tomorrow with Lomax who heads up the Harlem Originals. You know him. We're going to provide some information regarding the death of the previous leader, one Deontay Johnson. Are you with me so far?"

"Yes Mr. Dixx, all ears."

"I'm going to inform him that the people behind the killing of Johnson are the ABN. (Almighty Black Nation) Knowing Lomax as I think I do, he's not going to buy what I'm selling one hundred percent.

That's where you come in. I'm going to introduce you as a member of my organization that successfully infiltrated the ABN as an initiated member. The ABN and the HO's are not exactly kissing cousins and there are some major flare-ups that have occurred between them in the past.

We're going to play on that. You'll be introduced as Grady Robinson, and there is an initiated member of the ABN with that name. Lomax will check to see if someone by that name is a member. When he does, once it's confirmed, he'll accept conclusively the information we've given him.

Lomax isn't going to ask for a photo. Once he receives confirmation of Robinson's gang membership, he'll believe what we told him and then we just sit back and watch the fireworks.

Are you okay with what I just laid out, Jadyn?"

"Absolutely, Mr. Dixx. I know of the ABN's number one, a dude named Cleotha 'Mean Jean' RaJean. I'll make sure to get his name into our talk."

"Okay, we'll meet tomorrow. I'll bring Lord up to date. See you here at one."

———— ✦✦✦✦✦ ————

"Is everything okay?"

"Yes. I know you've been busy with Xavier and Colby and other matters, so I didn't want to bother you."

"You're not bothering me, You never do. You're always in my thoughts, so tell me what's happening."

"Nothing really. Dixx has been okay with me. That's probably because he's got a lot on his mind as you know, so there hasn't been much time for us to be together. That's just fine by me. I've been spending most of my time at my condo, and I hope…"

Lord interrupted. "I've got to take this call, Madison. It's Dixx. We'll talk later."

"Yes, Mr. Dixx."

"We're meeting at my place at one p.m. tomorrow. We have a sit-down with Lomax at two. I'll fill you in then."

"Okay, Mr. Dixx."

"Perfect," and then Dixx pressed the end button.

<hr />

His eyes followed the maitre d' as he led the three couples to a reserved table. Once they were seated, the tall black man placed something in the hand of the maitre d', then spoke briefly.

The maitre d' bowed slightly then turned and walked to where Y K Shin was waiting behind the bar.

"A bottle each of Dom Perignon and Remy."

Shin set both bottles on a tray, then placed eight champagne flutes and six smaller glasses on a separate tray. Then he motioned to a waiter, and pointed to an ice bucket.

"Wait until I come from behind the bar, and then we walk together so that everything is placed down at once. I understand he a good tipper, so let's get it right."

They walked slowly toward Lomax and his party. Once they reached the table, the maitre d' placed the bottles in front of Lomax. The ice bucket was placed slightly to the right of where Lomax was sitting.

Shin placed a champagne flute and glass in front of each person and then took a step back as the maitre d' uncorked the champagne bottle and began the ritual of filling each glass. After he placed the champagne in the ice bucket, he left with the waiter.

Shin began to turn away, then turned back and stared at one of the glasses. He said, "Excuse me. I think one of the flutes is cracked," and he pointed.

He moved around the table and when he reached one of the seated men said, "Pardon me, may I see flute please?"

Mims lifted the glass and held it at eye level. "You're right, it seems to have a slight crack. You have excellent eyesight," and he chuckled as he handed Shin the glass.

"I have another here, sir. It will just be moment."

Shin turned and placed the cracked flute on the tray. Then as he reached for one of the two extra flutes, he pressed his thumb nail against the small glassine packet in the palm of his hand and emptied the contents into the flute. Still keeping his back to Lomax he lifted the bottle out of the ice bucket and filled the flute.

After placing it in front of Mims, Shin said, "Enjoy yourselves. If you need anything, I am behind bar and at your service."

As Shin turned to walk away, Mims siad, "Wait a moment, please."

Shin placed the money in his pocket without looking at it, and said, "Thank you."

Mims smiled back and nodded, then he turned toward Lomax. "May I propose a toast?"

"Go ahead."

Mims lifted his glass and said, "To the good life. May we all enjoy it for a long time to come."

After Lomax placed his empty flute on the table, he said, "I think we need another bottle to get this party started." Then he laughed.

When he caught the bartender's eye, he held up the champagne bottle with one hand and his index finger with the other.

—11—

CHAPTER

LORD PARKED THE BENTLEY COUPE CURBSIDE AND WAITED.

He lowered the passenger side window and watched as the remaining few patrons left the club. Some of the men, aided by their wives or girlfriends, walked unsteadily toward the parking garage or the line of waiting taxis.

A few minutes after one a.m. Shin, together with a fellow colleague, walked out, and Lord tapped lightly on the horn.

Shin walked over and leaned into the open window. "This surprise, Nicholas. We supposed to meet at Grace's."

"I thought this would be easier. Please get in."

After Shin closed the door, Lord started the car and drove several blocks before he pulled over again.

After turning off the engine, Lord asked, "How did everything go?"

"No problems, Nicholas."

"Which one of the three did you send on vacation?"

"Don't know how to describe. They all look same to me."

Lord couldn't help himself and laughed. Shin smiled back, unsure of why Lord was laughing.

"That's funny Y K, what you just said about all the blacks looking alike. I remember when I first arrived in Korea and went to the Seoul Club, the expat club, (A person living outside their native country) and someone said to me, 'Don't worry about telling them apart. Right now I'm sure they all look the same to you.' That's why I was laughing."

Shin smiled and then said, "Michaso, you michaso namja, Nicholas. " (Crazy, you crazy man-Korean)

Lord laughed again. "I guess I am crazy. Maybe we both are Y K, but would you want it any other way?"

"No, Nicholas. All Americans are crazy, and now I American."

They both laughed in a way that friends do.

"Well, we'll see over the next few days which one it is." Then Lord reached into his pocket and handed Shin an envelope. "As I've always said, my hyeong, (Brother-Korean) I wouldn't know what to do without you."

"I feel same, Nicholas. You will always be my chingu." (Friend-Korean)

"Okay, I'll drive you home."

"I don't know about that. How much cost?" Then Shin laughed and Nicholas joined in as he started the car.

———— ✦✦✦✦✦ ————

Nicholas Lord, Colby and Jadyn sat at one side of a table facing Xavier Dixx.

"That's it. That's the way it will go down. If Lomax buys it, we've created a diversion for a while longer. If he doesn't, we're no worse off than we were before."

Dixx stopped speaking for several seconds and then started again. "As you've explained it, Nicholas, nothing will happen to either Lomax or one of his lieutenants for several more days. Symptoms, as you've stated, will develop first and then death. Let them wonder how that death was orchestrated. Some heat should be taken off us and placed on the Almighty Black Nation, but we'll see if that happens."

Dixx looked over at Jadyn and then said. "Don't let us down. Pull this off, and you'll never look back. If everybody is ready, let's go."

As Dixx and Lord exited the vehicle, Colby touched Jadyn's shoulder and said, "Wait on the sidewalk until I come around."

Jadyn nodded, opened the Maserati's door and then stood quietly with his back to the storefront entrance.

After Colby walked around the rear of the vehicle, he pointed at the car door and said, "Close the damn door, and get your brains unscrambled."

Dixx and Lord entered the storefront with Colby and Jadyn several steps behind. As Colby passed by the tall black man standing again at the door's right side, he motioned with his thumb back at the parked Maserati Quattroporte, and said quietly, "Eat your heart out."

The black quickly responded, "I'm looking forward to the day when I'll be driving that car to your funeral."

Colby smiled, "Your mother should have swallowed you," then laughed as he and Jadyn entered the building.

They followed Dixx and Lord into the same room where the previous sit-down was held. Lomax motioned to the chairs on the opposite side of the table where he, Baxter and Mims were sitting.

As soon as they were seated, Lomax pointed at Jadyn and asked, "Who the fuck is this dork?"

Jadyn started to get up when Colby reached out and placed his hand on his shoulder and then looked over at Dixx, who nodded back.

Jadyn kept his eyes on Lomax as he brushed Colby's hand away and then sat back down.

Once Jadyn was again seated, Colby said, "That's no way to begin a sit-down, Mr. Lomax, but since this is your territory, I guess you can pretty much do and say what you want."

Colby looked at Dixx who shook his head again in a way that indicated, continue you're doing just fine. "We've requested this sit-down because we've developed some directory assistance (Gang slang for information) that we believe can be of value to you, and this dork, as you've referred to him, obtained the DA."

"And by the way, Mr.Lomax, the dork's name is Grady Robinson, an initiated member of the Almighty Black Nation."

Lomax was on his feet, and two of his heavies (Bodyguards) standing behind the table drew the weapons and pointed them at Colby and Jadyn.

Colby held up his hand and said, "No need for that. Nothing of a threatening nature intended. I'm just telling you he's an initiated member of the ABM, but in reality he works for me…us. He's undercover there and not a threat to you or your organization, Mr. Lomax. So put…please put away those fucking guns and listen to the rest of what I'm trying to tell you."

Lomax bristled as he sat down, then waved his hand in the air as a signal to put the guns away.

"This better be good, Colby. You all got my attention and what you tell me better be good or I'm going to fry some cracker ass today."

Dixx started to speak, when Lomax waved his hand in a no motion.

"I don't want to hear from you, Uptown. Let Colby speak and if it ain't what I want to hear, you can then try to save the day, because I'm raging at about one hundred degrees inside me and that is going to spill over on you all very soon."

Colby stared at Lomax for a number of seconds. When he felt the gang leader's anger subsided somewhat, he began speaking.

"Grady Robinson has been an initiated member of the ABN for a number of months. I know the…" and then Colby paused for a few seconds as he tried to think of the proper word. When he began again he said, "…problems you've had with the ABN. Since you are our only distribution outlet in Harlem, we want to keep it that way.

The murder of Deontay was as much of a shock to us as it was to you. Something has given you cause to think that we are involved. That's bullshit, and ain't correct. We have more, or as much to lose as you do. When we asked for the previous sit-down it was because we wanted to make sure you knew where we stood…where our loyalties were.

When we left that meeting all of us felt that you still harbored some misguided beliefs that we had something to do with the blow away. (Killing) We brought our man here to set the record straight for you once and for all."

Colby pointed at Jadyn.

"My name is Grady Robinson. I work as part of Mr. Colby's team and we are all part of the organization that Mr. Dixx is head of. Our organization likes to know everything about everyone so that we're not surprised by something or someone who wants to change things as they presently exist. When I was asked to infiltrate the ABN, I didn't hesitate. They were the enemy, our enemy just like they are yours. I started to hang at the bar that the ABN controls, you know the one, the one with the fuck up name, the 'Candy Rabbit.'

I got to know a few of the ABN and after a month or so, I was asked to join. After the jump in (Ritual of initiation) I did the usual shit...sit around, drink, sell drugs, shake down a few..." then Jadyn stopped speaking, and a second or two later said, "...dorks, and jacked a few cars. It was petty shit but it got me closer to my so-called brothers.

At the meetings, the Elder, which is how they refer to Cleotha 'Mean Jean' RaJean, the conversation always came around to the Harlem Originals. Mean Jean felt that if they could take out your main man, Deontay Johnson, they would weaken you significantly so that they could take over the drug distribution.

I wasn't privy to how they planned to do the bump, (Killing) but it was definitely orchestrated by Mean Jean and the ABN. This is only the first bump. The ABN is planning another against you, and it's already in progress."

Jadyn stopped and looked at Colby, who nodded his head slightly.

"If what you say is true, I...we, the HO's owe you," and then Lomax looked at Dixx. "If I find out, and I will, that you all been planking (Lying - gang slang) us, we gonna do some dancing on your fucking heads."

Lomax locked eyes with Dixx, then with Lord, Colby, and finally Jadyn.

"If there's nothing else, this sit-down is over. We'll be in touch, guaranteed!"

———— ✦✦✦✦ ————

As soon as they pulled away from the sit-down, Dixx tapped Jadyn's shoulder. When the young black man turned, Dixx said, "That performance was definitely worthy of an Oscar. However, since I don't have any, this envelope should suffice and then some. You did extremely well, and you have a definite future with us."

Jadyn smiled. "I had a few moments if you know what I mean, Mr. Dixx."

"I do, but you managed everything well. They'll check to see if a Grady Robinson is an ABN member. Once they determine you exist, it should end there. If it doesn't, we'll know soon enough."

When Colby brought the car to a stop at the entrance to Dixx's building, Dixx leaned forward and said, "After you drop Jadyn off, please come back to the apartment. We have some additional matters to discuss."

"Will do, Mr. Dixx," then Colby waited until Dixx and Lord disappeared through the building entrance.

"Where to, Jadyn?"

"I don't need a ride anywhere, Mr. Colby. I'm okay. Thanks for everything," then Jadyn waved the envelope as he got out of the car.

Colby watched Jadyn walk away, then he started the car and drove into the building's parking garage.

—12—

CHAPTER

NICHOLAS LORD FOLLOWED DIXX INTO THE PENTHOUSE. AS HE WALKED through the doorway he moved his eyes in a one hundred and eighty degree sweep, but didn't see her.

Once he was seated on the penthouse deck, he thought about the last time he'd spoken with her, justifying the inaction by thinking about what he had to do over the last several days. Then he thought, what a crock, of course there is always time. All I needed to do was make it happen.

Dixx asked, "Is there something wrong, Nicholas. You have that far away look in your eyes?"

"No, Mr, Dixx, just going over the events of the past several days."

"And what have you concluded?"

"Lomax is no fool. He didn't get to where he is now because he's stupid. We helped him secure the number one position by vacationing Deontay Johnson, but he was always a strong number two. You don't get there unless you do it all, from all the strong arm stuff to the blow-aways." (Killings)

The dude is crazy smart. He'll check to find out if our Grady Robinson is the real thing, and he'll get the confirmation, somehow, that Robinson is an initiated gangbanger of the Almighty Black Nation. That may satisfy him for the moment, and convey that we were trying to help him. The last thing he wants or needs is a rumble, (Gang war) and that will happen if he retaliates against the ABN. He'll bide his time, wait it out to see what occurs next with the ABN and us.

We're not out of the woods yet as far as his suspicions go. He still feels, believes, that we're somehow connected with what happened to Johnson. The way Johnson died is a bit too sophisticated for the ABN. Then again, his brain might register that it was a molotov cocktail, not necessarily a remote explosive device.

When one of his lieutenants or even Lomax himself meets his maker," and then Lord smiled, "whoever is left will think first of the ABN, and then shift to us. We have to wait and see which one of them journeys to another world. My man said, and I'm quoting here, "I don't know which one was poisoned. The blacks all look the same to me."

Lord laughed and Colby, who had just stepped onto the deck, joined in along with Dixx.

"Nice summation, Nicholas," then Dixx looked over at Colby who said, "I heard some on the way in and I'm okay with it. We need to wait and see what happens after the unfortunate demise of another Harlem Original."

"Okay, if there's nothing more, you gentlemen can enjoy the rest of your Sunday."

Lord said his goodbyes, along with Colby, and then they took the elevator together to the parking garage.

As they stood next to Lord's car, Nicholas said, "Nice job with Jadyn. I think he just might have pulled it off."

Colby nodded, "Maybe we lucked out for a while. Once the second HO is vacationed and word gets around, anything could happen. We need to be careful and stay alert. Just maybe, whether they believe we are or aren't involved, they may try to send a message to us by bumping one of us. What does a dead cracker mean to them, one way or another?"

"I hear you. Can Jadyn be trusted?"

"A hundred percent, never! That goes for most of who we know and some who work for and with us."

Lord smiled. "Right on! Okay, I'm out of here, Enjoy what's left of Sunday."

Nicholas drove the forty-five plus minutes to Connecticut and when he entered his cul-de-sac, he saw the Mercedes convertible parked in front of his house. He thought, great timing!

He pulled into the garage and then walked through the laundry room, the kitchen and into the living room where Madison was seated at the piano trying to pick out the melody to 'Over the Rainbow.'

"Sounds pretty good. And you're a welcomed surprise."

"Oh yeah! How so?"

"I was thinking about you earlier today."

"Only earlier today? I would have thought, Mr. Lord, that you would be thinking of me constantly. I am somewhat addictive."

"Oh, indeed you are, Madison," and then he bent down and kissed her.

"Like wow! That was definitely worth the trip," and she smiled.

"How did you get away and how's it going with Dixx?"

"So many questions, Nicholas. Well, Dixx is a busy man right now, as you well know. I've been at the penthouse less than usual, but he seems okay with it. Maybe he's just a good actor and storing up whatever he's feeling for the right time."

"If he believes, and he does, Madison, that there's something going on between you and me, he's definitely going to act at some point. Right now he's up to his ears in alligators and he's got to tame them or kill them before we're a consideration."

"And how much time is that?"

"No idea at the moment, but it isn't something that's going to happen tomorrow or the day after tomorrow. I'll have a good feeling for when it seems likely, and I'll handle it."

"Will you, Nicholas, handle it in time?"

"I think so. My life and yours depends on it. Now to change the subject, what would you like to do?'"

Madison took hold of Lord's hand and led him toward the bedroom.

————————— ✦✦✦✦✦✦ —————————

Colby pressed down on the TV's volume button, then picked up his cell phone. After looking at the name, he said, "I was expecting to hear from you."

Serenity thought, yeah guess you did, then said, "Lomax left here in a rage, a real shit-fit. After cursing up a storm and throwing a few things around, Baxter was able to calm him somewhat. Seems Mims' girlfriend called and he's in North General Hospital on East 122nd Street. Seems he has a high fever and some other stuff. That's all I know. Baxter and some of the boys went with him to the hospital. Me, I'm going back home. This isn't gonna be a good day to hang around here."

"Give me a minute. I'm thinking.

"No, Serenity, stick around there. Lomax will return and you might pick up additional information that will be helpful to us. He isn't gonna bother you. He has other things on his mind," and Colby chuckled. "I, we, won't forget what you're doing for us. Just act natural, stay calm and don't worry. Talk to me later today if you have anything further, and thanks again. You'll be very well compensated."

Serenity hung up without saying anything further.

Colby dialed Lord's number. "It's happened. Mims was the target and he's now in North General on 122nd. Seems he was taken there with a high fever."

"That's only the beginning of his problems," and Lord laughed. "Was it Serenity who told you?"

"Yes."

"Okay. I'll clue in Dixx."

"There's another thing, Mr. Lord. Serenity wanted to go home. Seems when Lomax heard the news, he went bonkers and it scared the shit out of her. I think I calmed her down okay, and told her to hang around until Lomax and his crew returned.

Told her she might pick up some additional info that could be of value to us. I tried to insure her that despite the fact that Lomax is somewhat fucked-up now over Mims, she's not in any real danger. Told her to play it cool, act natural, let events happen, and that she'd be well compensated."

"Okay, I got it. If there's anything up after I speak with Dixx, I'll be in contact. If you don't hear from me, it's just that we're waiting for whatever happens to happen, and you'll probably know that before we do."

"Okay, Mr. Lord. Talk with you soon."

"I prefer to meet one on one if you know what I mean, Nicholas. These cell phones, any phone is subject to who knows what and any conversation could be monitored. Maybe I'm old world, but nothing like face to face conversations."

Lord shook his head yes as he listened to Dixx, then replied, "The woman, Serenity, telephoned Colby. In short Lomax went ballistic when he heard Mims was taken to North General. The Thallium Sulphate we used was the same poison that vacationed Santaigo Perez.

Right now Mims has a high fever which will be followed by a coma and then death. I doubt if he'll survive the day. Lomax will want revenge and I'm betting that the Almighty Black Nation is going to get a taste of it first. Based on Jadyn's performance the other day, Lomax will check to see if Grady Robinson is an ABN gangbanger and once that's confirmed, and it probably already is, he'll buy what we told him. When Mims dies, the rumble starts. We just sit back and see where the dust settles."

Dixx moved his hand to his chin and held it there for several minutes. Then he lowered his hand, and smoothed his eyebrow with two fingers. "Yes, I guess we wait and see. Based on what transpires, we can then decide how and when we move."

"One more thing, Mr. Dixx. The girl, Serenity, is our source of information on how Lomax is reacting. We want her there and Colby has been smoothing her feathers and propping her up by telling her how valuable an asset she is. We need to pay her something. I need some money to pass to Colby. It'll show her that we're the real deal and what we say, we do."

Dixx nodded and then got up from his chair. "Be back in a moment."

After handing Lord an envelope, Dixx said, "Keep me updated. Also, Nicholas, you'll have to tell me how you managed to poison Perez and Mims. Maybe you can introduce me to your associates."

"One day for sure, Mr. Dixx."

As Nicholas rode down in the elevator to the parking garage level, he thought about the strange request Dixx made regarding meeting his associates. Maybe he wants to know all the players so when the time comes, the spider will entrap all of us in his web and then eat us alive.

Lord laughed as he entered his Bentley Continental Coup. Then he said just above a whisper, "Yes indeed, the spider is always hungry, but sometimes the spider underestimates his prey."

13

CHAPTER

JAMAL LOMAX SLAMMED HIS FIST AGAINST THE TABLE AS HE SHOUTED, "NO ONE does a blow-away (Killing) against us and lives. Mims is dead. I don't have a fucking clue how it happened, but that ABN (Almighty Black Nation) plant that 'Uptown' brought with him on the last sit-down told us who was gonna do it. If the fucking ABN wants a KU, (Gang war) we'll give 'em one."

Thirty plus Harlem Original gang members crowding the room, shouted in agreement as they stamped their feet, cursed, and made gang signs with their hands.

"We gonna do a 'lil payback and it will be one them fuckers will never forget."

———— ♦♦♦♦♦ ————

Lomax telephoned Xavier Dixx that same afternoon.

"Uptown, I'm gonna need a favor. I need a sit-down. I need to discuss something with you and it can't be done on the phone. You wanna meet me at grandma's house (My place) or somewhere else?"

"I'm always willing to listen and if I can help, I will. Let's meet at grandma's house as you suggested. When?"

As Dixx waited for the reply he couldn't help smiling at the way Lomax described his headquarters.

"Like now. How soon can you get here?"

An hour later, Dixx, Lord and Colby sat with Lomax, his number two, Baxter, and a new lieutenant, Elijah Carter, and three soldiers.

"I appreciate your coming. Ain't gonna forget this. Let's finish the drinks and I'll get down to business."

A minute later, Lomax began. "Mims is dead. How the fuck it happened I don't have a clue. But based on what your man Robinson said, it's the ABN that's responsible."

Dixx shook his head, feigning surprise as he looked at Lord and Colby, then back at Lomax. "We just talked about this happening and I'm surprised it happened so quickly."

"When shit happens, it always happens quickly. We aim to settle a few things and I need some help from you."

After a brief pause, Lomax started again. "I wanna make a connection tonight. I need a white dude to drive a soccer mom (Van) which I'll provide. I'm gonna rattle Mean Jean's cage by taking out a few of his homeboys who operate between 120th Street and 142nd Street. It'll work better with a white dude driving because how many brothers are gonna be drivin' soccer moms to Harlem to buy drugs?"

Lomax laughed. "Right on, but funny, right?"

When no one spoke up Lord said, "Sounds right to me."

"Okay, now let's map out where we're gonna hit them. The snatch and grab should be over real quickly, then we'll..." Lomax stopped talking.

When he started again, he said, "TMI (Too much information) ain't good. Let's say I'm gonna deliver tonight and if it's okay with you, Mr. Dixx, I'd like either of your boys here to drive."

Dixx looked over at Lord. "Are you okay with that, Nicholas?"

"I have no plans for tonight, so I'm available."

Dixx smiled as he looked at Lomax. "I leave you and Mr. Lord, work out the details. Nicholas will bring me up to date when it's over, won't you, Nicholas?"

Lord nodded a yes, then watched as Dixx and Colby walked out.

Lomax turned to Lord. What do we call you?"

"You can call me Lord, Nicholas, Hey You, or any other thing you want. I'm easy," and then Lord laughed.

Lomax wasn't sure what Lord was trying to state, but he smiled and nodded.

"Okay Lord, this is the way it's going down. You be drivin' the soccer mom with Baxter here riding shotgun and his crew in the back. The interior lights in the van have already been disconnected. Elgin," and Lomax pointed to a tall black dude, "and Gaynor over there, are gonna be in two shadow cars following the soccer mom. All three vehicles have been twocked (Stolen) and the license plates switched. Nothing is gonna be traced back here.

After you make the snatch, you drive the soccer mom as close to the ABN clubhouse as you can. If the clubhouse or the surrounding area is hot with ABNers, you find a place to ditch the soccer mom where you ain't gonna get burned.

Once you ditch the soccer mom, leave the van running. If it's jacked before any ABN shits checks it out, too fuckin' bad. If the jakes (Cops) nail whoever it is that jacks the soccer mom, that's life in the fast lane and it's their tough luck if they go up the river for killing those shits. The dead bodies may take some time to identify, but word will eventually filter back to Mean Jean regarding the unclaimed cargo in the back."

Lomax shook his head and laughed. "He'll know what happened to three or more of his gangbangers, but the shit won't know who bumped (Killed) them. You do the usual with the two cars.

Okay, now all of you, get the fuck out of here. It's party time."

———— ✦✦✦✦ ————

Lord drove slowly along 123rd Street until Baxter pointed and said, "Pull over at the corner. The shit standing in the shadows will come out and walk to your side after you stop. Tell the fuck you wanna buy a nickel bag of horse, (Heroin) then we'll take it from there. You just sit tight, no matter what, understand?"

Lord nodded as Baxter left the passenger seat and moved into the back of the van.

Once Lord pulled over, it was a minute or so before the man moved from the shadows and walked into the street stopping at the driver's side window.

"I need a nickel bag of horse."

"That's gonna be one hundred green."

Lord reached for his wallet, removed two fifty dollar bills and held them up.

"Place them in my shirt pocket."

"Okay, I'll be back in a few seconds white boy. Sit tight."

Just as the candy man (Drug pusher) turned, the van door on the driver's side opened and four masked men pounced on the surprised man before he had a chance to react. Beaten until he was unconscious, they quickly loaded the inert body into the van where they duct taped his mouth and tied his hands and legs together with wire rope.

"Get moving Lord…like burn some fucking rubber."

"I'm moving, but it's got to be in the normal way. I don't want some cop looking to alter his bored routine to stop us for speeding. You got that, Mr. Baxter? Also, reach into that dude's shirt pocket and hand me back my two fifties."

Baxter handed Lord the money as he moved again into the passenger seat. "Keep driving to 131st Street. We're gonna repeat the action movie again."

Baxter laughed and then the crew joined in.

"How are you enjoying things so far, Lord?"

"I'm having the time of my life."

"I bet you are. You uptown folks, don't get much opportunity to enjoy what we POCs (People of color) have to offer," and then he started laughing again.

"It's a fun night, Baxter. We'll definitely have to do this more often," and Lord started laughing.

As they neared the end of 131ˢᵗ Street, Lord stopped the van at the corner before Baxter had a chance to say anything.

"As he moved into the rear, Baxter said, "You're a fast learner, Lord. Might even make you one of my crew."

"Can't wait," then Lord watched as two men walked over to his side of the van.

"Looking for a nickel bag of horse."

"That's one fifty green."

Lord removed his wallet and held up three fifties.

The other man waited until Lord handed over the money, then said, "Wait. We'll be back with the brown sugar in a few…"

Before the man could finish, the driver's side door opened and four men with ski masks and drawn guns surrounded the two men.

Baxter smashed his pistol against one of the men's skulls. As he fell, another of Baxter's crew slammed his face with brass knuckles he was wearing on his right hand, breaking the nose and cracking the cheek bone. The other man was punched repeatedly until he was unconscious.

Both bodies were quickly loaded into the van, taped and wire tied. Seconds later the van's door was slammed shut and the van was moving toward the Almighty Black Nation's clubhouse on 125ᵗʰ, considered one of the most dangerous streets in the United States.

Baxter sitting in the passenger seat again turned to face Lord. "A very productive night, wouldn't you say, Lord?"

"Depends on what you're measuring it by."

"You some kind of college boy, Lord, with all this and that shit talk?"

"I've got a piece of paper that says I am, but to tell you the truth Baxter, I only went there to hook up with the ladies so I could spread my charm."

"You are one funny white cracker, Lord. I'm definitely gonna ask Jamal if I can have you as part of my crew," then Baxter laughed until one of his crew called out, "It's over."

Baxter nodded and raised his arm, then pumped it a few times.

"Maybe I'm becoming too inquisitive, but do tell, what's over?"

Baxter answered, "The surgery."

"Okay, I give up. What surgery?"

"Marcus and the boys slit their fucking throats and packed them for FedEx delivery in some nice garbage bags."

Lord shook his head as he said, "We're coming up on 125th Street."

"Stop now. The shadow cars are behind us about fifty or so yards. The boys in the back will exit now and walk to the cars. We're gonna continue. Keep the headlights off."

Once the three men were out of the van, Baxter pointed. "Go slow and make a right turn at the corner. If everything is okay we park this soccer mom and go back home. Easy now, as I take a look see."

"Don't seem like there are any shits walking the line. Guess the fucks are partying up inside or whatever. Stop here but keep the engine on."

The two men, ski masks covering their faces, got out and walked quickly to the shadow cars.

"You get in this one with Elgin. He'll take you where you want to go. See ya around, Lord, and until we meet up again, don't do anything to get yourself in trouble." Then Baxter laughed as he closed the door.

Elgin put the car in gear and started driving as he asked, "Where do you wanta go?"

"Please drive to 5th Avenue. I'll direct you from there."

Lord waved as he walked away from the car and down the ramp into the parking garage of Dixx's building.

Once he was inside his car he sat staring at the windshield and contemplating whether he should update Dixx. After looking at his watch, he said above a whisper, "It can wait until morning."

Lord started the Bentley and headed toward the Hutchinson River Parkway, which would take him home to Connecticut.

As he drove, he wondered why Dixx was so quick to volunteer him instead of Colby who usually did the heavy lifting. Then an image of Madison floated across his mind screen and he knew. If something happened, a problem would be eliminated, and Dixx's hands would remain clean.

— 14 —

CHAPTER

GRADY ROBINSON TURNED TO HIS FELLOW GANG MEMBER AND HELD out two marijuana cigarettes. "Do you want to fire these up, DeAndre?"

"Sure why not. The beer ain't givin' me no buzz."

"Let's go outside, too much noise in here between all the talking and the rappin'. If they don't turn the damn volume down, we all gonna be fucking deaf."

DeAndre laughed as he followed Grady Robinson out the back door of the clubhouse.

Robinson handed one of the cigarettes to DeAndre and watched as his friend lit up.

When DeAndre let the smoke out he said, "Good shit, Grady. Must be someone else's grass, 'cause all we sell is bamboo. (Low quality marijuana)

"Yeah, this is AK47 (High quality marijuana) that them Park Avenue crackers like, and are willing to pay bookoo bucks for. Enjoy!"

"I tell ya, DeAndre, we ought to cut and go to one of the cubs and hook up with some skirts (Women) and do some dancing in and out of bed."

Robinson laughed, and then said, "Yep, we are wasting ourselves away here. Ain't nothing going down except drinking and wasting a good night away."

"Yeah, you right, Grady, let's cut out and find some skirts."

As Robinson turned he saw the outline of a parked van near the corner.

"Wait a minute! Look back the way I'm pointing. What do you see, DeAndre?"

"Yeah, okay. I see it. How the fuck did we miss it when we came out. I think the engine is running. Listen."

"Yep, you're right. Shouldn't be here. I'm gonna take a look see. You coming?"

"Yeah, I'm coming."

Both men walked slowly toward the van. You carrying, DeAndre?"

Never without it, bro."

"Get it out."

It's already in my left hand."

"Shoulda known," and Robinson chuckled. "Careful now. We don't need no surprises. You take the passenger side. I'll do the driver's side."

After they cleared the van's cab, Robinson said, "Go in the back and open the doors."

Moments later the doors opened. "You ain't gonna believe what's here."

Robinson moved closer and looked inside. One of the three green garbage bags was opened and as DeAndre pointed, Robinson stared at the body of one of his fellow gang members.

"Open the other two."

DeAndre opened the other two bags and then stared in disbelief. "Mother fucker...who the fuck..." and then his voice trailed into silence.

"I'm getting, MJ."

Gang members shoved and pushed their way out of the clubhouse and ran toward the van. When Mean Jean held up his hand, the group became quiet.

"Let me have a look and stay quiet until I see what we've got."

After a number of seconds, Mean Jean RaJean turned and faced his fellow gang members.

"Okay, somebody did a blow away on us. Labond, Fenton and Kool-aid are dead. We gonna find out who, and then we'll make some pay-back. Meantime you all stay cool. You don't do shit unless I or Travor or the Ghost here, tells you to. Do all of you understand that?"

A chorus of yeahs and okays pierced the night air.

"Okay, the party is over. Go and do whatever, and we meet here tomorrow morning at nine. If any of you develop anything I wanna know like yesterday. Otherwise, I'll clue you all in with what I have then. Keep it quiet as you leave and no rumbling, ya hear?"

MJ pointed to Robinson and DeAndre. "Get this motherfucking van outta here, and like quick. Can't be ditched near here, understand? Now go!"

Robinson shifted the van into drive. As the van moved toward 124th Street, he turned to DeAndre in the passenger seat. "Got any ideas?"

"There's a vacant lot near 1st Avenue."

"Don't wanna drive that far. This is one hot vehicle and I wanna ditch it as quick as I can. Keep your eyes open for somewhere, anywhere. I got a bad feein' about this one."

As the van approached 125th street, the red light of a police cruiser flashed and the siren blared.

"We're in deep shit. I ain't going back to the wire city." (Jail)

"Don't be stupid, Grady, We can't kill a pig." (Cop)

"Why not. With what we have in the back, we're dead meat. We gonna get life or they'll burn us."

"When the cop moved slowly toward the van he called for backup. Placing his right hand print just below the tail light on the driver's side to show that he was there in case something happened, the police officer said, "Driver, open the door and exit the van. Keep your hands up and don't do anything unless I tell you. Now do it!"

Robinson opened the door and moved out slowly, lifting the back part of his shirt with his left hand to show he had no weapons.

"I said both hands in the air. Do it now."

Robinson let go of his shirt with his left hand as he dropped quickly to a kneeling position, twisted his body toward the police officer, and as he fell sideways, fired several shots.

One of the bullets was stopped by the officer's armored vest. The other impacted his neck and severed his carotid artery. He bled out quickly and was dead when his backup arrived moments after the shooting.

The network TV and print media who monitor the mobile police communication system arrived on the scene just as DeAndre and Grady Robinson were taken into custody.

——————— ⋅✦✦✦✦⋅ ———————

"Okay Mr. Dixx, see you at ten."

Lord placed the cell phone in his pocket then walked through the kitchen and into the garage. Fifty-five minutes later he was seated with Colby and Dixx on the penthouse deck.

After Madison placed the coffee and pastries on the table, she smiled at Lord. "Nice to see you again, Nicholas."

"Likewise, Madison."

As Lord turned back and reached for his coffee cup he wondered what must be going through Dixx's mind, but let the thought dissipate when Dixx began speaking.

"Did you have an interesting night, Nicholas?"

Lord thought immediately of the Chinese proverb, that when they wish ill upon a person they say, 'May you live in interesting times.' Lord wondered whether there was a connection of sorts.

"I guess you could say that. It was a productive night for Lomax. The ABN are minus three gangbangers. Left the van near their clubhouse, lights off and motor running. Went home and that's about it."

"There's more, Nicholas," and Dixx moved a folded newspaper across the table.

As Lord opened the paper he asked, "What am I supposed to see?"

"Look just under the lead story on the front page. The headline is, 'Murder in Harlem, Police Officer Killed'. Two men were arrested. Take a few minutes and read the article. Also look at the two photographs and zero in on the names of the two gang members they arrested."

Lord scanned the article then stared at the prison photos of the two gangbangers. After a moment he looked up and locked eyes with Dixx.

"Yes. One of the bangers is Grady Robinson, the real deal. Maybe, Nicholas, Lomax didn't get past second grade, but Baxter or Lomax's new lieutenant, Elijah Carter, might be able to read. Either way, Lomax is going to see this photo and the name under it.

He'll know that the man we said was Grady Robinson wasn't so, and he'll connect the dots and those dots will link us to the killings of Deontay Johnson and Mims. Lomax will figure we played him and suckered him into a gang war with the ABN.

I'm still out two hundred and fifty thousand dollars, and no closer to recovering it than I was when all this started."

"Maybe, just maybe, Mr. Dixx, you're jumping to conclusions. These gangbangers don't read newspapers. Their IQ is in the single digits. Shootings in New York, especially Harlem, is a daily occurrence. So if someone reports to Lomax that two ABN gangbangers were arrested and one was named Robinson, he'll figure it was our plant.

The way his mind likely works, is he'll think we lost our man in the ABN, and that's tough bananas for us. In a few hours, certainly another day at most, it's yesterday's news."

Dixx moved his right hand to his chin, stared at the skyscrapers that dotted the New York skyline, and then turned back and looked at Lord.

"Could be you're right, Nicholas, but what if you're wrong?"

"Let's wait, see what happens over the next few hours. If I'm right, we're okay, and if I'm not we'll figure out something to do to make it right."

"Maybe we should nip it in the bud. Contact Lomax and give him the info as if we're doing everything we can to help him."

"I'm just not sure we should move anything along that could cause us a problem. If it happens on its own, then we react." Lord looked over at Colby. "What's your take on the situation?"

"I don't think we should tell Lomax anything. The news about the killing of the cop supposedly by the two gangbangers in custody, will be history shortly. We should just stay loose and let things happen naturally."

Dixx shifted his eyes away from Colby and looked again at Lord.

"Okay Gentlemen, then let's leave things as is. If there's nothing more, have a pleasant day."

Colby and Lord rode the elevator together to the parking garage. As Lord started walking to where his car was parked, Colby called out, "Wait a minute."

Lord turned and met Colby half-way.

"I'm not comfortable with how things stand, meaning there's going to be trouble and I think we're going to find ourselves in the middle. Dixx isn't street smart. He's plenty smart, but coming from the mean streets makes a difference. He can't feel things like I can and maybe you. He can't relate to a minor this or that as a sign of bigger shit to come. He lives in the stratosphere of the good life and lets us do the down and dirty for him.

I don't have a problem with that and I guess you don't either since you're still here and working for the man. He pays pretty good and so far we're all in one piece, but I tell ya, Mr. Lord, it feels like it's all going to come crashing down."

Lord rubbed his right eye with the back of his hand, then looked at Colby. "I agree with you in part. Things are going to boil over shortly. Dixx is still out two hundred and fifty thousand because he agreed to take payment in crypto.

I'm a college boy and I don't fully understand that crypto shit. Maybe Lomax is smarter than we think, and he managed to take the money back somehow. How, I don't have the foggiest idea, but someone opened that so-called wallet and emptied it.

I'm still thinking that Lomax is the primary problem we face, and now that the ABN gangbangers have surfaced, we, you and me, have some real problems. I can't help thinking that somehow we're going to get that accusing finger pointed at us. Then some tall tales about murder are going to circulate, fingering us as the ones who made it happen. Then we're open season for both the HOs and the ABNs."

Colby let several moments pass, then asked, "What about the shipment from Mexico? It's due to arrive in the next several days?"

"That's not my area of responsibility. Even if Dixx changed his plans, he probably wouldn't inform me since I'm not in that loop. But he should keep you clued in. Why not telephone him now and ask him if you can come back up for a few minutes and find out."

Colby shook his head in a way that indicated he agreed with what Lord just said. "I'll do that. Let's continue this conversation. I'll telephone you later today regarding what Dixx says, okay?"

Lord nodded. "I'll look forward to your call," then turned and walked to his car.

— 15 —

CHAPTER

CLEOTHA RAJEAN HELD UP HIS HAND AND THE GROUP BECAME QUIET. My contacts came up empty, nothing out there that they could find that pointed to any group or anyone that took out Labond, Fenton and Kool-Aid...not a damn thing and that's real strange. Anyone here got anything?"

No one responded and RaJean muttered, "Fuck."

"This ain't sittin' right. We lost two candymen (Drug street sellers) and a block lieutenant to some mother fuckers, got Robinson and DeAndre in the can (Jail) and no one here or on the streets has a clue who and why it happened. It just doesn't jive right."

A gangbanger standing at the back called out, "MJ."

RaJean looked toward where the voice came from and then said, "Yeah, Sparrow, you got something?"

"Don't know for sure. Some wannabes who live at the project tell me that Lomax has been visited by some upscale crackers over the last few weeks."

"Okay, Sparrow, stick around. I wanna hear more. Anyone else got anything?"

When no one replied, RaJean said, "Okay, you all got work to do. Hit the streets and get me something."

The gangbanger called Sparrow waited until the clubhouse emptied and then he walked up to where RaJean was standing. After motioning to his second in command, RaJean led the way to a small room, then pointed at a table.

Once the three were seated, RaJean pointed at the gangbanger.

"I have some okay relations with some wannabes who live at the project. They ain't our type material, but I keep string 'em along for whatever skinny (Information) they can give me. Seems some crackers been visiting the HO's clubhouse more than just a couple of times. The dude that doing the talkin' didn't know why, but tells me that it ain't the usual with these honkies (White people) to be visiting that often.

They're driving a fancy car but he didn't ID the car. Based on that, and what's gone down with our two candymen, the block lieutenant, and Grady and DeAndre, I'd say the HO's are involved."

After a few moments passed, RaJean asked, "Anything else, Sparrow?"

"No MJ. I'll massage the wannabes to get more skinny. If there's anything else I'll let you know."

"Okay, Sparrow. Well done. Ain't gonna forget it."

After the gangbanger left, RaJean turned to his second in command. "Whatja think, Adwin?"

"Maybe a connection with the HO's. Everything is possible and I think we ought to set up a lookout and see if those white boys pay another visit. We get the license plate number and run it through the PoPo (Police Officer) we have on the payroll at the two five precinct."

"Yeah, agree, You set it up. Meantime I'll continue to push at my end. We'll get something, got that feelin' and it'll happen soon."

———— ✦✦✦✦✦✦ ————

Colby dialed Xavier Dixx's cell number as he stood watching Lord's car exit the garage.

"Sorry to bother you, Mr. Dixx. I'm still in the garage and was thinking that we didn't discuss the shipment."

There was a pause, before Dixx said, "Come up."

Madison opened the door for Colby and pointed toward the deck. "Where's Lord?"

"I think he's heading home to Connecticut."

Dixx picked up his phone and dialed.

"Nicholas, I have Colby with me at the penthouse. If you're not too far along, please come back. We need to discuss a matter."

"I'm not that far. Give me about fifteen or twenty minutes and I'll be there."

"With everything else going on, we're…" then Dixx corrected himself, "I'm…not addressing certain issues that need addressing. Colby here jarred my memory that we're days away from receiving a shipment from Mexico."

Payment has already been made to Delgado by wire transfer. The shipment will be delivered to Hudson Salvage as usual. We'll get a fix on exactly when, when the driver is twenty-four hours away.

Colby and his crew will handle the receiving and transfer. Right now I think we should pay another visit to Lomax and discuss the payment arrangements. There isn't going to be any more cryptocurrency crapola. The pills are to be paid for in cash, just like before I was talked into that crypto crap."

"I think you made that clear to Lomax already."

"I did, Nicholas, but are you willing to trust Lomax?"

"I don't see what choice we have. Colby and his crew will be at Hudson Salvage and nothing is going to be exchanged before they verify that Lomax's people have the money. Maybe a simple phone call to remind him is all that's necessary."

Dixx shook his head no. "Can't take a chance that a phone is tapped or some other mechanical screw up that can happen with phones nowadays.

Okay, that's settled. Let me call Lomax. I'll be back in a minute or so."

As Dixx left the deck, Madison entered. "Would either of you like something? It's five o'clock somewhere in the world."

"Sure is. I think I'd like vodka," and then Colby looked over at Lord.

"It's too early for me. I'm an after six o'clock drinker," then he chuckled. "How about a cup of black coffee, Madison?"

"Coming right up, gentlemen."

As she walked away Colby couldn't help commenting. "That's a wonderful looking Lady. Dixx is fortunate."

"Yes indeed, fortunate indeed," and then Lord smiled at his play with the word indeed. "You should be doing okay in that department. There's plenty of lookers out there for the taking."

"You're right, but my type is usually wrapped around a pole. You know, the strippers who give as good as they take. Trouble is, they're rough around the edges instead of sophisticated like Dixx's lady. Maybe in the next lifetime, when I come back, it can be different," and then Colby laughed. "Until then I'll take what I can get."

Madison placed the vodka and coffee down, then left. As she passed Dixx, she asked if he wanted anything, mentioning that she just served Colby and Lord a drink and some coffee.

Dixx shook his head no and continued toward the deck.

"It's arranged. I informed Lomax that you'd be there within the hour Nicholas. The cash is to be handed over before the product is exchanged. It's that simple. Make sure he understands. Contact me only if there's a problem. This sit-down shouldn't take more than ten or twenty minutes of your time, then you can continue your trip back to Connecticut."

Lord looked over at Colby. "Are you ready, Colby?"

Dixx spoke up, "I need to talk with Colby about the delivery and several other matters. You're handling Lomax alone. Have fun."

+++++++

Lord parked the Bentley in front of the HO's clubhouse and walked toward the entrance.

The two tall blacks were on either side of the doorway and a number of gangbangers were standing around talking and watching.

Their eyes turned toward the car and then focused on the white dude who parked it.

When he was a few steps away from the black on the right side of the doorway, Lord nodded.

The gangbanger continued to stare straight ahead.

Lord walked through the doorway and then a gangbanger moved out of the shadows and motioned him toward a room.

Once inside, Lord nodded to Lomax who was pointing to a chair.

Sitting on either side of Lomax were his lieutenants, Baxter and Elijah Carter, and behind them were six gangbangers, weapons clearly visible.

As he sat down, Lord tried to figure out why the dramatics…why were the foot soldiers (Lowest rank in the gang organization) in the room with weapons on display? He couldn't reach a conclusion and the moment passed as Lomax began speaking.

"Your Mr. Uptown, tells me that we are getting a shipment in the next couple of days."

Lord nodded, as Lomax continued. "He tells me no more crypto, but he didn't tell me why. Maybe you can enlighten me?"

I don't know. Mr. Dixx tells me only what he thinks I need to know to do my job, and that's all."

"And what is your job?"

"To follow instructions when they're given."

"Obviously you do since you're still in one piece," then Lomax turned toward Baxter who was shaking his head up and down and smiling.

"You're the one with the names, right?"

Lord wasn't sure what Lomax was referring to, then he recalled the meeting before they went hunting for a few ABN gangbangers.

"Yeah! I'm the one with a few names. Like I said before, you can call me Nicholas, Lord, Hey You, or anything else you want. I'll answer to most."

"Okay Lord, to repeat myself, Uptown said the shipment is coming in a few days. Now what?"

"As you said a few moments ago, Mr. Uptown, as you refer to him, doesn't want payment in crypto. Why he doesn't want to get paid that way, he didn't tell me. It's called, 'need to know,' and as far as he's concerned, I don't need to know."

"My instructions were to tell you that this transaction will be in cash, sixty thousand large on delivery. I need a yes if it works, or a no, that's not going to work. It's that simple."

"How many pills?"

"Twenty-five thousand."

"Tell Uptown that we'll have the cash when he tells us the merchandise is here. Now if there's nothing else Lord, I'd suggest you get the fuck outta here before one of my boys decides to make you his play thing."

The room erupted in laughter as Lord stood up, smiled and walked out.

———— ✦✦✦✦✦ ————

Sparrow watched from the corner of the intersection as the Bentley coupe parked in front of the ABN clubhouse. After the white guy disappeared inside, Sparrow started walking again on the opposite side of the street.

As he came parallel to the car, he stopped, then casually crossed the street. When he was a few steps away from the front of the car, Sparrow leaned over as if he was picking up something he dropped, and glanced quickly at the license plate before a blow to his head knocked him momentarily unconscious.

He was pulled up, slapped and punched several more times.

"What are you doing here motherfucker? Get your fucking worthless peanut brittle ass outta here before we cut you up. Now you listen up cause I ain't gonna say this more than one time. You stay in that fucking projects where you belong with all them other Nancies. (Slang for gay men who speak and behave like women) Now get the fuck outta here while you still can."

Sparrow ran as quickly as he could, the pain from the beating resonating with each step he took. When he was a block or so from where he parked his car, he stopped, looked for a place to sit-down, then moved onto a bus stop bench.

The woman who was already sitting there stared at Sparrow's face, then moved to the opposite end of the bench before she got up and walked away.

As his eyes followed the woman he thought, just as well. I don't need any company.

After several minutes, Sparrow got up, and began walking toward where he left his car.

"Hello Mr. Dixx. I don't think we need to meet again. I can relate what happened quickly."

"Go ahead."

"It's agreed. We just need to let him know when. I think we need some extras there for effect and just in case, if you know what I mean."

"Everything is understood and I concur. I'll let you know when," and then the phone connection ended.

As Lord crossed over the border separating New York from Connecticut, his cell phone rang.

"I'm about fifteen minutes from your house."

"Me too, Madison. If you get there first, you can make the drinks."

"I had something else in mind."

Lord laughed. "See you in a bit."

Lord saw the Mercedes convertible in the driveway and parked his car behind it. Just as he turned off the ignition, his cell phone rang.

"It's Colby, any chance we can connect sometime today? If you're home, I don't mind driving to Connecticut. It'll give me a chance to get away from New York for a while. If you're still around town maybe we can hook up here."

"I'm in Connecticut and I'm busy today, sorry. Try me again in a couple of days."

"Okay. Whatever it is that's keeping you busy, do it well."

"Will do," and then Lord pressed down on the end button.

The front door was unlocked and Lord walked in calling out, "Anyone home here?"

A voice from the den called out, "In here and please get some ice."

Lord diverted to the kitchen, filled a bowl with ice, then walked to the den. Madison was sitting on the leather sofa holding a glass in each hand.

"Are you surrendering, or do the upraised arms signal something else?"

"The surrender comes later. The raised arms are telling you where the ice belongs."

Lord chuckled. "You're in a good mood."

"Why not. I'm where I'm supposed to be."

Lord similed. "You're something else."

"Of course I am. That's what makes me so alluring," and then she laughed.

"Indeed. How did you manage, Dixx?"

"Told him the usual. Need some girl time. Needed to go to the beauty salon, a fancy word for beauty parlor and all that kind of stuff. He seems preoccupied these days. Maybe it's the upcoming delivery, maybe the gang-bangers, and then there's you, Mr. Nicholas. I don't think you and I, as an item, are far from his thoughts. He's going to act on his feelings, and I'm thinking soon."

"Agree it's going to come. I'm wondering whether it's as soon as you think. He still has problems with Lomax and the HO's plus now he, most likely, has a few problems with the ABN. There's also Mexico.

Remember one of their boys, a dude named Perez met his maker and I can't help thinking the Mexicanos believe it's foul play. But with all that said, we just can't assume that time is on our side. I guess Madison, we need to make some decisions."

Madison shook her head yes. "But not now or today. Let's enjoy each other, and put them all out of our minds for today and tomorrow. You're going to have me for forty-eight hours. Do you think you can handle that?"

"I'm not sure, but I'm willing to try."

They both laughed.

"Cheers, Madison. To a new dawn down the road."

"I like that toast, Mr. Lord."

"By the way, Madison, do you know why people say cheers and touch their glasses?"

"To be honest, no. I never thought about it until just now when you mentioned it."

"Well, Miss Madison, cheers originates from the French word chiere which means 'face' or 'head.' By the eighteenth century, it meant 'gladness,' and was used as a way of expressing encouragement. Today it evolved to a symbolic and succinct way of toasting with a wish."

"Wow! Not only are you a handsome and suave member of the opposite sex, but you are one of the intelligent species as well."

Lord couldn't contain the laughter. "I never had anyone express what I am so eloquently. Thank you for making my day."

They touched glasses and sat in silence looking at each other. After the second drink, Madison stood up, took hold of Nicholas' hand and led him toward the bedroom.

— 16 —
CHAPTER

SEVERAL GANGBANGERS BRACED THEMSELVES AGAINST A WALL AT the rear of where Cleotha 'Mean Jean' RaJean sat together with his second in command, Adwin.

Across the table was the ABN gangbanger known as Sparrow.

"I'm waiting Sparrow. Ain't got all day and make sure you include what happened to your face. Looks like someone did a dance on it," then RaJean laughed.

"I'm gonna get to that. Got a call from one of the wannabes that a fancy black car was parked in front of the HO's clubhouse. The douche bag was too frightened to check out the license plate and type of car. Said there were too many HOs millin' about.

I figured I'd check it out myself. Parked my whip (Car) about a block or so from the Ho's clubhouse and started walking on the opposite side of the street. Once I was about thirty or so yards from the clubhouse I saw the car. I kinda walked in a zigzag way toward the middle of the street, leaving an okay distance between me and the car and the clubhouse.

When I was a little past the middle of the street, I pretended to drop something. I reached down, glanced at the car and the license plate, then the next thing I knew, several HOs were tap dancing on my head and face. They didn't tag me as an ABN. Wasn't wearin' any colors or clothing that could make me. The motherfuckers just didn't like that I was anywhere near them or their clubhouse and they needed to teach me, and any onlookers something, besides havin' a little fun at my expense.

The car is a Bentley and the license plate is Connecticut, NAK26."

"Very good, Sparrow. I like the way you did what you needed to do and came through with some solid skinny. (Information) We'll run that plate number through our boy at the two five precinct. And by the way, Sparrow, I'm gonna move you up. Gonna give you a crew to play with. Think you can handle that?"

"Absolutely, MJ, and more."

"Okay, Sparrow, get yourself some down time. Find a skirt (Woman) and then get some. We talk later."

⁺⁺◆◆◆⁺⁺

After Madison left, Lord let his mind freewheel. As he sat on the couch, he thought about the all too brief time they enjoyed together. The dinner at Roscoe's in Greenwich, Connecticut where she insisted he play the bar's piano to the delight of the patrons and staff. The dancing, following dinner, at the Lion's Disco. It all seemed like a moment in time, too fleeting, and now the utter loneliness without her.

Then he thought, that will change. I guarantee it.

He was jarred out of his mind fog by the ringing.

Momentarily unable to find his phone, he moved his hand around where he was sitting. As his fingers brushed against the protective cover he took a breath, brought the phone up to his ear and said, "Yes."

"Dixx here. Please come to the Penthouse. Need to talk briefly."

"I'm on my way."

⁺⁺◆◆◆⁺⁺

"The merchandise is arriving Thursday morning between one and two a.m. at Hudson Salvage. We'll meet there at midnight. They, the HOs, should arrive at two a.m. On your way back to Connecticut, Nicholas, stop by the HOs clubhouse and inform Lomax. You might want to mention payment again.

That's it. There's nothing more until we meet at midnight two days from now. Enjoy the free time," and then Dixx stood up.

"Excuse me, Nicholas, for rushing off. I have a few things that need taking care of. You know your way out. Ciao."

————————— ✦✦✦✦✦ —————————

Lord parked the Bentley in front of the HO's clubhouse. As he approached the entrance both gangbangers on either side of the doorway moved in front and assumed a blocking position.

"No one told us to expect you and you ain't gettin' in till we clear it with Jamal. You can wait here or cuddle up in your Bentley."

Lord smiled and remained in place as the tall black went inside.

A few minutes later the gangbanger reappeared and motioned Lord inside.

As Lord walked the familiar corridor he was again motioned into a room by one of the HO soldiers who was leaning against a wall.

Lomax and several other HO bangers were scattered around the room. Lomax pointed to a chair and watched as Lord sat down.

"You don't come here, ever, without a call to let us know. You understand?"

Lord thought about replying that he thought Dixx had done it, but let the thought fade.

"Now my time is valuable and I don't have a lot of it to waste like you and Uptown do, so get to the fucking point and make it quick."

"Why the hostility? We're on the same side. In case you've forgotten, I was part of a little payback on the ABN a few nights ago. And another thing, when you talk to me, you speak in a civil tone. Do you understand?"

Lomax fought hard to restrain himself and keep the rage inside from spilling over.

"The shipment is coming, two days from today, on Thursday. The transfer will take place at Hudson Salvage as usual. Be there at two a.m. and make sure you have the sixty large. Come in one car only. This meeting is over," and Nicholas stood up, turned, and walked out and back to his car.

As soon as Lord disappeared, Baxter turned and faced Lomax. "You're King Shorty and no one is disputing that. You run the HOs and establish policy, but I think you just made a serious mistake with that cracker."

As soon as Baxter finished the last syllable, Lomax screamed, "When I want your fucking advice, I'll ask for it. Until then, keep that fucking trap of yours shut. Ya hear me?"

Then Lomax made eye contact with several other gangbangers before storming out of the room.

⁘

Dixx answered the phone but before he had a chance to say anything, Lord said, "I'm in the garage...coming up. We need to talk," then the disconnect.

Lord shook his head no when Dixx offered coffee or a drink.

"Lomax was in a rare mood. Lectured me on never making an appearance without calling him first and getting an okay. Made some veiled threats about a day of judgment stuff, using his limited knowledge of the English language to get the point across," and then Lord laughed.

"Something has got him a little stir crazy. Maybe it's the ABN, but I didn't like his attitude. I think there could be trouble coming at us, but can't figure out why. He doesn't have any other supply channel as far as I can determine, so why cut the umbilical cord with us before he's got an alternative source."

"What about the upcoming shipment?"

"Informed him that the transfer would be made two days from today, Thursday at Hudson Salvage. Told him to be there at two a.m. and make sure he had the money with him."

Dixx shook his head in a yes motion, "I'll contact Colby and have him boost his crew a bit. A few more men can't hurt. We'll see how the transfer goes. If it's smooth, I'll suggest another sit-down with him and try to determine what's bothering his royal highness."

Lord smiled as he shook his head. "Maybe, just maybe, Mr. Dixx, we should cut our ties with the HOs and get a new arrangement. Lots of gangbangers out there from the Bloods to the Crips who would like to handle what we're peddling."

"You just triggered something, Nicholas, and that's the crypto. I don't think it was the Mexicans as we suspected initially. What you just related about Lomax makes me feel that the son of a bitch was, is, behind the theft. Wasn't he the one who proposed payment in crypto? I'll answer my own question. Yes he was, and I'm still out the money with no possibility for recovery in sight.

And while we're on the subject, I think we should pay a visit to Delgado. I doubt if he'll ever be able to figure out what happened to his man Perez and maybe that was a mistake on our part. But what's done is done, and we can't go back. Let's give it some thought and we'll decide after the transfer."

+ + + + + + +

Colby and Lord, flanked by four heavily armed men, stood secluded behind an immense mound of scrap metal. The two Land Rover vehicles with their running lights on, were positioned to their right side.

A four door Buick was parked behind the two Range Rovers and behind the Buick were three more men armed with MAC-10's. (A compact, blowback operated submachine gun)

At three minutes past two a.m. a Chevy Suburban slowly made its way toward the two parked Range Rovers.

Once Lomax, Baxter and three other men exited the vehicle, they began walking toward where Colby and Lord stood.

Colby called out. "Stop there and tell your men to remain where they are, then move to us."

When Lomax and Baxer were standing in front of Colby and Lord, Lomax asked, "You afraid of somethin'? Do my boys frighten y'all?"

"Not in the least," and Colby turned in several directions and looked at his contingent of heavily armed men.

"I noticed them," and Lomax moved his head slightly. Why are you comin' with all the heavy artillery?"

"Never know when you're going to need them. Better they're here, than wishing they were. You know what I mean, don't ya Mr. Lomax?" and then Colby half smiled.

"Time is wasting away, Where are the pills?"

"There here, twenty-five thousand of them," and then Colby looked over at one crew members and nodded.

"Where's the money?"

As Lomax looked toward Baxter, he handed him a large black doctor's bag.

"Take a look. Sixty thousand large and it's all there."

"Never doubted you for a moment. You don't mind if I take a quick look."

Colby opened the bag and moved the bundles of banded onehundred dollar bills around. You'll hear from us if it's short, but you wouldn't want that would you, Mr. Lomax?"

Lomax just smiled as he held out his hand.

When nothing happened, Lomax said, "The pills!"

After a signal from Colby, several crew members placed two cardboard containers on the ground next to Lomax.

"Mimicking Colby's words, Lomax said, "You don't mind if I take a quick look?"

"Suit yourself, we have plenty of time, nothing on tap," and then Colby laughed.

Lomax opened both containers and stared at the plastic wrapped packages of off-white pills. Then he again mimicked Colby's words. "You'll hear from us if it's short, but you wouldn't want that would you, Mr. Colby?"

Lomax and Baxter laughed as they turned away.

After the cardboard containers were loaded into the Suburban, Lomax and his entourage entered their vehicle and drove out of the salvage yard.

Lord and Colby walked toward the Buick sedan as Colby's crew loaded into the two Range Rovers.

When the vehicles left the Hudson Salvage yard, the Range Rovers turned right while the Buick continued straight ahead for the seventeen minute drive to the upper West side and Dixx's penthouse.

17

CHAPTER

"IT'S ALL HERE!"

"You're not surprised are you Mr. Dixx? Lomax wouldn't, couldn't be stupid enough to try and short change us."

"No, I'm not surprised, Colby, just relieved in a way. There's always the doubts and with those doubts comes the thought of unnecessary problems."

Now speaking of problems, real or imagined, there's the Mexicans. It may well serve our interests to pay Ramon Delgado a visit. Play nice and cement our relationship with a few drinks and whatever the circumstances call for. I want you to lead on this, Nicholas, and it would be a good idea to take Colby along. Get him exposed to the supply side."

Lord moved his shoulders in a way that conveyed indifference. "If that's what you want, Mr. Dixx, that's okay with me. The only drawback is Colby doesn't speak Spanish."

"Then you can translate for him, Nicholas, or Colby can get a long haired dictionary and learn the language from her."

Dixx couldn't help himself and laughed. Lord smiled and Colby shook his head yes.

"Okay, I'll contact Delgado, and let you know when and where. Meantime, take some downtime," and then Dixx handed an envelope to each of them.

———————— ✦✦✦✦✦ ————————

As both men stood in the parking garage of the Fifth Avenue penthouse, Cobly said, "Ya know, Mr. Lord, that wasn't any of my doing up there...the Mexican thing."

"Relax, I can always use the company. Ever been to the sunny south before?"

Colby shook his head no, "And I never planned to. Plenty of chickie poo on this side of the border."

Lord laughed at Colby's choice of words to describe women.

"Yeah, I know what you mean. It's not a picnic over there, lots of drug cartels vying for territory and control. I can't be sure what we're going to face. Their man is dead and we're the only ones who know how, why, where, and when. Chances are his death appeared as a respiratory thing, meaning he died because his heart gave out. Shit happens. It's that simple."

"By the way, you wanted to talk to me? Sorry I wasn't available when you called a few days ago."

"That's alright, Mr. Lord. Just wanted to feel you out on something. I'm getting some real negative vibes, the HOs and the ABNs and what seems to be an attitude with the HO's King Shorty. That dude Lomax, he's a low life mother fucker if there was ever one. Despite the fact that we supply him, the SOB is a disrespectful piece of shit.

If I were running this thing, I'd cut his ass off and go with the Daybreak Boys, The Whyos, The Forty Thieves or The Aces. There's gangs a'plenty out there. It's just a question of choosing one that we can control.

As I see it, Mr. Lord, things are going to continue downhill until Lomax decides he doesn't need us any more and puts out a marker on all of us just to beef up his rep. Or he gets Dixx to do some more of his dirty work until one or more of us gets blown away. I wouldn't put it past him to try and hook up with another spic supplier and cut us out. It ain't that hard, the way I see it. What's your take, Mr. Lord?"

"What you say makes sense. I've got the same negative vibes. Each time we've had a sit-down with Lomax there is always a feeling of contention… always one sided and that's Lomax's side. Can't understand why Dixx doesn't see it the way we do, but maybe he does and just maybe he's waiting for something to happen.

That's my main concern, that 'something' he's waiting for. When it happens, it isn't going to be pretty, and I'm not willing to get hung out to dry."

"Yes, Mr. Lord. That's what I mean, that's exactly what I mean."

"Okay, we're on the same page. Let me do some thinking and we'll discuss this again. By the way, have you been in contact lately with that woman, Serenity?"

"No, but I'll connect with her today."

"After you do, if there's anything you think we should go over, contact me. Meantime that talk about chickie poo, as you call those feminine creations, has aroused my male interest. I think I'll hook up and suggest you do the same. It'll take your mind off what we've been discussing for a while."

"I like the way you think, Mr. Lord. See ya!"

* * * * * *

Lord dialed the number as he started his car.

When the connection was made, he asked, "Got any free time for somewhat of a stranger?"

"I could make some, if it's worthwhile."

"I will spare no effort to ensure that it's worthwhile. Do we play the New York or Connecticut scene?"

"I'm in New York. Please come by."

Fifteen minutes later, Lord was entering Madison's condo.

She tugged at his jacket and when he moved closer they kissed passionately. "Wow! I needed that."

"Me too. Is it too early for a drink?"

"It's never too early. It's five o'clock somewhere in the world so that makes it okay. What'll it be?"

Lord brought his hand up and held out a silver gift sleeve wrapped bottle.

"My oh my, how sweet and kind of you."

"It's chilled Roederer Champagne, Brut Premier, for a young lady that I happen to love."

Madison laughed. "Those words and the champagne will get you everywhere and where would you like to get Mr. Lord?"

"Well for starters, how about inside."

Madison moved to one side, and then closed the door.

"Make yourself comfortable. I'll get the flutes."

"Let me help."

"No, you'll just get in the way and I'm a pro at opening champagne bottles, pouring, and drinking. Sit!"

As Madison and Lord sat side by side on the couch, their eyes locked onto each other, their thoughts only of the present moment. Then the mood changed when Madison asked, "How much longer?"

Lord knew exactly what she was referring to and was about to answer the question humorously, but after a few seconds he nixed the idea.

"I'd like to make it now. This very moment when we cut and run from it all, but..."

Madison interrupted before he could finish the sentence.

"Then what's holding us up? There will always be just one more thing to finish or whatever. If we don't decide when, and do it, we may never..." and then her voice trailed off.

"Never, is a long time and that word doesn't fit into anything we have between us or what we intend to do. It will happen," and Lord motioned with his hand to stay quiet for a few more moments and then said, "I promise."

"It's becoming harder and harder to be with him. I hate the times I am and despite those times becoming more infrequent, they do happen. I want out, a new life...a life with you. Please, Nicholas, make it happen," and then she began to sob.

"Please, Madison, don't do that. It hurts me to see you cry. Please darling, don't."

She dabbed her eyes with a handkerchief, and then faced him.

"I'm sorry. I love you and feel my life is so wasted. I'm afraid of him and what he can do to me and you. We only have each other. No one is going to care what happens to either of us, no one. He will take revenge on me and you, and if ever there is a guaranteed happening in this f'ing world, what I just said, is it. He will kill us both, Nicholas. Do you understand, he will kill us both?"

Lord reached out to touch her but she shook her head no. "I need only one thing from you, an answer. When?"

"Dixx mentioned something about Colby and I visiting with the Mexicans, and talking..." he was about to say shit, but changed his mind quickly and said, "junk with them. I was thinking it might well be an opportunity to suggest to Delgado that it might be better to play ball with me and eliminate Dixx."

Lord saw the startled look in Madison's eyes, but before he could continue, she said, "That's not what I had in mind, Nicholas. I want us out of this drug stuff. If it isn't Dixx that's a threat, it'll be the Blacks, the gangs who you use to move the drugs."

"I can handle that part of it, and the Mexicans too."

"I'm sure you can, until you can't. One day, the cops, the feds, the gangbangers or someone who thinks he can, will put a marker out on you and maybe me, and that's the end game. It'll be over and final for both of us as we push up daisies.

I want us out and a new life somewhere, anywhere but here. I have some money saved. It won't take us far but you're a college boy, a vet, and you're one of the most intelligent men I have ever known. We can make it happen, even if we have to work at Walmart or Burger King, we'll have each other and we'll make it work because we'll be alive."

Lord laughed, "Burger King sounds interesting and they even provide a uniform, then he laughed again, and Madison joined in.

"I need some time. I need to put the house up for sale. It's worth about eight-hundred thousand. The Bentley will bring in another one hundred and thirty-five thousand, and I have some off-shore savings accounts. That should be enough to get us somewhere and start a life."

"That's what I wanted to hear, Nicholas. You've made me so happy."

"I need to meet with Dixx to get a feel for what he's thinking about Mexico, the Blacks and a few other things. Once I get a fix on where his mind set is, I can better plan what we have to do, and when.

I'm not going to screw around indefinitely. I'll set up a time-table of sorts, like a military maneuver and stick to it. I'll pay Dixx a visit over the next day or so, unless he contacts me to come sooner.

Now young lady, meaning now, right this minute, let's party," and he smiled and the smile was reciprocated."

18

CHAPTER

"I'VE SPOKEN WITH DELGADO, AND HE'S OKAY WITH A SIT-DOWN."

Dixx stopped speaking and asked, "Do I detect something not quite right, Nicholas?"

"I was just thinking, is this really necessary, the meeting? They don't know we were involved with Perez's untimely departure. The autopsy would show cardiac arrest. His heart suddenly and unexpectedly stopped pumping, and he stopped breathing. It's that simple. Nothing is traceable back to us."

"It's not really about that, Nicholas. It's been a while since we've had a sit-down with Delgado and relationships are maintained not only through business interaction, but by friendship as well.

We, you and Colby, that is, will meet with Delgado and assure him that our relationship is just peachy.

You'll tell him that we look forward to continuing and growing the relationship as we enlarge our presence in New York and soon in Connecticut and New Jersey. There's a growing appetite for what we have to sell, and that should please our mutual friend."

Lord looked over at Colby, then back at Dixx. "When is the sit-down?"

"I informed him you'll arrive this Saturday or Sunday. You have his cell number and once your plans are firmed, I suggest you contact him directly and let him know where, when, etc."

"Okay, I've got some things to take care of first, then I'll let you and Colby know. If there's nothing else, I'm outta here."

Lord waved as he walked toward the penthouse door.

A few minutes after Lord left, Colby stood up, nodded toward Dixx and started to walk out when Dixx said, "Please wait a moment. I have a proposition that might be of interest to you."

Once Colby was seated, Dixx began. "You've been with me a number of years now, about twelve isn't it?"

Colby was about to correct Dixx but instead said, "About that."

"I'm very satisfied with how you perform, Colby. How you run and handle the crew. Your second in command," and then Dixx paused, "I have a momentary lapse. What's his name, Colby?"

"His name, Mr. Dixx, is Joko Rapolo."

"Yes, that's it. Thank you. Could he handle the crew and your duties while you're in Mexico?"

"Yes, he's very capable."

"That's what I wanted to hear. Now about that proposition I previously mentioned. What I'm about to offer is strictly between us. If you decline, nothing changes, but if you divulge anything I am about to state to anyone...ANYONE..."

Dixx stopped talking and locked eyes with Colby. "Do I need to spell it out for you further?"

Colby shook his head no.

"Okay, we have an understanding, don't we?"

Colby nodded yes.

"Listen carefully, At any time you can stop this conversation, and it's over at that point. I am offering you Lord's position in the organization. With it goes a sizable increase in the money you will receive."

Dixx again stopped speaking and watched Colby, for any reaction, negative or positive to what he said so far.

"I know what you are thinking at this moment. "Where is Lord going, or perhaps a better way of putting it, is what's going to happen to Nicholas Lord?

It's very simple, Colby. You are going to kill Nicholas Lord during your trip to Mexico. How, when and where exactly, I leave to you. The contract is worth thirty-thousand dollars. Do we have an understanding? Do we have an agreement?"

Colby didn't answer, instead looked questioningly at Dixx.

"Is there something wrong with your ability to speak, Colby? Or, are you having trouble processing what I've just said?"

"Perhaps I've overestimated you, Colby. I have a habit of doing that with people on occasion."

"You haven't overestimated me, Mr. Dixx. I'm a person who likes to think about things before I make a decision. I like to weigh the pros and cons as a means of reaching that decision. Once I commit to doing something, I'm all business until whatever it is, is concluded satisfactorily. You can understand that, can't you Mr. Dixx?"

Dixx bristled at how Colby spoke his last sentence.

When he did reply, Dixx kept his tone civil. "Yes, I can certainly understand that. It makes sense and once again you've shown me that you think carefully before making a commitment. A very necessary trait in our line of work. You have five minutes to make your decision, Colby. That should be more than ample time to…" and then Dixx enunciated the words, "consider the pros and cons of what I've proposed."

Dixx stood up. "I'll be back in five minutes."

———— ✦✦✦✦✦ ————

Nicholas Lord sat across from Y K Shin at a table in Grace Park's Bar & BBQ, a bottle of OB beer in front of each of them.

"Are you ready for another beer, Nicholas?"

"The answer is yes, but let's wait until I've finished telling you what I need. As I mentioned, I need a clean car to drive into Mexico. The car won't be coming back with me. That's number one. Number two, is I need a weapon, preferably a Glock 9mm, and four, fifteen round magazines. Can you contact the Lee brothers in San Diego to arrange the car and weapon?"

"Yes, I am sure they be very willing to help old friend like you, Nicholas."

"Good, I need to know as soon as possible. I'll be flying in on Saturday with someone else, and then we'll both drive to Mexico that same day. Can you arrange it so that they'll meet me at San Diego International Airport this Saturday?" and then Lord handed the Korean a slip of paper together with an envelope.

"The details regarding my arrival time, the airline, etc., are all there," and Lord pointed to the paper. "This envelope is for your trouble. I'll take care of our friends, the Lee brothers, when we meet up."

"Consider it done, Nicholas. Are you now ready for that second beer?"

Dixx stood facing Colby who was still seated. "Your answer please."

"Okay, I'll do it. May I ask you a question?"

"Certainly, but I may not answer it. Go ahead."

"Why?"

"It doesn't matter. It has no bearing on what you have to do. Lord is not a friend of yours or a family member. He's just another one of my employees. Employees get fired in corporations. In our line of work, they get terminated differently. Either way, they're gone."

When Colby remained quiet, Dixx said, "I believe our meeting is over. I'll expect to hear from you when the business has been concluded. Now I suggest you contact Lord and find out when you leave and by what means. Goodbye, Mr. Colby."

As Colby drove away from the Fifth Avenue penthouse, the entire scene that took place there replayed across his mind. His constant thought was that if Dixx would eliminate his number two man, a man like Nicholas Lord, it's only a matter of time before his own number was up. Obviously everything is momentary and deluding himself into thinking otherwise was foolhardy.

Then his thoughts shifted. Just maybe there's something more. Could Lord have stolen money or drugs from the organization? Then he thought, it could be anything and now I've cast my lot with Dixx in a way that will either shorten or increase my time on earth. I'll know soon enough.

Colby pulled his car to the curb and then dialed Lord's number.

"Hello Mr. Lord, it's Colby. Just checking in. When do we leave?"

"Tomorrow. I'll pick you up at six a.m. We've got a flight at JFK leaving at seven-thirty a.m. Pack for about three or four days. I'll go over the drill with you on the way to the airport."

————— ✦✦✦✦✦ —————

I'll be leaving tomorrow morning on the early bird special to San Diego. Mexico is a three or four day trip, then it's back here, and you and I become history shortly after that. Do what you have to do while I'm gone. Stay cool with Dixx and get yourself ready. I'll finish up as soon as I can, then…well you know what the 'then' means."

"Be careful. Mexico is dangerous."

"And New York isn't?"

They both laughed. "Yes, Nicholas, New York is dangerous in many ways."

"Spoken like an experienced woman."

Oh yes, a very experienced woman. Now be careful, and come back in one piece."

"I intend to do that. See ya, and remember, Madison, I love you."

"Ditto, Lord. I'll be waiting for your call."

————— ✦✦✦✦✦ —————

As Lord and Colby disembarked at San Diego International Airport, two Korean men waved and motioned them over to where they were standing.

"Good to see you again, Nicholas," and both men extended their hands. One asked, "Jal jinae issuayo?" (How have you been - Korean)

"Jeon guaenchanayo." (I'm okay)

Lord turned slightly and said, "This is Colby.

The men shook hands.

"These two very fine men, Colby, are the Lee brothers. This handsome devil is Mun Jae, and the other good looking dude is Hae Won."

All four men laughed, and then Mun Jae Lee said, "I think we should start moving away from here unless we want to get crushed to death."

They laughed again and Mun Jae Lee made a motion to follow him.

They took the elevator to the fourth level of the parking garage and walked to the far end where a gray Chevrolet Malibu Coupe and a White Lexus SUV were parked. Hae Won Lee pointed to the Chevy. "That's your chariot, Nicholas. I need to talk with you for a moment. Let's go to the car and talk inside."

Lord nodded okay, then Hae Won turned toward Colby. "Please excuse us for a minute or two. I need to catch up on a few things with this man," and then Lee smiled. "My brother will entertain you meanwhile," and Lee smiled again.

Once they were in the car, Lee opened the glove compartment and handed Lord a gift wrapped box.

"Very pretty, Hae Won."

Lord tore the wrapping and opened the box. He reached for the 9mm Glock and placed the weapon under the seat, Then he took the four magazines and placed them back in the glove compartment and covered them with the box and ripped wrapping paper.

"Gamsahamnida, Hae Won." (Thank you-Korean) What about the car?"

"It has been borrowed Nicholas and the owner won't miss it. Do not bring this car back."

"I didn't intend to," and then Lord removed an envelope from his pocket and handed it to Lee. "I think this should cover everything. I appreciate what you and your brother did."

"What are friends for, Nicholas, unless they can be helpful from time to time."

Lord smiled, "And friends like you, your brother, and Y K are not easy to find."

"We are all brothers, Nicholas. How many happy days did we have when you lived in Seoul, Korea and all the good business we did? My brother and

I, together with our families, will always be grateful to you for helping us get to America. We will never forget that, my brother Nicholas, never. Perhaps when you return, we can have a family get together. Our wives and children would like to see you again, Nicholas."

"We'll try to make that happen, Hae Won. Until then, be well and thank you, and Mun Jae, for the car and the other items."

Lee smiled as he opened the car's door, and then he and Lord walked to where his brother and Colby were standing.

After the goodbyes, they entered their respective vehicles and drove out of the parking garage.

Once they crossed the U.S. border to Tijuana, Mexico, Lord turned to Colby and said, "Only about 16 hours more to Sinaloa."

"Wouldn't it have been better to take a plane?"

Lord pictured the 9mm Glock under his seat and the magazines in the glove compartment and knew he couldn't take them on a plane. The car was his only option. Then he thought, maybe it might have been better to go by plane, forget about carrying anything and let Delgado handle whatever it is that needed handling.

He dismissed that thought as quickly as it came and then reflected on something that was a core part of his character, I didn't get this far by relying on anyone other than myself.

Lord answered, "What's the hurry. Besides, I like to have my own wheels. Then we come and go as we please."

Colby wasn't sure what Lord was trying to say, but nodded anyway. As he stared at the passing panorama of people and buildings, his mind focused on the possibility that the drive to Sinaloa might well present an opportunity to do what he committed to. He thought about fate and how it always played a part in everything that took place, the car versus the airplane being one of them.

— 19 —

CHAPTER

"WE'RE NOT TOO FAR FROM SAN BLAS, MEXICO. MY STOMACH TELLS me I'm hungry. How about you, Colby?"

"Sure. Do you have a place in mind or do we just take our chances at one of those taco stands along the road?"

"Your American stomach will never be able to digest the food from those stalls. You'll have the runs for days. I have a better place in mind. It's in a hotel in San Blas, the Hotel Posada del Rey." (King's Inn)

After they were both seated, Colby remarked, "Not a bad place. Obviously you've been here before."

"Obviously, and the food is very edible."

They small talked through their meal and the after Lord paid the check, he motioned with his hand toward the main entrance. "Time to go. We have about seven more hours of driving left and I want to reach Sinaloa State before nightfall."

Both men stood up and as Lord turned and began walking, Colby reached down, took the knife off his plate and shoved it into his pocket.

After some meaningless discussion about the lousy countryside, the boring scenery, and the hordes of poverty stricken people, all of whom seemed to be in need of a bath, Lord and Colby fell into a comfortable silence.

The traffic was light as they drove along highway 15D, so Lord pressed down on the gas pedal and increased the speed to a little over 80 miles per hour. (130 Km/h)

"Are we off to the races, Mr. Lord?"

"I guess you could say that. The police here usually don't get excited about speeding, assuming you're not doing over eighty. But you're right about the races. Thanks for saying something. No need to go this fast and take a chance of something happening that we'll…I'll regret."

As they rounded a curve in the road, Lord pointed at the windshield. Seems we have a checkpoint of sorts up ahead. Good thing you spoke up and I slowed down. I don't think those boys in uniform would appreciate a vehicle going 80 miles per hour coming at 'em."

Colby laughed and Lord joined in.

When Lord brought the car to a stop, one of the three uniformed soldiers approached the driver's side.

"Sus documentos por favor. (Your documents please) And move your car off the road near those trees."

"Un momento. Necesito traducir para mi amigo." (One moment. I need to translate for my friend)

"I need your passport, Colby."

The three soldiers followed the car as it moved off the road and stopped near several large trees.

Lord opened his driver's side window and handed the passports to the soldier in charge.

After he examined both passports, he looked back at Lord. "Por favor sal del auto. Ustedes dos." (Please get out of the car. Both of you)

"Necesito traducir de nuevo." (I need to translate again)

Lord turned to Colby. "He wants us out of the car. When you open your door, drop down below the window level and stay there. Don't move no matter what happens. I need to do something. Understand?"

Colby nodded and started opening his door.

As Lord pushed his door with his left hand, he reached under his seat and pulled out the Glock 9mm, then fired a three round burst through the open window at the soldier standing several feet away. The rounds tore through the soldier's chest, killing him instantly.

Quickly maneuvering out of the car, Lord continued firing over the roof at the two soldiers who were now in a panic run to their rear.

One stumbled, then fell. The other continued to run until another burst drove him into the ground where he remained motionless.

"I think it's over. Get up, Colby."

"Are you fucking crazy, Lord? You just killed three soldiers or police or whatever the hell they are. Where did ya get the gun? Are you crazy?"

"Relax, and you asked that before."

"What did I ask before?"

"If I'm fucking crazy. And by the way, no, I'm not crazy. They're not police or soldiers. They're fucking dead bandits, like in gangbangers. You understand?"

"No, I don't understand. How do…how did you know?"

"Look at the sandals and shoes the shits are wearing. Police and soldiers wear boots. Got it?"

Lord walked over to the dead soldier lying near the car and took the passports out of his hand. "There's some blood on your passport Colby. Clean it up when you can. Now get back in the car before someone comes along that road and nails us. Make it quick."

As Lord sped away from the scene of carnage, Colby's thoughts were of how close he came to getting killed. When he realized Lord was speaking, he turned in his seat and tried to focus on what was being said.

"…and we're damn lucky. Once we exited the vehicle, we would have been stripped of everything and then killed. That's the way it works down here."

"Thanks, Mr. Lord. I like to think that because I'm a kid who grew up on the mean streets and what I now do for Dixx, that I am a pretty savvy guy. But you just showed me, I don't know it all. I'm grateful for what you did. You saved my life."

♦ ♦ ♦ ♦ ♦ ♦ ♦

Cleotha RaJean, flanked by his underboss, Adwin, looked down at the paper in front of him and then at Sparrow, who sat across the table.

"Our jake (Cop) at the two five precinct came up with nothing much regarding that car and license plate that was at the HO's clubhouse. Seems the dude by the screwed up name of Lord, Nicholas Lord, lives in Connecticut and is a consultant for so-called new business ventures. Classy huh?

Nothing in his background that our guy could find that will help us. Usual parking tickets but nothing else to give us a clue about why or what he's doing at the HOs. So, I gotta assume that he's connected with the food (Gang slang for drugs) they're getting from somewhere. We gonna keep an eye on the HOs and that's where you come in."

RaJean paused for several seconds then asked, "You with me so far Sparrow?"

"All ears, MJ."

"Good. I want you to arrange with your crew to keep eyes on the HO clubhouse. I wanna know when that dude shows up again and then you make sure you have wheels to tail him wherever he goes. Maybe you get two sets of wheels so you can alternate as you follow the mother fucker and he don't catch on that you're tailing him. We develop a pattern of what and where he does whatever he does and then we are better equipped to know what we should do. You understand what I just said, Sparrow?"

"Completely, MJ."

"Okay then, times a'wasting. Get movin'."

♦ ♦ ♦ ♦ ♦ ♦ ♦

"It won't be long now. We've just entered Culiacan, officially known as Culiacan Rosales. I mentioned that, Colby, in case you're ever on a quiz programs and they ask that question."

Colby chuckled, "Doubt if I'll ever be on a quiz program and damn if I remember what you just said."

Lord laughed. "I'm figuring another ten minutes or so."

As Lord waited for the wrought iron gate to open, Colby remarked, "That's some palace."

"They believe in living the high life since they never know how long they've got to do it. Despite the bodyguards, the fences, the cameras and all the other stuff, life is momentary at best. They're always distrustful and looking over their shoulder, if you know what I mean?"

"Yeah, I got the picture all right."

"Once we get inside, Colby, stay loose and don't do anything unless I tell you. Delgado speaks okay English, but I'll open up in Spanish and translate for you when I feel necessary. Just stay cool and let things play out."

Lord parked the Chevy and motioned to Colby to exit the vehicle. Two men holding AK-47 type weapons beckoned them forward. After a quick pat down, one of the men said, "Ve a la parte superior de los escalones." (Go to the top of the steps)

Once they reached the landing, they were patted down again. Once inside another man motioned them to follow. After a short distance the man held up his hand, then knocked lightly on the door.

After the command to come in was given, the man opened the door slowly and then pointed. Once they were inside, the door was closed.

Lord stood several steps from the entrance and waited until a man came from behind an immense desk and began walking toward them.

"Es bueno verte de nuevo, Nicholas." (It's good to see you again Nicholas)

"Asi mismo, Senor Delgado." (Likewise here Mr. Delgado)

"Este buen hombre es mi socio, Senor Colby." (This fine man is my partner, Mr. Colby)

Delgado offered his hand and Colby shook it.

Delgado said, "Un amigo de Nicholas es un amigo mio. Bienvenidos." (A friend of Nicholas is a friend of mine. Welcome)

After Lord translated, Delgado said, "My apologies. I assumed Mr.

Colby spoke Spanish. I think we'll continue in English since I need practice. May I offer you gentlemen some refreshments, a drink or perhaps coffee."

Lord waited for Colby to reply and then said, "I'll have the same but make mine black coffee only, no sugar."

Delgado turned toward one of his men standing nearby and nodded. Moments later three cups of coffee were placed on a table.

"And how was your trip to Culiacan?"

Lord thought of responding with a simple okay, but realized there are few secrets in Sinaloa State and decided to relate what happened.

After Lord finished, Delgado sat quietly for several minutes then replied. "Mexico is dangerous, but the roads to Sinaloa even more so. You both are extremely fortunate. Others in a similar situation would most likely be dead, but I never have underestimated you, Nicholas. You are a survivor."

"Well, at least up to this point, but one never knows what the future holds."

Delgado shook his head acknowledging what Lord had just said. Then he added, "That's why you must never trust anyone completely, whether a woman or a man."

Lord laughed and Colby joined in then added, "Especially a woman. Can't live with them, and can't live without them."

That brought more laughter.

"Where did you acquire the gun, Nicholas?"

"Arrangements were made when we picked up the car north of the border, and by the way, the weapon is yours now, a Glock 9mm and several spare 15 round magazines. They're under the driver's seat. Also the car is un regalo. (A gift) We'll take a flight back to the states and avoid a repeat episode of what took place enroute here. I don't think my delicate heart could stand the excitement again."

Delgado roared with laughter, and managed to say, "Your delicate heart...very funny. I never was sure you had one," and then he laughed again.

"And how is Mr. Dixx doing these days?"

"Busy. He's planning to expand into two additional states that border New York, called Connecticut and New Jersey. That should increase our business nicely and help you get rid of additional fentanyl. Is it still coming from China, Ramon, or are you now producing it in Mexico?"

"Yes on both counts. The Chinese are supplying us and we have opened several labs in Culiacan. The demand is ever growing," and then Delgado smiled. "So many people in the world, and so little fentanyl."

Delgado laughed. "Let them all lose their souls to drugs."

Lord smiled but his thoughts were of the over one hundred thousand drug overdose deaths in the United States each year, and he felt the sudden heaviness behind his eyes as he knew that he was part and parcel to these deaths.

It seemed a long way from a promising career as a financial intern at that prestigious wall street firm where he interned, and then left due to re-deployment as a Reserve Infantry Lieutenant to Afghanistan. Then the cocktail party after he returned where Dixx was a guest. The conversation between them and then the offer. It all seemed surreal.

Lord continued to think Madison was right. Sooner or later, and probably sooner, I'm going to meet my maker in an untimely event. This trip seems to be the eye opener. That happening enroute and now sitting here with this drug kingpin talking about supplying an opioid that will kill thousands.

Lord caught the last few words Delgado was speaking and replied, "No Ramon, one cup is enough. Gracias."

"Okay gentlemen. I am on my way to visit one of my laboratories. Please come along and observe. Bring your things. We'll drop you at your hotel on the way back."

The twenty minute drive ended at an open pasture with a considerable number of cows milling about. As men exited from several cars and SUVs, Delgado pointed toward the field.

"It's quite ingenious, isn't it?"

Lord wasn't sure what Delgado was referring to, then he continued. "It's quite ingenious because we have set up the lab in the middle of the cows," then he chuckled. "And because there is so much police activity in the area right now, those cows provide a perfect cover."

Delgado stopped walking and raised his hand, then one of his men handed Lord and Colby a respirator and goggles.

Delgado pointed to the respirators and goggles. "You need to wear these gentlemen because fentanyl is very toxic and many of the cooks have died just from inhaling it. However, some of our cooks work without protective equipment. They believe in the myth here that drinking beer will disable the high that comes along with being close to the heated substance.

We're close enough. You can watch the operation from here."

Lord, Colby and the others watched as several of the cooks threw handfuls of dirt into the air to gauge the way the wind was blowing. It was explained that this procedure was extremely important work, because one gust in the wrong direction or any mistake in the delicate process of making fentanyl, could lead to death.

Pointing in the direction of several men, Delgado said, "They, the cooks, are self-taught chemists."

Delgado continued to explain that his drugmakers aren't using poppy plants as their raw materials. Instead they start with a synthetic powder, which is cooked over an open flame. The resulting drug is called fentanyl.

"We mix the fentanyl with cocaine, methamphetamine and other opiates. Fentanyl is sold as a competitor to heroin. After processing here, it's packaged and then sold in America. The further a package of fentanyl travels, the more valuable it becomes, but you already know that, don't you, Nicholas?"

Lord shook his head yes,

"If you'll excuse me I need to confer with my foreman."

Delgado walked over to a man standing a respectable distance from the cooking pots, then after several minutes walked back.

"Okay gentlemen, it is time to leave. Enrique here, will drop you off at your hotel and then tonight we shall go to a place where there are some very beautiful mujeres. (Women) I know Nicholas likes women. Do you, Mr. Colby?"

"I don't only like women, Mr. Delgado, I love them."

Delgado smiled and Lord laughed.

"Excellent, then we shall meet again tonight. Goodbye gentlemen."

— 20 —

CHAPTER

COLBY SAT ON THE SMALL BALCONY OUTSIDE HIS FIFTH FLOOR HOTEL room, staring at the sunbathers and swimmers at the pool area below.

As his eyes watched their movements, the fingers on his right hand rubbed the knife he'd stolen from the restaurant. His thoughts were of Lord and the ways he could use the knife to carry out the commitment he'd made to Dixx.

Then his thoughts shifted to the road incident. The ensuing calm he felt after the killing, and then the realization that Lord saved his life.

He thought that even if he did make the connection at the roadblock, as Lord did to who those men actually were, he had nothing to neutralize them with. Lord, on the other hand, had the means, the savvy, and he did what was necessary to save them both.

As a result, didn't he owe his life to Lord?

Colby inadvertently moved his head in a slight up and down motion. This was the second, third or fourth time he thought about whether he owed Lord anything. It was playing on his mind continually, but why? Wasn't this just another thing he had to do to survive and move up in the world he made for himself?

He didn't have an answer. Or was it that he didn't want to reach one?

Colby's mind again pictured Lord, his Bentely, his Connecticut home, his custom made suits, and he wondered whether he could fit into that world.

His world was carved out of the mean streets where he was born and grew up. His schooling, his formal education outside of what he learned from the streets, was limited, and he certainly didn't have the polish Lord projected. He was covered with body art, tattoos, which in the opinion of many, marked him as a member of the underclass.

If Dixx would eliminate a man like Lord, what would it take for Dixx to get tired or become dissatisfied with someone like him. Lord fitted nicely into the world Dixx lived in. The penthouse and everything else it entailed. But he was a breed apart from that. Dixx would never accept him entirely into that world, as he did with Lord.

Then Colby wondered if Dixx at some point would approach his second in command, Joko Rapolo, and issue orders to do the same thing to him that he had committed to do to Lord. The one word answer, sure, flashed across his mind.

Dixx, on the surface, projected a loyalty to those who worked for and with him, but underneath it all, it was apparent that he had little if any loyalty to anyone other than himself. When he determines that the usefulness of someone has reached its maximum, or that person becomes a threat, he reacts the only way he can feel safe. And that way is to eliminate that person or persons. Hadn't he witnessed it often enough?

Maybe Lord did something which placed Dixx and his organization in a precarious situation. Obviously, whatever Lord did, tried to do, or was suspected of doing, was enough for Dixx to want him dead.

Colby moved forward in the chair, placed the knife on a small table and then rubbed his eyes. As he brought his hands down, he said in a whisper, "What's happening to me? I have no problem with killing anyone. I've already earned my ticket to Hell, so why am I wavering about this one?"

His mind was racing now as images of Lord, Dixx, Rapolo, Lomax, Ramon Delgado and some of the faces of those he killed flashed quickly by.

Colby screamed out, "NO...STOP...NO MORE!"

Then realizing what he was doing, lifted himself quickly out of the chair and bolted inside his room as startled people below looked up to determine where the screaming came from.

He walked quickly to the bathroom, turned on the cold water at the sink, and washed his face repeatedly. After drying his face with a hand towel, he tossed it aside, walked to the bed and then drifted into a troubled sleep.

At quarter to five p.m. Colby was startled awake. Reaching awkwardly toward where the hotel phone rested on the night table, he finally managed to bring the receiver to his ear.

"Caught you sleeping, or were you doing some entertaining?"

He registered quickly to Lord's voice and answered, "The former. Saving the latter for tonight."

"And since you brought up tonight, be downstairs at six fifteen. Delgado will pick us up and then we're off somewhere. See you then," and the connection ended.

Now fully awake, Colby once again thought about what he had committed to do and then made a promise to himself that he would reach a decision by the following morning. Tonight he would relax, forget about everything except the beautiful mujeres, (Women) that Delgato promised to provide.

◆◆◆◆◆

When Colby stepped out of the elevator he paused and then glanced around the crowded lobby. He spotted Lord standing near the concierge's desk and began walking in that direction.

Lord's appearance, his gray tailored slacks, white silk shirt and custom made blue blazer, defined for anyone interested, that this was a man of some influence. Someone with exceptional taste and the money to go with it.

Immediately Colby felt ill at ease as he thought of himself. He was dressed in a red and white plaid shirt and khaki pants. The clothes placed him in sharp contrast to Lord's attire. It marked him as part of the lower strata of whatever group or organization he considered himself part of.

He thought about Dixx, the penthouse and the lifestyle he lived. Then he thought about Lord and where his station in life was. It was certainly on a similar level to Dixx. Then he realized, at that very moment, that no matter how well he did whatever it was that Dixx wanted, he would never be accepted the way Lord was.

Colby shook his head slightly as he knew what his decision regarding Lord would be.

"Let's wait outside. Delgado should be here any minute."

Colby nodded but didn't say anything. He followed Lord through the main entrance to the hotel and past the line of taxis.

"Let's wait here. Delgado will see us. Your shirt will act as a beacon for him," and then Lord laughed.

When Colby didn't join in, Lord said, "Hey Colby, I'm only pulling your chain. I'm too dressed up for what's going to take place tonight. I should've followed your lead and dressed down."

+ + + + + +

The car and two escorting SUVs parked in a reserved space in front of the restaurant entrance.

Delgado and seven of his bodyguards waited with Lord and Colby on the sidewalk as several others went into the restaurant. After several minutes an okay signal was given.

"I think you gentlemen will like the food here. Very tasty for both the stomach and the eyes." He smiled and then laughed as Lord and Colby joined in.

As they walked inside, the maitre d' and owner stood apprehensively and then welcomed Delgado in a manner reserved only for the moneyed and the feared. After several more moments Delgado was escorted to a large table at the rear of the room. Two smaller tables on either side were reserved for his ten bodyguards.

Once they were seated, Delgado asked, "Do you like this place, Nicholas?"

"What's there not to like? Nice decor, nice music and the eye candy looks interesting."

"What is this eye candy you refer to, Nicholas?"

"Lo siento. Eye candy, Ojos dulces, es una forma en que nos referimos a las mujeres hermosas. (Sorry, eye candy is a way we refer to beautiful women)

Delgado laughed, "And it is a very excellent way to refer to beautiful women Nicholas. I must remember it."

Lord translated for Colby, who shook his head as he smiled.

"Let me order some food, Nicholas. I think first we satisfy the stomach and after that we satisfy other things."

"Perfect."

After the meal was finished and the dishes cleared away, Delgado ordered several bottles of Dom Perignon champagne and a bottle of Hennessy cognac.

Moments after the bottles, glasses and champagne flutes were in place, three very attractive and well attired women approached the table.

After a brief exchange with Delgado, the women sat down next to each of the men.

Delgado looked at Lord. Your eye candy speaks only Spanish, Nicholas, but that is not a problem for you."

Then Delgado turned his head and locked eyes with Colby. "Your companion knows some English but I don't think you should concern yourself. You will, I assume, not be doing too much talking later," and then Delgado smiled as Colby shook his head from side to side and smiled.

After the drinks were poured, Delgado asked, "What shall we drink to, gentlemen?"

Colby looked at Lord who nodded yes. Then he looked at Delgado and said, "I think we should drink to life. May we all have health, happiness, wealth, and the time to enjoy them."

"A very nice toast, Mr. Colby," and then Delgado lifted his champagne flute. Lord, Colby and the three women did the same.

After Delgado placed his champagne flute on the table, he pointed toward the dance floor. "I think I'll stretch my legs out there. Would either or both of you care to join me?"

The three couples made their way through the crowd and onto the dance floor as the band played the up tempo song, 'No se va.' (It doesn't go away)

After several more songs, Delgado waved his hand. "I need some more liquid fuel. I'm running out of gas."

Lord and Colby laughed while the women just stood there confused. After Lord translated, they laughed as they made their way back to the table.

After a few minutes Colby and his companion returned to the dance floor and the other two women excused themselves, leaving Delgado and Lord alone.

"Have you ever considered changing the scenery, Nicholas?"

"I'm not sure I understand your question, Mr. Delgado."

"I mean changing jobs. I could use someone like you, Nicholas. Someone who knows the distribution side and has an understanding of the supply end. Besides, the weather here is much better than in New York."

"The weather for sure, but la policía federal y local son un problema, no?" (...the federal and local police are a problem)

"Los pagamos. Asi de simple. Hay algunos problemas con las organizaciones rivales, pero también son manejables." (We pay them off. It's that simple. There's a few problems with rival organizations, but they're manageable too)

"And an added benefit Nicholas is the hermosos dulces para ojos que tenemos aqui," (...is the beautiful eye candy that we have here) and Delgado laughed.

Nicholas smiled and then chuckled. "You're a fast learner Mr. Delgado... eye candy, ojos dulces," and then Nicholas smiled again.

"Yes, that is the way I will refer to them from now on. When I say it, it always makes me smile and I will think of you. So, Nicholas, now back to the other subject. Please consider what I have offered you. I think you will find this arrangement attractive. Everyone needs a change occasionally in their life."

Lord spotted the women walking toward the table and replied quickly, "I will definitely consider it, Mr. Delgado," and then he turned and smiled as the women took their seats.

After more hours of drinking, dancing and conversation, Delgado started to lift himself up from his chair when he stopped and sat back down. "I think it is time I said goodbye to you fine gentlemen and ladies."

Then Delgado looked at Lord. "When are you planning to leave?"

"The day after tomorrow," then Lord looked at his watch and said, "It's already tomorrow."

"I'll see you at my office then today say about eleven a.m. Enrique will pick you up at your hotel about a quarter to."

"That works. Colby and I will be waiting outside."

Then Delgado looked at Colby and asked, "How is your Spanish coming?"

"Slowly Mr. Delgado, but I plan on getting some practice tonight," then he laughed, and Lord and Delgado joined in.

"Until tomorrow Gentlemen. The check has been taken care of. Enjoy the rest of your evening."

Delgado stood up and moved slightly away from the table. He was joined by his female companion and they were immediately surrounded by his contingent of bodyguards. As they walked toward the entrance, Delgado lifted his hand and waved.

"Well, Colby, shall we dance and drink some more, or do we call it a night?"

"I think I'll call it a night, Mr. Lord." Then Colby stood up, pointed at the woman who had been his gal pal since the evening began and said, "I'm ready. Let's go, okay?"

The woman just stared.

Colby looked at Lord. "I think I need some help. Can you translate what I said?"

"Can do. Then Lord motioned with his hand toward the woman. "Este hombre encantador quisiera irse contigo. Estas listo?" (This charming man would like to leave with you. Are you ready)

"Si,"

"She's ready Colby. I'll be outside the hotel at quarter to eleven. See you then."

Colby nodded, then looked at the woman.

After they both left, Lord turned his attention to the woman he spent the evening with.

"Gracias por una velada encantadora. Tal vez nos volvamos a encontrar." (Thank you for a lovely evening. Perhaps we'll meet again)

"Por cierto, ¿cuantos años tienes?" (By the way, how old are you)

"Cuantos años tenga, doce, quince, veinte? (How old do you want me to be, twelve, fifteen, twenty)

Lord couldn't help himself and laughed. "Eres toda una joven sin importar la edad que tengas." (You are quite the young woman no matter how old you are)

The woman smiled, but Lord saw only the face of Madison. He reached into his pocket, took out his wallet and removed a one hundred dollar bill. He handed the money to the woman.

"Para ti. He disfrutado de tu compañía pero desafortunadamente tengo que irme. Buenas noches." (For you. I've enjoyed your company but unfortunately I have to leave. Good night)

Lord stood up. Smiled at the somewhat startled woman, then turned and walked toward the door.

Once outside, he stopped for a moment as he thought, good decision Nicholas, good decision, and then continued walking until he reached the first taxi in line.

Lord opened the back door and got in. Then he leaned forward and said "Los Tres Rios Hotel." (The three rivers hotel)

The driver started the ignition and eased his way into the surprising heavy traffic.

Lord asked, "¿El tráfico siempre es tan malo?" (Is the traffic always this bad?)

"Si, y más cuando brilla el sol." (Yes, and more so when the sun shines)

Lord smiled as he leaned the back of his head against the leatherette seat covering. When he closed his eyes he saw Madison smiling back. His thoughts were of when he would be flying back to civilization, to Connecticut and Madison.

He heard a voice or what sounded like a voice in the distance, He was suddenly jolted awake and heard the driver telling him they were at the hotel.

"Lo siento. Cuento?" (Sorry. How much)

Lord paid the fare, left the taxi and walked into the hotel. Seventeen minutes later he was fast asleep.

—21—

CHAPTER

COLBY LOOKED AT HIS WATCH AND THEN STARED OUT THE TAXI WINdow.

A panorama of the night's events played across his mind. The woman was everything he imagined she would be and if circumstances were different, who knows where it could lead. But that wasn't going to happen. In a scant seven hours they would be meeting with Delgado and then tomorrow, it would be back to New York.

The matter regarding Lord was still open. He needed to stop procrastinating and make a decision…make a decision as to how, when and where it would happen. A decision that was now delayed because of the events of last night.

He needed to do what he committed to, or face the consequences.

Colby was brought back to the moment as the taxi driver jammed down on the brake pedal. The abrupt stop caused Colby to be thrown forward and he impacted with the plexiglass partition that separated him from the driver's seat.

"What the fuck…" escaped from Colby's mouth just as the street erupted in military grade gunfire.

Colby shifted his body so that he was lying on the back seat.

The shattering of the windshield and then a piercing scream from the driver, told him all he needed to know.

He reached for the door handle and slowly pushed the door open. He crawled across the seat and maneuvered his body through the partially opened door and onto the street,

He crawled as quickly as he could back to where the taxi made its turn, and then once clear of the intersecting street, he lifted himself up and ran as fast as he could.

After a hundred yards, Colby stopped running. He leaned over as he tried to bring quantities of air into his lungs. When his breathing normalized, he started walking again, indifferent to where he was going as long as it was away from the mayhem in front of the hotel.

Suddenly, the sound of sirens filled the air. Colby moved from the street and onto the sidewalk, then watched as a number of police cruisers and SUVs sped past.

After several minutes, Colby decided to walk toward the hotel. When he reached the corner, he'd make a visual as to whether he should continue, depending on the police activity or lack thereof.

He walked slowly, apprehensive, wondering whether what he was doing was the right thing. Should he stay in place and wait a while longer? What was the hurry, and then he pictured Lord and knew that time wasn't on his side. Whether he met his end by whoever was creating the havoc around the hotel or from Dixx or his crew, it didn't matter. He would be dead.

As he walked, he thought, fuck it. I need to get back to the hotel and do it.

As Colby rounded the corner he stopped and watched the police activity. There were at least ten or more vehicles, several ambulances and a substantial number of police and federal officers. A number of men were laying in the street, bodies and blood everywhere. Others were handcuffed and beaten as they were dragged toward police vans and trucks.

He walked slowly toward the hotel entrance and then several uniformed officers motioned him to stop.

"No puedes entrar aquí." (You cannot enter here)

Colby pointed to himself and said, "American." Then he thought of the derogatory word the Spanish use for Americans, and said quickly, "Gringo," as he again pointed to himself and then toward the hotel.

In a few moments another police officer was motioned over.

"Who are you?"

"My name is Colby and I'm a guest in that hotel."

"Let me see your passport."

Colby removed his passport from his shirt pocket and handed it to the officer.

After a comparison between Colby and the passport photograph, the passport was handed back and he was told to continue to the hotel.

Colby walked quickly through the hotel's main entrance. A number of guests and employees were milling around the various windows watching the activity that had disturbed their sleep and complicated their normal morning routine.

Once inside his room Colby removed his clothes, went to the bathroom and showered. As he was toweling dry, the hotel telephone rang.

"Figured you were up. Nice street show, wasn't it?"

"That's one way of putting it, Mr. Lord. I was in a small way part of that show."

"How so?"

"I was coming back to the hotel when the shit hit the fan. The taxi driver was probably killed. Can't be sure, and I didn't hang around to find out. Made my way here after the local 5-O's did what they had to do to get things under control. Just showered and I'll meet you downstairs at quarter to eleven."

"I think you and I should meet before Delgado's man picks us up. You wanna come to my room or meet somewhere else?"

"Your room works. Give me another twenty and I'll be there."

As Colby shaved, he thought about the opportunity this meeting would give him. He could do what had to be done, then leave. How he would get away was open ended. Whether it was by plane, car or some other way, he'd figure it out.

Colby dressed, then walked to the bureau, opened the top drawer, lifted several shirts, and picked up the chrome knife he'd taken from the restaurant. He rubbed his thumb against the blade, then slipped it into his pant's pocket.

A few minutes later he was knocking on Lord's door.

"Come in, Colby. Make yourself comfortable," and Lord pointed to a sofa in the upscale room.

"Quite the room, Mr. Lord. Rank has its privilege," and then he laughed.

"It's not that. Delgado and I go back a ways. He thinks by doing things like this, I'll leave Dixx and work for him."

"Doesn't seem like a bad deal, Mr. Lord. Only one thing to worry about and that's staying alive."

"Yeah," and then Lord smiled.

"Do you want something to drink?"

"I could use some coffee."

"Well, you're in luck. I have a fresh pot here which I ordered from room service a few minutes ago."

Lord poured Colby a cup and then did the same for himself.

"Not bad coffee."

"Agree. A bit hairy out there this morning."

"That's one way of putting it, Mr. Lord. I felt naked without a weapon. Nothing to defend myself with. I was lucky the way it worked out. I could have been killed, and I'm assuming the taxi driver is now meeting his maker all because I was his passenger and this was my destination. Interesting how fate always has a hand in everything."

"Yes, to a degree always, and by the way cut the Mr. Lord bit. Call me, Nicholas."

"Okay, that'll work. And you can call me, Colby."

Lord smiled.

"I wanted to meet here before we get together with Delgado. I'm going to make it quick. I've known Delgado for a while. He's smart and that's why he's survived in a place where killing is a happening every five minutes. The business, our business is brutal, and good people that can be trusted are few and far between."

Lord paused for several seconds and then began again.

"You and I, Colby, work for a man who is not too different from Delgado. They both live the good life because of the people like us that protect them and produce for them. You're good at the heavy stuff and what you do, you do well. Me, I'm part of all this because I said yes to a proposal a long time ago. I had the education and mindset to do other things, but the proposition offered was something at that time, I couldn't turn down."

Lord paused again.

"You and I have benefitted from our association with Dixx. But now, I've reached the point where I'm thinking, and probably will, retire from it all. Delgado offered me a position with his organization. I didn't tell him anything, in detail, about my intended plans...what I've just related to you. What this all leads to Colby, is I'm going to recommend to Dixx that he makes you his number two.

I know you're tight with Joko Rapolo and he functions as your second in command. I don't know him well and can't make a judgment regarding his capabilities. You can make that judgment...whether you keep him or replace him."

After a few more moments, Lord continued. "I plan on telling Dixx when we return to New York that I'm out and you should be my replacement."

Lord picked up his cup and sipped, then placed it down again. "I like your style, Colby. If you want a change of scenery, I'd be willing to recommend to Delgado to hire you, but I know you'd be better off with Dixx as his number two."

"Take a moment to digest what I've said. I'm going to the bathroom."

Colby watched as Lord left the room. He thought about what was said, and then the scene on the road enroute here came flashing back. His thoughts again were how Lord saved his life and now this conversation. His hand rubbed the pocket where he placed the knife and then Colby shook his head from side to side.

He wasn't aware that Lord re-entered the room, until he heard Lord asking, "Is there anything wrong? I saw you shaking your head."

"Yes, there's something wrong. Please sit-down Nicholas."

"I appreciate you're opening up to me regarding your plans. You didn't have to do that. Now I have to open up to you.

First off, I know that you saved my life back at the road incident en-route here."

Lord was about to say something when Colby held up his hand.

"Please, I know you were doing it to save yourself, and I just happened to be there," and then Colby smiled. "It doesn't matter why or how. The fact is that I'm still in one piece because of you and what you did. Now I gotta level with you on something.

Why did Dixx want me along on this trip? It might not be what you think. It wasn't so that I'd get an understanding of the operations down here. It was for an entirely different reason. Dixx told me that he wanted you killed and he wanted me to do it. If I was successful he offered me your position in the organization," and then Colby stopped and stared at Lord to gauge a reaction. When none came, he continued.

"During our time together on this trip, I wrestled with what I had committed to. I've always fulfilled every contract I've undertaken, except for this one. As I've said, you saved my life and that's worth something in my book. You've been a decent guy with me all through your time in the organization…always treating me respectfully and as an equal, despite where I came from and my lack of polish. That's no little thing as far as I'm concerned and it was always appreciated.

That's it. I've said it and…" then Colby just stopped.

Lord remained quiet for a number of seconds, then said, "That took some real courage, Colby.

Okay. Now we need to plan, you and me, but it's got to wait until after we finish up with Delgado. Meantime it'll give us both a chance to think. Are you okay with that, Colby?"

"Yeah, makes sense."

⸻

The meeting with Delgado was short. Lord mentioned, again, their plan to extend their territory into New Jersey and Connecticut, and Delgado reconfirmed the supply side.

"Don't forget the offer, Nicholas, and that offer can include Mr. Colby here."

Delgado looked over at Colby. "Nicholas can explain for you. And if you decide to take up the offer, Mr. Colby, you can always learn to speak Spanish quickly. We have many long hair dictionaries available for just that purpose," then he laughed. "Nicholas can explain that to you also.

If there's nothing else, Nicholas, Enrique will drive you back to the hotel, and thanks for the car and pop gun. It's appreciated. Ten un buen viaje." (Have a good trip)

After they entered the hotel, Lord said, I need to arrange for tomorrow's flight. You can come with me, wait at the bar, or in my room."

"I'll wait for you at the bar."

"Okay. Order me a vodka on the rocks with a twist of lemon."

Colby nodded as Lord turned and began walking toward the concierge's desk.

Fifteen minutes later he was seated next to Colby at a corner table.

"I've had a chance to do some thinking about the problem, Colby, and I've reached a possible solution that will eliminate the immediate threat, one Xavier Dixx.

For your info, I've paid cash for our two tickets back to the states. We're going to travel separately on different airlines. My flight leaves later this morning, and your flight is tomorrow at eight a.m. When Dixx checks the passenger manifest, he won't see my name on your flight. Dixx is cautious to the extreme and he'll check it out, trust me.

Here's how I see it playing out. You'll telephone Dixx after you arrive and inform him you're back and would like a meeting. You reconfirm during your telephone call that what you agreed to do has been done, and you'll discuss the details when you meet, then you…"

After twenty-five minutes, both men stood up and shook hands. "I'll see you in New York, Colby. Have a good flight. If there's anything that needs to be discussed again, you know how to contact me."

22

CHAPTER

LORD DIALED MADISON'S NUMBER.

When the connection was made he said, "Hi Madison. Remember me?"

"Very funny. I've been worried about you. Why didn't you call before?"

"Been busy, Madison, but that's all buttoned up now, and I'm out of here early this morning on Aeromexico with a connecting flight to New York. Should be back about two p.m. Might be easier if we meet up at your condo. Does that work?"

"Yes. Call me when you land, just in case."

"Understood. See you then."

Lord touched the end button, looked at his watch then said out loud, "Might as well go to the airport."

+ +◆◆+ +

"Hi. I'm on terra firma (Firm ground) once again. Are you home?"

"Yes, and I'm waiting for you. Hurry and be careful."

"Yes on both counts. See ya in a bit."

When she opened the door, he smiled as he held out a gift-wrapped package.

"Oh! Is that for me," and she giggled like a schoolgirl. Then kissed him and pulled him inside.

"Now let's see what this handsome man has brought me."

She removed the wrapping paper and stared at the five ounce bottle of Louis Vuitton 'Atrappe-Reves Eau de Parfum."

"This must have cost you a fortune."

"Only a small fortune and you, my dear, are worth a small fortune."

"Words like that will get you everywhere. Do you want a drink?"

"That'll work for starters."

They sat close together on the sofa as Lord related what he felt necessary about the trip, and embellished other things to keep the description on the lighter side.

When he finished, she nodded her head and then said, "It sounds so boring."

"It was. I'm happy to be back here with you."

"Have you thought about us, Nicholas?"

"I've thought about nothing else."

"When do we put it all behind us and leave?"

"As soon as we can. There are several important things I have to do to ensure that nothing will interfere with us when we…" and then Lord stopped as he thought of the words, then he continued, "…separate ourselves from all of this. It won't take long but it's got to be done correctly or we'll always be looking over our shoulder. Trust me. I've never lied to you. I'll get what has to be done, finished as quickly as possible. Then you, Miss Madison, and yours truly, will start living."

She threw her arms around his neck and kissed him. "That's part payment for the perfume and now let me complete the payment."

She stood up, still holding his hand and then they both walked toward the bedroom.

Lord was up early the following morning and on the telephone.

"Hello, Federico, it's Nicholas Lord."

"It's been a long time, Nicholas. I was getting the feeling you didn't love me anymore."

"Nothing like that Federico," and Lord chuckled. "I know it's been a long time. Maybe a few drinks to catch up would be in order."

"I can always make time for a few drinks, Nicholas, so don't be a stranger. Now, what can I do for you?"

"I need a good bounty hunter, Federico, someone who can trace about two hundred and fifty thousand in stolen Crypto, and you're the man. Whatever you recover, there will be a bonus, and you know when I say something…"

Federico interrupted. "You don't have to go on. I've known you a long time and consider you a friend, so just tell me how I can help."

Lord carefully related the details as he knew them and then waited for a reply.

"I'll see what can be done. It may take more than a few days before I can get back to you. Is this the number I can reach you, and is it secure?"

"It's the number you can reach me, and it's as secure as it can be."

"Okay. I'll be in touch."

Nicholas pushed back in his chair and thought, one less problem maybe. Let's see what happens. Nothing ventured, nothing gained.

Madison walked into the kitchen and asked, "Did you finish the call?"

"Yep, but I need to make one more, and please don't look at me that way. I need to take care of what we discussed and then we can go out and get something to eat, if you want to. It won't take long."

Once the connection was made, Lord said, "It's me. I'm in New York. Were you able to set up anything?"

"Yeah. After I told him I completed what I committed to, he wanted to meet immediately. I stalled him, saying I was sick as hell from the stinking food in Mexico, and needed a few hours to get my shit together. He bought it, and we're gonna meet at his place this afternoon at four p.m."

"Okay, I'll be waiting near the parking garage around three-thirty. Don't drive into the garage. They have cameras. Park somewhere else and walk. Make sure you wear a mask to cover your face. Everyone does because of Covid, so you won't stand out. If you need anything or if there's any change, call me pronto…like quick."

Lord placed the phone in his pocket then looked up at Madison. "Do you want to do an early dinner or a late lunch?"

"Sure, let's do an early dinner. A change of scenery always helps."

<hr>

Lord was standing in the middle of the block when he saw Colby.

He waved his hand and waited.

Colby acknowledged with a head shake, and then pointed toward the garage.

"In a minute. We need to cover a few things. First off, keep your Covid mask on until you get to Dixx's apartment. There's cameras everywhere including inside the elevator. The masks are simply another layer of protection so we're not readily identified. We'll walk in separately a few minutes apart. Meantime take this." He handed Colby a wallet.

"You're going to need it. Dixx will want proof that I'm history and this is as good as it gets. He knows you would never have my wallet with the cash and credit cards inside, unless what you stated happened. Make sure you watch what he does with the wallet. I want it back intact.

Let's go over it one more time. You ride up first. Dixx opens the door, and you walk in. He'll close and lock the door, then you'll either go to the living room or out to the deck to talk. Whichever, it doesn't matter. A few minutes into the conversation you go into your act, then head for the bathroom and the rest you know. Do you have any questions?"

Colby shook his head no.

"Good. It's just about showtime. See you in a few minutes."

Colby took out his phone and dialed Dixx. "I'm here. Coming up."

Fifteen seconds later, Lord walked to the elevator and saw the dial indicated that it had reached the penthouse level. He waited an additional fifteen seconds before he pushed on the up button.

As the elevator started its descent, Lord moved back a few steps and angled off to his right. When the door opened, the cab was empty. He moved quickly inside and pressed the button for the penthouse level.

⁘⁘⁘⁘

The apartment door was open when Colby stepped out of the elevator and took off his mask.

Dixx held out his hand and after a few words of greeting, Colby was motioned into the apartment.

After Dixx locked the door, he pointed toward the outdoor deck.

"Please make yourself comfortable, Colby. Would you like anything to drink?"

"No thank you."

"Then perhaps you can provide me with some of the details of your trip to Mexico."

Colby thought, not a bad way to phrase it.

"It was shortly after…" and then Colby began coughing and pointed to his throat. He choked out the words, "Sorry, Mr. Dixx, it's that Mexican food again…it's causing me a bit of trouble. Can I use your bathroom for a moment?"

"Of course. Do you need help?"

"No, I'll be okay. I just need to wash my face with cold water and rinse out my mouth. I'm really very sorry, Mr. Dixx. Just give me a minute, then I'll be okay."

Colby moved slowly in the direction of the hall bathroom. When he was no longer in the line of sight, he went quickly to his right and unlocked the penthouse door.

After entering the bathroom, he turned on the cold water, flushed the toilet several times before reopening the door. Then he walked unsteadily back to the living room.

"Dixx stood up when he saw Colby. "Are you sure you're okay?"

"Better now, thank you. That damn Mexican food plays havoc with your stomach and everything else. So does the damn water."

"So I heard. If you're okay, shall we continue?"

"Before I do Mr. Dixx, I think you'd like to have this. It's the late Mr. Lord's wallet."

Dixx took the wallet from Colby's hand and opened it. He removed Lord's driver's license, several credit cards, and a medical insurance card. He studied each one and then placed the wallet, license and cards on the wrought iron table.

"You don't have to go into any detail Colby. The wallet tells me all I need to know. A job well done, and this is for you."

He reached into his jacket pocket and removed an envelope. As he was handing the envelope to Colby, Nicholas Lord walked through the open glass door and onto the deck, a .357 magnum pistol pointed at Dixx's chest.

"You look surprised, Xavier. Did you think it would be so easy?"

The petrified look on Dixx's face spoke volumes.

"Colby, stand up and move to your right. You, Dixx, just sit quietly and keep your hands where I can see them."

"Stay where you are Colby, don't move," then Lord walked closer to where Dixx was sitting and smashed the pistol against the right side of his head. The force of the blow toppled Dixx to his left, but somehow he remained in the chair as both hit the deck together.

Lord stared down at the unconscious Dixx who was bleeding from his right ear and leaking a clear fluid from his nose, probably cerebrospinal fluid which normally surrounds the brain.

Lord placed the pistol back into his holster, then lifted Dixx up and dragged him to the deck's railing. "Okay Colby, give me a hand. Grab his feet."

Once Colby held Dixx's feet, Lord said, "The late Mr. Dixx is about to go flying. We'll lift him together, swing him back once, then continue forward. Once we've cleared the railing, we let him go. Are you ready?"

Colby nodded.

Twenty seconds later Xavier Dixx disappeared over the penthouse railing.

Lord picked up his wallet from the table, replaced his driver's license and the credit cards inside, and then slipped the wallet into his pant's pocket. He smiled as he thought, what the Lord giveth, the Lord taketh.

"Get a towel from the bathroom Colby, and I'll do the same. Wipe down the door knobs and anything else you touched like the door lock. Let's do it quickly and get the hell out of here, and don't forget to put the mask back on. Make sure you take the towel you're using with you and get rid of it and the clothes you're wearing. I'll be in touch with you tomorrow."

A half hour later, Lord was back at Madison's condo.

"I think we should go out tonight, Madison. Let's go to dinner. How about 'Michaels' and then go dancing at 'The Music Lounge'?"

"What are we celebrating?"

"Us."

— 23 —

CHAPTER

THE SUDDEN RINGING STARTLED LORD FROM THE DEEP SLEEP HE WAS
experiencing. As he tried to focus on where the ringing sound was coming
from, he glanced at Madison whose eyes were open and staring up at him.

As he reached for his cell phone, he mouthed the word, "Sorry."

He moved out of bed and he brought the cell phone to his ear and replied yes.

"It's me, Colby. You sound like you're still asleep. Did I wake you?"

"A matter of fact you did."

"Well you don't want to sleep the day away. It's already past eight-thirty
of a brand new day."

"It was a late night, Colby. I was celebrating."

"And I wasn't invited?"

"It was skirts only," and despite himself Lord laughed. "What can I do
for you at this early hour?"

"Got a call from Serenity, the woman who's now hanging with Lomax.
She said Lomax is having a shit fit. Seems the pills we sold him are bamboo

shit (low quality) and word is out on the street which means his business is down. He wants us to return his money."

"Give me a second, Colby, to process what you just told me."

After several minutes with no further response from Lord, Colby asked, "You still there Mr…err, Nicholas?"

"Yeah, I'm still here. I'll telephone Lomax and arrange a sit-down. I'll call you back as soon as it's confirmed. It might be a while so stay cool."

"I'm sorry, Madison. Seems there are a few more loose ends to tie up."

"It seems to me, Nicholas, that there are always going to be a few more loose ends to tie up."

"At the moment, it certainly seems that way and I wish it wasn't, but it is. I need to meet someone with Colby. After that I'll have a better fix or what you and I can expect. I want to assure you, Madison, I want out of this as badly as you do."

"I love you, Nicholas, and I trust you. Please…please get whatever it is done and let's get away from it all before we're in a situation where all of this swallows us up."

Lord nodded. "I feel the same way."

Lord walked into another room and dialed Lomax. When the connection was made, Lomax came on strong.

"Okay, I don't understand how that happened. Let's have a sit- down and discuss it face to face."

"Be here at two 'Hey You', and you better come with some answers, and you better bring Uptown along."

Lord looked at his watch. It was ten after nine.

Lord dialed Colby. "We have a sit-down with Lomax at two this afternoon. Pick me up on the corner of Broadway and Lafayette at one-thirty sharp. That'll give us some time to discuss a few things before we meet him."

Lord walked back to the bedroom. "I don't know if you heard the conversations but Colby and I are meeting with Lomax, the head gangbanger of the Harlem Originals at two this afternoon. Seems there's some problem with the recent shipment of fentanyl Dixx sold him. Not to worry, Madison. I'll handle it somehow."

"And what if you can't?"

"That's not a consideration. I'll handle it."

———— ✦✦✦✦✦ ————

Lord moved toward the curb when he saw Colby turn the corner.

Once he was inside the car, Lord said, "We've got a problem. If Lomax wants his sixty large back, I'm not sure I can raise it quickly, but more importantly, I'm not so willing to give him back anything. You saw Delgado's operation. We've been doing business together too long for him to ship us bamboo.

I think Lomax is trying to yank our chain, but I can't think of what advantage that would give him. When we're there, let me take the lead and you can add-in whenever you think it's necessary.

Whatever happens, stay cool. We're on his turf and he has all the advantages. Okay Colby, I'm ready if you are?"

Colby put the car into gear and edged slowly into the Lafayette Street traffic.

———— ✦✦✦✦✦ ————

After Colby parked the car, they walked toward the storefront entrance. The tall black gangbanger on the right side of the door held up his hand and Lord and Colby stopped.

"No Bentley today?"

When no reply came, the gangbanger said, "My friend here is gonna frisk you both. No weapons allowed inside."

After the pat down Colby and Lord walked inside. They were pointed toward the same room they'd used a number of times previously.

After they were seated, Lomax asked, "Where is Uptown? You were supposed to bring him."

"He couldn't come. Some kind of health problem."

"Well he's gonna have some real health problems if this bamboo shit mess ain't fixed, and fixed soon."

"Colby and I were just in Mexico visiting with our supplier. I've personally known the head of this cartel for years. He doesn't make or ship bamboo, so I don't understand how the quality is anything other than what he always supplies. Where are you getting the feedback that this is substandard fentanyl?"

"It's comin' back from the streets."

Colby spoke up. "Did you ever think that the ABN might be putting out the word that your material isn't quality so you have problems? If you're taking business, market share, away from them whether it's fentanyl, blow (Cocaine) or smack (Heroin) they're not going to sit quietly and watch what they built disappear.

I was with Mr. Lord in Mexico. I can vouch that the material I saw being made is exactly the same quality as you always get. We value our connection with you and wouldn't do anything that stupid to jeopardize it. It's that simple. The material is first quality."

"We gonna do some more checking, and if we find out that what we're hearin' is true, you and him and Uptown are gonna have some real major problems."

Lomax looked over at his number two, Elijah Carter, who nodded, smiled and then said, "We going to come down on you like a hammer if we find out this fentanyl is bamboo. We'll test it and then you'll be hearin' from us."

Lomax stood up. "This here meeting is over. Tell Uptown he should start worrying big time, 'cause his health problems are about to get a lot worse. Now both of you leave while you still can."

Colby put the car in gear and pulled away from the storefront. After several blocks, Lord motioned to pull curbside.

"About what I expected. How do you read it, Colby?"

Colby chuckled. "To put it simply, the yob (Tough guy) thinks we've shafted him. But he doesn't have the brains to figure out why we'd sell low grade fentanyl and close out our primary sales channel in Harlem. He's too fucken stupid to understand that there's nothing for us to gain by doing what he claims we've done."

Lord nodded, "He thinks or he knows, that his street sales are down because the word is out there that his 'China white' (Fentanyl) isn't up to par. We know differently, but that's not enough, as long as Lomax believes otherwise."

"Based on what you've just said, Nicholas, do we have the time to wait?"

"No, time isn't on our side, but what's the alternative? Lomax is one confused dude and that makes him dangerous. If the dude can't think clearly, he's prone to do all crazy shit."

"That's exactly what I mean. The son of a bitch is likely to come after us just for the hell of it. To do something, anything rather than see his drug sales go down and his leadership threatened."

"Nothing more we can do now, Colby. Table it for today and we'll reconnect tomorrow or sooner."

"Okay, Nicholas, do you want me to drop you off at Lafayette Street?"

"That would be appreciated. Thanks."

Sparrow sat with Cleotha RaJean and several ABN associates.

"As I said MJ, Clement was eyeing the HO's headquarters for that Bentley car, but it hasn't shown up for a week or more. Clement did say that a Chrysler four door car pulled up about two this afternoon and two honkies got out and went into the storefront entrance."

"I asked him if he could ID them and he said one looked like a honky that's been there before. He couldn't tell me whether it was the guy who drove the Bentley or someone else. Too far away."

"Okay, Sparrow. Stay on top of it. Keep eyes on their headquarters and let me know what I should know. You understand?"

"Yes, MJ. I understand."

"And keep the word circulating on the street that their candy (Drugs) is second rate. Saying it enough times makes it true, right Sparrow?"

"Right MJ."

Lord dialed then placed the phone against his ear. "Hi Madison, I'm downstairs. Buzz me in please."

When Madsion opened the door to her condo she pointed to the newspaper she was holding in one hand and said, "You won't believe this."

After Lord sat down, she handed him the paper.

"Look at the top right hand column."

Lord eyes scanned the headline. 'Xavier Dixx Dead In Suicide At Penthouse, Spurring Inquires.'

After a few minutes, Lord put down the paper, and looked at Madison who was still standing.

"Holy Hannah, but why? Why would he jump off the deck? I wonder if he was drunk, or maybe slipped looking over the railing? We won't know until after the investigation, and may not know much even after that. Whether he fell accidentally or whatever, you can't live after falling sixteen stories. It's just that simple."

Lord moved his head from side to side slowly then said, "Wow! that changes things a bit."

"No, Nicholas, it changes things a lot. It takes a lot of pressure off you and me. I can't say I'm sorry about it, although I wouldn't have wanted him to end his life that way. I'm not a heartless person. He was good to me and I was good to him for a long while. Then…" and Madison locked eyes with Lord. "…you know the rest."

"I'm going to make a call to Colby. It'll take just a minute. Please stay here.

When Colby answered, Lord said, "Get yourself a copy of the Post. Second page, top right hand column. Seems Dixx killed himself. Jumped off or fell off the deck of his penthouse."

"Holy shit," then Colby chuckled. "I wonder what he looked like when he made contact with the street."

"You don't want to know. I'll get the word to Lomax. Better he hears it from me than someone else, although I don't think it really makes any difference. You know, a difference regarding what he told us about during our meeting. I'll be back to you if I have anything more."

"One more call and that's it. Please stay."

"I need to go to the bathroom. Be back in a few."

Lord dialed Lomax's number. "Yeah. What you want, Hey You?"

"I just want to tell you Uptown committed suicide. Took a swan dive off his penthouse balcony. You can read all about it in the Post."

"So he felt guilty about selling me bamboo candy?"

"That's pure bullshit. He had health problems like I told you and the future didn't look too bright. So I'm guessing he took the easy way out while he could. What I told you about the quality of our merchandise is a fact. Nothing but top grade comes to us and you get what we get. Check out why the word on the street is otherwise. You have the foot soldiers to find out. When you do, you'll see we've been straight with you. Have a good rest of the day!"

Madison was walking back when the ringing of a phone sounded. "I think that's mine, and I left it in the bedroom."

As Madison was turning away, Lord's cell rang.

"Hello Federico."

"Hi Nicholas. Just wanted to update you. Making some progress but it's slow, very slow.

"Okay, thanks, Federico, appreciate."

Lord looked up as Madison walked back holding her phone in one hand. "That was Mel Peterson, Xavier's lawyer. He wants to meet with me preferably tomorrow. I made a tentative appointment for eleven in the morning. Does that work for you?"

"Sure, did he indicate what he wanted to see you about?"

"Yes, it's about Xavier and his will."

"Eleven works."

"Okay, I'll confirm it and I'll inform him that you'll be accompanying me. It should be interesting."

—24—

CHAPTER

THE TALL, MUSCULAR, HO GANGBANGER POSITIONED AT THE RIGHT side of the entrance to their headquarters, turned slightly so he was facing the man standing on the left side.

"Hey, Labond, take a good look at those two brothers off to my right about a half a block down. They're standing near the variety store. They been there for a while talking shit, but they keep looking at us. I've seen them or others like 'em around almost every day for a while. I think we need to talk with them. Get Marvis and several of his boys, and bring them both back here."

Labond shook his head once. Okay, Marcel, I'll get Cleever to take my place here. Where do you want me to put them?"

"Take 'em to the store room and let me know you have 'em. We're gonna find out a few things."

Twenty minutes later, Sparrow and the teenager were seated in two chairs facing Baxter, Carter, Marcel, and ten more HO associates.

"We're gonna ask ya some questions. If we don't like the answers, you won't like what happens to you. You can play tough for a while, but I guarantee we'll rearrange your body parts so your mothers won't recognize you. Yeah, I know what you're thinking...you feed us some shit, and then walk out of here. Well, think again. Personally, I don't give a rat's ass whether you walk out of here or the boys here carry you out. Now let's get started."

"Two questions for that pea brain of yours. Who are you and why are you watching us."

Sparrow answered. "My name is Kordel Washington, and my friend here, Cornell, said a white honky drives a Bentley car and parks it in front of this storefront. I wanted to see it. I don't have a job so I hang around the streets, hustle here and there and that's it.

That variety store across the street and a ways down, has a fair amount of traffic in and out, and that's where I can get an odd job once in a while. So, like I said, I hang there with Cornell or some others from the project."

"That's a crock of shit. I told you what we'd do if you start lying..."

Before Marcel could finish his sentence, another HO gangbanger delivered a punch to the side of Sparrow's head, toppling him off his chair and onto the wooden floor.

He was picked up roughly and slammed against a wall. Two HO gangbangers held him up as Marcel and several other HOs pounded his face and body. After several minutes, they let the bloodied body of Sparrow fall back to the floor.

Marcel looked at the other man. "Now it's your turn."

The man held up his hand. "Don't, please don't. I'll tell you whatever I know."

Marcel leaned toward the seated man. "If I don't like what you're saying, I guarantee that you are gonna get twice what we did to that piece of shit laying on the floor," and then Marcel punched him several times in the face. Okay, now that we understand each other, let's start off with a name, like your name."

"I'm Cornell Commings. I live in the projects with my mom."

"Who is that?" and Marcel pointed at the motionless body of Sparrow?"

"That's Sparrow. He's a member of the ABN, the Almighty..."

"I know what the ABN is. No need to tell me. Are you a member of the ABN?"

"No. I hang around them and they give me things to do sometimes, but mostly Sparrow does."

"Why ain't you a member?"

"They don't think I have what it takes…that's what Sparrow hinted to me."

"Okay. We'll leave that for a moment. Why were you eyeballing us?"

"What Sparrow told you was partly right. We're watching for that Bentley car. Seems the ABNs wanta know why a white guy is comin' to your headquarters. That's not the kind of car that's seen in the neighborhood and they want to know the connection. That's it, so help me, that's it. Sparrow pays me to watch and tell him when…if I see the car. There isn't anymore. I swear it on my mother."

The blow knocked Commings off the chair. One of the HOs placed the chair upright while another gangbanger yanked Commings up and slammed him back into the chair.

"I told you not to lie. Now tell me why you and Washington are watching us?"

"I swear on my mother, what I told you is the truth and that's all I know. The ABN don't trust me to be a member, so what more could I know? Sparrow is a decent guy. He doesn't treat me like the others do and he gives me some work like watching for the white honky and his car.

You can beat me more, but I don't know anything more than I just told you. I didn't do nothing wrong. I just want to make some change and Sparrow always gives me jobs like the one I just said…like watching for a car."

"Going to ask another question, Commings, and you better tell me straight. We're gettin' feedback from the street that our TNT (Fentanyl) is bamboo shit. Where is that comin' from?"

Cornell Commings took several deep breaths and then said, "From what I hear and I can't swear to it, the ABN is spreading the word around the street that your stuff is low quality, bamboo shit."

Marcel looked over at several HO associates and smiled. Then he looked back at Commings.

"You got ID, Commings?"

"Yes,"

"Give it here. I want to take a look."

Commings removed his wallet and handed it to Marcel.

After a number of seconds, Marcel handed the wallet back.

"Okay Commings I know where you live. I'm going to let you go, but with the following understanding. Anything, anyone associated with the ABN wants you to do that involves us, or you hear about, you come here on the quick. Ask for me, Marcel, and then you tell me what you got. Do you understand me?"

"Yes, I understand you."

"As far as this one called Sparrow is concerned you don't know anything. You play dumb. Shouldn't be too hard for you. Understand?"

"Yes, I understand."

"Okay, Cornell. You're one lucky Nig. Now get the fuck out of here while you can still walk, and keep outta sight. Stay with momma until your fucking face heals. Don't want no one asking what happened. Understand?"

"Yes, I understand."

After Commings was thrown out of the rear doorway, Marcel pointed to the still unconscious Sparrow. "Make sure this piece of shit gets deliver back to the ABN mother fuckers in the proper way. Then we go on alert. Never can tell if we're going to war, so let's get prepared. I'll fill King Shorty (Lomax) in about all this. Labond, you come with me."

A little after three a.m. a city garbage truck stopped in front of the ABN headquarters. Two men, their faces covered with Covid masks, lifted a large canvas bag and placed it on the sidewalk. Then they remounted the rear portion of the truck as it continued driving south on 126th Street.

—————— ✦✦✦✦✦ ——————

Mel Peterson, Esq., greeted Madison with a hug and shook hands with Lord. After they were seated, Peterson went behind his desk, picked up a manila folder, opened it and removed Xavier Dixx's will.

"Our meeting here today may seem a bit sudden in light of Xavier's recent passing, but I see no reason to wait. I have represented Xavier for many years. While I'm privy to certain aspects of his business, I am…" Peterson paused for several seconds then continued, "…I am not privy to everything. Xavier did tell me that he was considering changing some parts of this will, but whatever he planned to do will not happen, and this document will remain his last will.

To you Madison, Xavier leaves five-hundred thousand dollars. The Maserati Quattroporte automobile, the Fifth Avenue penthouse, stocks, bonds and other real estate, he is dividing among his ex-wife, and twin daughters. That's it in a nutshell. Within the next several days, please advise what financial institution you want these funds transferred to.

Xavier always spoke highly of you, Madison, and you also, Nicholas. If I can do anything for either of you in the future, please don't hesitate to contact me. May the money bring you good fortune, Madison."

"Thank you, Mel. I'll be in touch tomorrow. Quite a surprise."

Once they were in the elevator, Madison turned to Lord and wrapped her arms around his neck. "Can you believe what just happened? I never figured anything like that for a moment and I'm shocked, surprised and very happy, Mr. Lord. It takes some pressure off us, at least in the financial sense."

"Yes indeed, Madison. Quite a surprise. In the end, Dixx did right by you, his ex and his daughters. I have the distinct feeling that what Peterson was referring to about the changes Dixx wanted to make to the will, was that he was going to write you out. Obviously based on what he suspected or knew about your involvement with me."

Lord purposely left out any mention of what Dixx planned for him via Colby. He thought about telling her, but nixed the idea, realizing that nothing would be gained by her knowing.

"I think we should celebrate Nicholas. What do you say?"

"Okay but I think we should go to Connecticut. I need a real change of clothes. What I've been switching around doesn't seem to work anymore."

"Let's do it. We'll go to my place first. I'll get some glad rags and other girlie necessities and I'll drive you there."

"Deal, Miss Money Bags," and they both laughed.

— 25 —

CHAPTER

WORD SPREAD QUICKLY ABOUT THE BODY OF KORDEL WASHINGTON, aka 'Sparrow.' The discovery was made shortly after it was dumped in front of the ABN clubhouse.

Several anonymous calls were made to the 25th police precinct, and homicide officers were dispatched to the scene. After an examination of the body, the homicide detectives notified the Medical Examiner and then the body of Sparrow was transported to one of the three New York Forensic Pathology Centers.

The police questioned a number of stand arounds, and ABN members including Cleotha RaJean. Nothing definitive was developed regarding how the body got where it was, or the circumstances of the killing.

The detectives weren't surprised that no one saw or knew anything about the body. In this neighborhood, like those in other gang controlled territories, people of every stripe knew better than to talk to the police about anything.

After the police left and the street activity returned to normal, RaJean called a meeting of his lieutenants and crew leaders.

"Listen up. We all saw the same thing. Someone blew away Sparrow. They fucked him up pretty bad by the look of his face. The pigs ain't gonna find out shit about who hit Sparrow, but we are gonna do some serious diggin' and we're going to find out.

I want you to get the jacks (Another name for gang members) on the streets. Find out everything you can. Someone knows something and we're going to find that someone. That's it. Get moving!"

✦ ✦✦✦✦ ✦

Lord looked at the cell phone screen then answered, "Before you ask, I'm in Connecticut. Needed a change of clothes."

Colby chuckled. "I know the feeling. I'm wondering, Nicholas, with Dixx dead, shouldn't we be in contact with Delgado? He's going to want to know, and what's the story on our next shipment, and what are we going to do about Lomax, and…"

"Whoa, slow down Colby. Way too many questions. Haven't had that third cup of coffee yet," and Lord laughed. "Maybe too many questions, period. Let's take them one at a time. As far as Delgado goes, I'll make a call and tell him you're running the operation and I'll find out what he's scheduling for us. Second, regarding Lomax, I guess we need another sit-down and we'll inform him the same thing, that you're the new 'Uptown,' then Lord laughed again. Was there a third question Colby?"

"Yeah. Something over the TV. Seems a body was found in front of the ABN clubhouse early this morning. No other details were reported, but the chick giving the report speculated that it was some gangbanger."

"May have something to do with Lomax and that rumor circulating about the quality of our supply. That's the only thing that comes to mind, but with these rival gangs, anything is an excuse to bop someone. Guess we do need another sit-down and try to get a handle of what's happening or will happen. Guaranteed the ill wind is going to be blowing in our direction at some point."

"Yeah, I agree, Nicholas. Let me know when."

"Will do, anything else?"

"Yes, one more thing. I did a one on one with Joko Rapolo, asked him some specifics about Dixx while we were south of the border. Watched his body language which I'm pretty good at reading. Didn't get any negative vibes. Seemed Dixx stayed in the apartment most of the time.

Only thing Dixx asked him to do was get the Maserati serviced. I think Dixx was waiting for me to return and tell him the commitment was completed, then he'd decide what he'd do regarding me and Rapolo. Just don't know, but I haven't forgotten what you stated about Joko. That's it."

"Okay, I'll be in touch with you after I speak with Delgado. Stay loose."

"Always do, and you do the same."

✦✦✦✦✦✦✦

Stefon Walker, Mean Jean's third in command, motioned one of his crew leaders to move closer.

The crew leader looked at the man standing on his left and said, "Don't move until I tell you or he does."

Rhylan Davis moved forward and stopped two paces away the ABN's underboss.

"Speak."

Using his thumb, Davis motion toward the man standing at his rear.

"The wanksta (Wannabe gangbanger) says that he saw someone who looked like he was thumped (Beat up) and lives in the project with his mom or grandmother. Seems that person was a hang around with Sparrow. That's what's come back so far from my feelers after we put the word out on the pave. (Street) Might be worthwhile to hear what he says."

"Bring him over."

Rhylan Davis turned and moved his head in a way that conveyed move closer.

"Stop. Talk when you're told to. Otherwise you stay quiet. Understand?"

The teenage black shook his head yes.

Stefon Walker locked eyes with the boy then asked, "You have something you want to tell me?"

"I understand that you want information regarding the killing."

Walker shook his head yes, "And you know something?"

"Maybe."

"Talk. You don't have much time."

"Seems there's a bro that has been hanging with your man who was killed. Seems your man was using him for odds and ends. A short time after the body of your man was found, I had a chance meeting with him. I was visiting some skirt I was doing and who lives at the project. I was taking the stairway up as I didn't want no one to see me, and crossed with Cornell Commings who was coming down.

Saw his face was fucked up like someone did a dance on it. When I asked him what happened he just said some fuckers cornered him and punched him for the hell of it. That's it, then he continued down the stairway and outta the building. That's all I know, but it may be something, since he did know your man."

"Okay, take this," and Walker handed the boy some folded money. "If you hear anything more, you get in touch with Rhylan."

"I will and thanks for the paper," (Money) and he held up his hand as he turned away.

Stefon Walker looked at Davis. "Get busy, Rhylan, and let's find out."

+ + ◆ ◆ ◆ + +

"Do you want to go out for dinner, Madison, or stay home? I could order some pizzas."

"Let's stay home, and pizza from Mario's sounds yummy. Make my half with anchovies."

"I'll call it in and then pick it up. Easier that way."

After Lord called in the order, he looked at Madison. "The usual fifteen minutes."

Madison nodded her head. "I've been thinking Nicholas, the money Dixx left me and the fact that Dixx is no longer a threat, means we don't have to run and hide. We can live here in Connecticut and use the condo in Manhattan when we want to. There's no threat we have to worry about, is there?"

Lord shook his head no, "As far as I know, there's no threat against us. Colby will take over and he's already met with the Mexicans. It's just a question of assuring the Harlem Originals that everything remains as is, and they're the sales channel for Delgado's products."

"Does that mean you still have to be a part of all that?"

"Yes, until everything is clarified for everyone that's involved. It shouldn't take that long, and then I'm history as they say."

"How long is that long?"

"Not sure. A week, two at the most. Now I need to get that pizza. Sit tight, be back in the usual fifteen."

Rhylan Davis and four of his associates rode the elevator to the eighth floor. Then walked to a door marked 8E and knocked.

An elderly woman, using a cane, opened the door and asked, "Can I help you?"

Raylan answered, "We would like to see Cornell. We're friends of his."

"Oh! He's not here at the moment. He's on an errand for me. I needed some medicine. He should be back shortly. Do you want to come inside and wait?"

"No thank you. We'll wait downstairs."

"Okay. you boys have a nice day, okay?"

Davis smiled and said, "Same to you."

Once they were on the ground level, Davis pointed to two of his associates. "You two, along with Clipper, wait outside for him. Cover the back as well as the front. We'll wait inside in case he somehow slips by you."

Ten minutes later, Cornell Commings was shoved into the back of a car and taken to the ABN Clubhouse.

Commings sat alone on one side of the table while several ABN gang-bangers formed a semicircle at his rear.

Cleotha RaJean stood on the opposite side of the table. "Gonna ask you some questions, Commings. Depending on what I hear, you can walk out of here or some of the boys will carry you out. That's the only two options you have."

Commings coughed, and then some spittle dripped from his lips.

"I see we understand each other," then RaJean laughed.

"First question. How did you face get that way?"

"Someone used their fist."

"Why?"

"To show me what happens if I say anything."

"Who was that someone? Now think carefully before you give me an answer, and make sure it's what I want to hear."

"It was a gangbanger with the HOs."

"Make long words and tell me why the HOs think you're a threat."

"Cause I saw what they did to Sparrow."

RaJean's eyes widened, as a low, intense murmur filled the room.

"Keep talking."

"He was fucked up real bad…bleeding…laying on the floor. He was still alive then. The gangbanger who was doing all the talking asked for my wallet. He looked at my ID and then said he now knows where I live. Told me to say outta sight until my face healed and not to say anything to anyone or he'd make sure I got what Sparrow got. I liked Sparrow and we were friends. We were watching the HO's clubhouse for that Bentley when we was grabbed by some HOs. Then it happened like I just said."

"You're one lucky guy once again, Commings. You're going to walk out of here in one piece. If you want to stay that way, just stay outta sight for a while…a long while. We also know where you live. Now get your ass back to the project and deliver that medicine. And if that woman asks what took you so long to come back, you tell her you had to wait for the prescription or some shit like that. Now git!"

— 26 —

CHAPTER

CLEOTHA RAJEAN HUDDLED WITH SEVERAL OF HIS UNDERBOSSES after Commings left.

"Rhylan, I want you to get us some dingers. (Stolen vehicles) I'm thinking of a school bus and a van to take us back home. There's a private company located around 140th Street that has a contract with the city's school system. I think they go by the name of, "The Burton Bus Company."

They park their buses on their lot overnight. I want to pay the HOs a visit tonight. We load the bus with several jerry cans of gasoline, drive to the HO's clubhouse and torch the fucking place. We'll have five or six of our boys on the bus in case there's any HOs at home which will probably be the case. I'm going along on this one tonight. It'll be like old times."

At nine twenty-seven p.m. RaJean, Stefon Walker and four associates loaded onto the school bus.

"Okay, listen up. Make sure your weapons are loaded. Secondly, no faces. (Masks on) Third, after we crash this mother, we get out of the bus through the rear door. Stefon and Nugget hang back and lights the bus on fire. Then we get in the van, and we're outta there. Kill anything that tries to stop us."

Thirty minutes later, Cleotha RaJean drove the bus onto the sidewalk and then through the front entrance of the HO's clubhouse. He kept the accelerator pressed to the floor until three-quarters of the bus was inside the clubhouse. Then he opened the bus's rear door, and left with the others.

They quickly formed a cordon around Nugget and Stefon Walker, as the two gangbangers lit the rag wicks of their Molotov cocktails. Then both gangbangers tossed their bottles through the open rear door of the bus. The bottles shattered on impact, igniting the gasoline canisters.

The six men ran quickly to the shadow van, and moments later disappeared into the night.

— ✦✦✦✦✦ —

"Yes, I caught it on the morning news as well. It's going to change things, Colby. We don't have a sales channel anymore. Good thing I didn't make contact with Delgado yet."

"Yep, I agree. Just as well since this is now one screwed up situation. The news I saw only said that there were several dead and injured. Whoever did it, and I've got a feeling who it was, I've got to hand it to them. Using a school bus, that's a good one.

Seems the bus wedged itself in the front so no one could get out that way. Probably killed a few on impact. Whoever was still hanging around at the rear that time of night, got lucky and probably made it out the back."

"Did they ID any of the bodies on the news program you were watching?"

"No, Nicholas, didn't hear any names."

"I think I'll place a call to Lomax."

"Good idea. Clue me in after you finish your call."

"Will do."

Madison sat quietly watching Lord as he finished his call.

"Will this complicate things, Nicholas?"

"Unfortunately, yes. I'm going to call Lomax and try to figure this out before I bring Delgado up to speed. I want to get it right the first time. It's going to cause a slight delay in our plans, but we'll work our way through this somehow."

"Do you want more coffee?"

"Sure another cup can't hurt."

Lord dialed Lomax's cell and heard only one ring before a recorded message said that the number can't be reached. He called again and the same thing happened.

He thought that Lomax might be one of the dead or injured, and then, Lord, looked up and saw Madison holding two cups of coffee.

"Do you want to drink it here or in the kitchen?"

"Since you're already here, let's drink it here."

Madison walked to the sofa and placed the two cups on the coffee table. "Please sit, Mr. Lord. I assume you didn't connect with the person you were trying to."

Then she smiled. "I think I said too many words."

"Doesn't matter, and yes I didn't connect. A recorded message came on that said the number can't be reached. I have the feeling that the person I'm trying to connect with, is one of the dead or injured from that fire the news channels are reporting on. I need to call Colby and let him know. I'll only be a minute."

"Hello Colby, I called our mutual friend but only a recorded message came on. Seems his phone isn't working, or he can't answer, or both. Could be he's one of the dead or injured. Is there any way for you to check this out?"

"I'll try and let you know."

✦✦✦✦✦

Colby drove toward 116th and the HO's clubhouse.

The police and fire activity had the block and surrounding area cordoned off. He parked his car on one of the side streets, then walked the long way around so that he was approaching the scene from a block away.

As he walked slowly toward the cordoned off area, he recognized one of Lomax's underbosses standing on the opposite side of the street, along with a number of HO gangbangers milling around in various size groups.

He crossed the street and walked slowly toward where Elijah Carter was standing.

As Colby narrowed the distance, three HO gangbangers blocked his way, one of whom was the tall dude that always stood at the right side of the store front.

"I need to talk with Elijah Carter."

"Sure you do. Keep your feet planted where they are and I'll see if Mr. Carter wants to waste his time with you."

Marcel turned and walked to where Elijah Carter was standing. Motioning with a nod of his head toward Colby, Marcel said, "He wants to talk with you."

"Bring him here."

"Where are the others?"

"Uptown is dead and Mr. Lord is trying to keep our side from getting too nervous."

"What the fuck does that mean?"

"Well, from the looks of things around here, somebody fucked you up pretty good," and Colby pointed toward their burned clubhouse and adjoining damaged and destroyed buildings.

"No disrespect intended, Mr. Carter, but I'd like to see Jamal Lomax."

"We'd all like to see Jamal, but he ain't around no more. He was killed when that the fucking bus rammed us, then lit up like a Christmas tree and burnt the fucking building pretty good. Killed some of our soldiers as well. Baxter is gone and the skirt, Serenity something, that Jamal was doin' is dead too. You got anything to say, you say it to me."

"We're wondering…Lord, me and our supplier, how are you going to continue selling and paying us for our product?"

"That's our problem, isn't it? You don't need to concern yourself with our business."

"That's just the point. It isn't just your business. It's our business, like in the word, together. When one end of the business is fucked up like it is now, then it becomes my business. I doubt if you have much merchandise left from the last delivery, and I have serious doubts that you have enough bread to pay for any future shipment."

"That shouldn't be a concern to you. We've always managed."

"Things have changed," and Colby again pointed toward the burned, destroyed, and semi-destroyed buildings.

"That's no never mind. You tell me when the next shipment is arriving and where, and you'll have your money just like always."

Colby nodded. I guess our talk is finished."

"I guess so. Do you have my cell number?"

"No."

"Listen up. Program this number into your phone. You contact me and only me from this point on. Got it?"

Colby smiled, turned and walked away without saying anything further. When he was inside his car, he dialed Lord's number.

"Just met with Elijah Carter across from their clubhouse. Decided to drive here and connect one on one. The entire block is in ruins. Looks like the place was bombed. The HO gangbangers were huddled across the street. According to Carter, Lomax is dead and he's now in charge.

If their hang around money or their merchandise was stored in that building, it doesn't exist anymore. I mentioned to him that we were concerned how he would handle the next shipment and how we'd get paid. The shit told me it wasn't any of our concern. They always paid and will pay next time, and so on. I think that it might be to our advantage if we look for another sales channel."

"Like the ABN?"

"Exactly, Nicholas. I'm on my way back to my place. It'll give you some time to think over what I've said. If need-be, call me."

———————— ✦✦✦✦✦ ————————

Lord looked over at Madison, "That was Colby. He drove over to the HO's club house. The entire block is a mess and Elijah Carter now seems to be the new King Shorty." (Gang leader)

Lord smiled. "Don't you just love these terms they use for each other and everything else?"

Madison smiled as Lord laughed.

Lord's cell rang, shattering the moment. "Hello, Federico. What's up?"

"I have some pretty good news, Nicholas. I've managed to recover one hundred and twenty thousand worth of your crypto. The rest is, unfortunately, probably lost. As a point of reference, hackers have already stolen nearly two-billion dollars worth of cryptocurrency in 2022 and the year is only half over."

Lord laughed. "Is that supposed to make me feel better?"

"I wasn't thinking of it that way, Nicholas, but it could, couldn't it?"

"What makes me feel good is your recovery. I didn't expect it to be that much. Take thirty percent for yourself."

"My fee is the usual twenty percent of everything recovered."

"Yeah I know, but you caught me at a weak moment. Take thirty Federico. You earned it, and as always, I'm grateful. Thank you."

"You're a stand up guy, Nicholas. I'll continue to try to recover more, but like I said, it's an uphill struggle and highly doubtful at this point in time."

"Noted and again thank you. After you sell the crypto, have the funds transferred to the usual account."

"Consider it done, Nicholas, and again, thank you for the extra ten percent."

"Stay well, Federico. I'll be in touch at some point."

"Okay, Nicholas. It's been a pleasure as always. Take care!"

"Sounds like you had a good conversation with whomever it was."

"Yes, Madison, my guy was able to recover about one hundred and twenty thousand in crypto, less his fee which I increased by an additional ten percent. He'll sell it for me and then make the dollar transfer in one of my offshore accounts."

"Can you explain how the recovery of stolen cryptocurrency works? I'm just curious."

"I'll give it a try. The short version is you need a skilled computer programmer like I have with Federico. They use a variety of programs and devices to accomplish their recovery task ranging from specialized software to supercomputers. The software and supercomputers generate thousands of password combinations.

One method is termed a 'brute force attack' in which millions of passwords are tested in rapid succession to crack a wallet. A crypto wallet keeps your private keys. These keys are the passwords that give you access to your cryptocurrency, supposedly keeping the crypto safe and accessible, and allowing you to send and receive.

That's about it. Somewhat confusing, huh?"

"No. You've explained it well enough. Simple, yet not so simple. I guess Xavier didn't know about the Federicos of the crypto recovery world."

Lord smiled. "Maybe not."

"I think with your new found riches, Nicholas, and my gift from Xavier, you won't have to sell your cute little Bentley or this house. And I won't have to sell the New York condo. We can stay put, live an okay life, and not worry about anyone coming after either of us, right?"

"Yes, more or less. I still need to help Colby establish himself and then advise Delgado what's happening. There are a few more loose ends, but I can see the light at the end of the tunnel, and that light is going to shine on us."

Lord embraced Madison and they kissed.

— 27 —

CHAPTER

"I CAN ONLY ASSUME THAT PIECE OF SHIT WE LET GO...WHAT WAS HIS name, Marcel?"

"Commings, Cornell Commings."

"Yeah, that's it. Mistake, a big mistake letting him go. It was only a matter of time until someone got in the know about a connection between him and Sparrow. Then whoever, and I got a real good feeling about the name of that whoever, then pumped him dry and he told 'em everything he knew about our little dance party we had with Sparrow.

You know where he lives, Marcel. Take a few of the boys with you. Find out if he opened up to the ABN, then dump him somewhere. Now take a good look across the street. That used to belong to us. Don't forget that when you meet up with Commings."

Marcel nodded, then pointed at Cleever and Nugget. "C'mon, get the van and pick me up. We're going visiting."

Lord dialed Colby's cell. When it went to voicemail, he said, "Somewhat urgent, call when you can."

A few minutes later Colby called back.

"I was doing some serious reflection on our present situation and feel we need a new sales channel sooner, rather than later. Time isn't on our side. The channel we have is seriously flawed and it looks like there's going to be an on-going rumble between the HOs and the ABN for control.

Delgado expects his product to move without interruption. I've serious doubts whether the HOs are capable of either paying up for future products or moving the merchandise. They're having trouble moving the last shipment.

To sum it up, the HOs are drifting down a stream without a paddle. If we don't move product, there is no reason for Delgado to continue using us. The revenue stream dries up and you're unemployed. As for me, I'm getting out as I told you.

But if you want to continue this as the number one dog, then it's a matter of considerable concern. You've got to make the decision whether we change horses and hook up with the ABN, or you call it quits and find another line of employment.

The other alternative is to stick with the HOs and ride with them as they regroup and rebuild. However, there's no guarantee that either will happen."

"I hear you, Nicholas, and yes, there's more than a few problems. I'm okay with switching horses. How do we go about getting in touch with the ABN?"

"We drive the Bentley up to their clubhouse and ask for a sit-down."

"Ok. When?"

Lord looked at his watch. "It's now ten forty-seven. Give me forty-five minutes to an hour and I should be at your place before noon."

Nicholas looked over at Madison. "It's one of those loose ends I've got to tie up. I should be back by three this afternoon. Then dinner tonight at Michael's. I'm getting close to ending it all. Stay positive, Madison, don't worry. It'll be over soon."

Nugget knocked on the door of apartment 8E.

Commings opened the door part way.

"Some friends of mine would like a word with you out front."

"That's not going to happen and…"

Commings stopped in mid-sentence as his mother called out, "Who's there, Cornell?"

"Just a friend, Mom. Be finished in a minute."

"Like I was sayin' we'd like to talk downstairs."

"And like I was saying, that's not going to happen."

Commings pointed the pistol at Nugget's chest. "Now get the fuck out of here. No more talk."

"You're going to have to come out of that apartment sometime and we'll be waiting."

When Nugget came out of the building alone, Marcel yelled, "What the fuck? Where's Commings?"

"He's up at the apartment. The motherfucker pulled a gun on me."

Marcel pointed at Cleever. "We all going back up and drag that pussy out, mother or no mother. Let's move."

After they climbed the stairs to the eighth floor, Marcel held up his hand. "This is the way it's going down. Nugget knocks on the door. I'm behind Nugget, and Cleever is standin' off to my left side, away from the door. When Commings opens the door, Nugget moves right and I'm facing the pussy. If he still has the pistol we do what we have to do. Any questions?"

Before they could answer, Marcel said, "One more thing. You all packin' right?"

Nugget shook his head no. Cleever nodded yes. Then nugget moved in front of 8E and knocked.

The door partially opened and Commings stood part way behind it holding the pistol.

"Why are you back? Didn't you understand what I said before?"

As Nugget moved quickly to his right, Marcel kicked the door, driving it and Commings back. Then Marcel started edging toward the open doorway when Commings fired off two rounds striking Marcel in the shoulder and left arm.

Marcel managed to fire several rounds which went wide as Commings moved away from the door and into the interior of the apartment.

Several of the adjacent apartment doors opened briefly, then closed quickly.

Inside 8E, Comming's mother was screaming as she dialed 911, and Commings, now hunkered behind a threadbare sofa, was firing intermittently at the doorway.

Nugget grabbed Marcel and pulled him back through the doorway, then shoved him toward the stairwell.

As they moved, Nugget called out to Cleever, "Keep that mother fucker busy until I can get Marcel inside the stairway and then come over an give me a hand gettin' him down."

When Nugget, Marcel and Cleever reached the ground floor, the Police were waiting. Nugget and Cleever were taken to the twenty-fifth precinct and booked along with a screaming Cornell Commings. Marcel was handcuffed and transported, by a police cruiser, to North General Hospital.

✦✦✦✦✦

As soon as Lord parked the Bentley in front of the ABN clubhouse, the car was surrounded by ABN gangbangers.

"Looks like our welcoming committee, Colby."

"Yep, but they don't look too friendly."

"You want to get out first," and then Lord laughed.

As Colby opened his door, several gangbangers stepped back. Lord came around from the driver's side and stood next to Colby.

"We'd like to see Cleotha RaJean."

A voice called out from somewhere at the rear of the ever enlarging crowd of gangbangers. "And who the fuck are you?"

As Lord was about to reply, the crowd parted and a tall, muscular Black walked slowly through until he was a step away from where Colby and Lord were standing.

"Maybe you two crackers have gone deaf. Didn't you hear me ask who the fuck you are?"

"We think you know…" and Lord paused for a moment as he considered several replies, then continued. "We think you know who the fuck we are."

"Yeah, I think I do. You're the one who parks those wheels in front of the HO's now burned down clubhouse, ain't ya?"

"Bingo! You got it right."

"I got a good mind to have some of my boys whip your asses and take those wheels."

"You could, but if you did that, you'd lose out on a proposition that would get you and most of them wheels like the one I'm driving and one hell of a lot of pocket change to go with it. Think about what I just said. Maybe you and we can find some common ground. What do you have to lose…two of us against what you've got standing around here. We're hardly a threat as I see it."

"You two follow me, and we'll see what you got."

Colby and Lord followed the man into the ABN clubhouse and then into a surprisingly well furnished room.

"You two sit over there," and the man pointed toward several chairs. And don't worry about my boys standin' around. They're just here in case either one of you two gets frisky."

"Now for starters, who are you?" We'll start with the dude on the right."

"My name is Lord."

"Your name is Lord! Are you some kind of Lord?"

"Absolutely."

"And you, the other one. Are you one of the Lord's angels?"

Several gangbangers laughed, and made signs with their fingers.

Colby looked at Lord and then at the man doing the talking. "If you don't like calling me Angel, you can call me Colby. As far as this gentleman sitting on my left is concerned, he is indeed the Lord. He giveth and he taketh." Then Colby smiled.

"Okay, you are Colby and that isn't Lord. His name from now on is Bentley."

"Nice name, but I'm not sure my mother would like the change."

"We ain't worried about no mothers in here. Besides, mother is half a word. The other half is fucker," and then the man laughed.

"Okay, now that we got that outta the way, what do you want?"

Lord held up his hand. Before I go into that, who are you?"

"The name's RaJean, Cleotha RaJean, and if I like what you say, I'm going to let you call me MJ. Now talk!"

"We supply the HOs exclusively with 'Murder 8,' (Fentanyl) 'China White,' (Heroin) and 'Molly,' (Ecstasy) and just about anything else that keeps their customers riding the wave. (Using drugs)

It seems that the HOs are in a bit of difficulty right now. They've got a blown clubhouse, some deaths because of a bus accident which includes their number one, Lomax," and then Lord smiled, "and one hell of a lot of other shit. All of it is affecting our sales and is rattling the status quo."

"Wait a minute Bentley, what's this status quo mean? Are you some kind of college boy?"

"Yeah, I'm a college boy, and status quo means state of affairs, status, existing condition, and…"

Cleotha RaJean held up his hand. "Enough, Bentley, I got it. Now go on."

"What Colby and I are looking for is a new sales channel. A new relationship with a group that can keep and grow the clientele, the users. If it isn't you, it'll be some other group, guaranteed."

"What makes you think we'd be interested?"

"Our Murder 8, for example, is top grade. The best on the street, hands down. We can supply it in pill form, powder, eye droppers or nasal sprays. The product doesn't come from China. It's manufactured in Mexico by us from start to finish. We deliver what we say and when we say it. We're local and reachable, and we've been around for a long while, which tells you one hell of a lot about us. That's it."

"We'll think it over, Bentley, and be in touch. I need a number where I can reach you any time of day or night."

"Colby will give you one and our next meeting will be someplace else, not here. Someplace neutral."

"We'll consider it, and have a good drive back to Stamford, Connecticut."

⸺ ⋆⋆⋆⋆⋆⋆ ⸺

As Lord pulled away from the ABN clubhouse he said, "RaJean did some homework on me. He wants to tell us he's in the know about a lot of things. It's not too difficult to find out where I live and a bunch of other stuff, if you have the connections, and he obviously does.

He probably locked onto my license plate, somehow, during one of our recent sit-downs with the HOs, and then had his connection dig up some background info on me. We need to assume he's more savvy than he projects. Do you have any feelings, one way or the other, about the meeting?"

"You made a nice sales pitch, but these hoods are already hooked up. Why do they need to switch horses? With the HOs crippled, they're the big dog in Harlem."

"I understand your point, but whoever supplies them doesn't drive a Bentley. That RaJean dude might figure his future could look a lot brighter hooking up with us."

"Or he could play us, Nicholas, until he finds out our supplier, and then decides to go direct."

"That's always a possibility but I have a long standing relationship with Delgado. He knows he can trust me, and now you. He isn't about to work with the likes of a RaJean directly. No way of insuring anything with a gang-banger like him. We're a proven commodity, and besides I speak Spanish," then Lord chuckled.

"How about that name shit, the dude started with? Are you the Lord bit and am I one of your angels? Too bad we didn't have a documentary film crew with us. Could've put it on TikTok and made a fortune."

They both laughed. "I needed that, Colby. Laughing always helps. Okay we're home. Let me know if and when the gangbanger calls, and we'll figure out the next step then. I'm off to Connecticut. You can reach me there."

— 28 —

CHAPTER

"HOW DID IT GO?"

"About as I expected. An arrogant gangbanger but that's what we deal with in this business. Laid it out for their number one that we can supply everything he needs and then some. He understands that Colby is the man to contact, so I'm a step closer to breaking free."

"Are you really, Nicholas? Are you really a step closer to breaking free, or are you getting yourself in deeper?"

"It seems there's always just one more thing, but I've got to do this right, Madison. We don't need the Mexicans, or some scatter brained gangbangers thinking that we left them vulnerable to whatever. I'm trying to get Colby set up with the sales end here, then I'll advise Delgado that he's running the show.

After that, I'm out. We might have to leave here. Get away from New York and Connecticut. Away from all the temptations that if something goes wrong, they contact me for help. It's like an umbilical cord that is difficult to cut."

"And what happens, Nicholas, if this gangbanger you met doesn't want to do business with you?"

"Then I guess we have no choice but to stay with the Harlem Originals. Keep supplying them as long as they pay. And at the same time, placate Delgado until the HOs can get back on their feet and reestablish themselves."

"And if they can't?"

"Trouble for Colby and maybe me. Delgado isn't going to be happy if his product doesn't move."

"Why can't he just get someone else to handle things here?"

"He might well do that, but no one, especially his kind, likes to think he's been screwed over, and that's just the way he'll take any disruption in moving his product. It's one heck of a complicated mess and I feel, at times, like I'm in quicksand and sinking fast."

"You're scaring me, Nicholas."

"That's not what I'm trying to do. I love you and I'm trying to lay it all out so you can understand the delay. I want out, but I want out in one piece. I don't want them coming after any of us because I didn't tie everything up the way it should be.

Colby should hear something from the ABN in a day or two. If he doesn't, that tells me all I need to know about their intentions. Then, as I've said, we stay with the HOs."

Madison tried to smile, but didn't pull it off. "I think I need a drink. It's a bit early, but it's five o'clock somewhere in the world. Care to join me?"

"Sure, why not. By the way, it's a little past two in the afternoon here in Connecticut. That makes it a wee bit past seven in the evening in London. So we're beyond the five o'clock hour if you need an excuse," then Lord smiled. "Make mine a double vodka with a twist, please."

After Madison handed Lord his drink, his cell rang.

"Figures. I'll only be a minute."

"This is Colby. Hope I'm not disturbing anything. I'll only be a minute."

Lord chuckled. "Funny Colby, I just said the exact same words to the young lady sitting next to me. I'll only be a minute."

"Ouch! Really bad timing, huh?"

"No. I can always add more ice to my drink or more drink to my ice. Now what can I do for you?"

"We have a sit-down with the ABN's number one tomorrow at ten a.m. He wants it at his place, so I said okay. I know you wanted it somewhere neutral, but I figured I'd better lock it in rather than take a chance he'd cancel out. Can you pick me up enroute."

"Will do. See you tomorrow at about nine-thirty."

"Enjoy your drink and the lady. Sorry for the interruption. See ya tomorrow."

———————— ✦✦✦✦✦✦ ————————

Lord parked the Bentley in front of the ABN clubhouse, but this time the milling gangbangers remained in place. They just watched as Lord and Colby made their way through the front entrance.

There were a number of gangbangers braced against the walls as they continued walking toward the rear of the clubhouse.

One gangbanger pushed off the wall he was leaning against, held up his hand, and pointed at a door.

"MJ is waiting for you inside. Knock once and then open the door."

Lord complied with the instructions. Once the door was opened, RaJean motioned him inside.

They both took seats opposite the gang leader, who had an ABN member seated on his left and right side. Standing, at various positions around the room, were a number of other gangbangers.

"How was your trip from Connecticut, Bentley?"

"Uneventful."

"Perhaps so. Maybe we can spice that up a bit. While the HOs are without a building to operate from, they can still operate. They will expect you," and then RaJean moved his eyes from Lord to Colby and then back again, "to honor your commitment to them. That commitment is to supply drugs. How are you going to get around that, Bentley?"

"I'm not. You are."

"Oh, and how so?"

"That's up to you. But if it were my decision, I'd see to it that the HOs would be powerless to take any retaliatory..." and then Lord thought about the word he used and said, "...Revenge. I'd make sure they were incapable of striking back. I'd cripple them permanently."

"Are you and him capable of doing that?"

"Yes, Colby and I are quite capable, but we're in the supply business. The strong armed stuff is better left to professionals such as yourselves."

RaJean smiled. "You think so, huh? Don't you like to get those hands dirty?"

"As I've said, "we're suppliers, not smokers." (Killers)

"What guarantee do we have that you'll live up to your end of the bargain, Bentley?"

"You know where I live, don't you?" and then Lord smiled.

"Indeed we do, and one hell of a lot more."

"I suppose you do. Okay, now what?"

"You'll be hearing from us. We have some tidying up to do, then we can talk serious. And when we have our next sit-down, serious is the way it will be. No more jive. You dig?"

RaJean turned away as Lord and Colby left the room, and looked at one of the men sitting at the table.

"Stefon, you and Jahleel get together with Jaden, Baku and Marcus. I want the HO problem fixed. Tell Marcus to use the van, the one with the plumbing company logo and shit on the sides. It's a perfect fit with all the other construction vehicles coming and going on that block. If Marcus wants to do it differently, I'm okay with that but, I want him to run it by me first, understand? On second thought, after you pow wow with Marcus and the others, you run it by me."

Stefon Walker, RaJean's number two, nodded. "Will do, MJ."

Walker, Jahleel and the three others sat in various chairs scattered around the small room. Positioned outside of the door were four armed gangbangers.

Stefon Walker began speaking. "Okay, you know who the target is. We take out Elija Carter, the new King Shorty of the HOs and any other targets of opportunity. Carter will have bodyguards around him, probably one or more of his lieutenants, and other gangbangers scattered about.

They've been hanging out either across the street from their burned out clubhouse or at times on the corner of the block across the intersection. They're still looking for someplace they can call home that has four walls and a roof," then Walker laughed.

"There are some parked cars and several vans they're using for meetings and whatever else the fuck they do. You should take a look see and get a feel for yourself. You can take one or more of the cars parked at the back of the clubhouse. They're clean. Once you're okay with what you see and decide on when you'll do it, then MJ suggests you use the plumbing van. If that's not how you want to handle it, that's okay with MJ, but he wants a sit-down to go over just how you plan on carrying everything out."

Marcus nodded then turned toward each of the others. "Any comments or questions?"

They shook their heads no, or said the word.

"Okay this meeting is over. I'll let you all get on with what you have to do. Check in when you come back. I'll clue MJ in."

Two days later, Stefon Walker, Jahleel, Jaden, Baku and Marcus sat around a table with Cletotha RaJean. Marcus took the lead.

"I'm the shooter along with Baku. Jaden is driving the plumbing van and Jahleel is along as added security. We're going to dress in the plumber uniforms we've used before, the ones with the same logo and shit that's on the sides of the van.

In case we have to abandon the van, we'll peel outta the plumber's clothes or keep 'em on, depending, and disappear into the subway system or scatter into the neighborhood. We're all carrying pistols in case we're gonna do the foot racing bit out of there.

Obviously we're leavin' the rifles in the van if we gotta go. No prints since we're all gloved. Plan on parking as close to them as possible, ideally at the corner across from where they're usually hanging. I checked out the possibility of using a rooftop on the adjacent block, but that's a bit hairy. The van is the better option."

"Sounds okay. When do you plan on doing it?"

"Tomorrow, early. We'll be in position by five or six in the morning, latest. Then we wait."

+ + ✦ ✦ ✦ + +

Jaden parked the van at the corner diagonally across from where the HO gang members usually congregate. The block where their clubhouse was situated, remained cordoned off by police and fire department tape.

Fire department personnel had concluded their investigation during the past week, and were no longer at the scene. The police presence was reduced to traffic control as reconstruction was begun on numerous buildings.

Inside the van, Marcus and Baku were armed with a .308 Winchester rifle. Each weapon had a 1-4x mounted scope. (The first number identifies the magnification and the second number identifies the diameter of the object) The rifle had a range up to five hundred yards and they would be using 7.62 mm bullets.

Both men screwed silencers onto the end of their rifle barrels which would reduce the acoustic intensity of the sound of the gunshot.

Marcus opened the firing port embedded in the right rear door of the van and secured it. He then moved his eyes slowly from left to right. At the diagonal corner stood several HO gangbangers, but Elijah Carter wasn't among them.

Marcus shifted his eyes toward the taped off street and saw several policemen talking to each other and construction workers removing supplies and equipment from their vehicles.

"Carter isn't there yet. There are three jakes (Policemen) huddled together probably talking their usual bullshit and a bunch of construction workers doing what they do. We need to just cool it until Carter appears, then we decide on the timing.

Buku, get yourself ready. You take the left side of the van. Get your firing port opened and then start a visual. Let me know if there's anything I should know. Jahleel takes the right side of the van and does the same. Anything you see that shouts trouble, you tell me like quick."

Baku nodded, then opened his firing portal and secured it on the hook and eye clasp above the hole. After assuming a prone position, Baku looked through the portal and canvassed the street and as much of the surrounding area as he could. The street activity was minimal and normal.

Jahleel, at the right side of the van, removed his pistol as he dropped into a prone position and opened the portal.

Seconds later Baku whispered, "A metallic red car just pulled up at the corner. It looks like Elijah Carter getting out of the back. Do you see him, Marcus?"

"Yeah. I see him and I'm sighting in on him now. I'm going to take him out. You take out either one of the shits walking with him. I'll try to take out the remaining one after I do Carter."

"JADEN! Get this van started and ease us away when I say go."

The 7.62mm bullet's trajectory from Marcus' rifle tore through key blood vessels in Carter's brain. The rapidly expanding blood clot critically compressed important brain tissue, resulting in Carter's immediate death.

Baku's round tore into through the chest of the gangbanger on Carter's left, driving him forward and onto the pavement.

Marcus squeezed the trigger again and watched the bullet impact the back of the running gangbanger who was on the right of Elijah Carter.

"Okay GO Jaden! Get us the fuck out of here like quick, but not too quick. Easy on the pedal until we clear the next block"

Marcus continued to watch through the firing portal of the van's rear door as the van distanced itself from the shooting scene. The three policemen were turning in the direction of where the commotion was happening, but ignored the van.

Moments after leaving the shooting scene, the van was caught up in the slow moving morning traffic, typical of New York City.

"Just play it cool, Jaden. We're not being followed. We're just another vehicle going somewhere in this New York City traffic mess."

Twenty-seven minutes later, Jaden parked the van in between two other cars in the back of the ABN's clubhouse. Then after he placed a gray tarpaulin cover over the van, the four men walked in through the rear of the ABN clubhouse.

After Cleotha RaJean was notified of their return, the men sat together in the same room where the subject of Elijah Carter was originally discussed.

"I believe in patterns. Things should continue the way they started. I'm superstitious. We began in this room and we are going to finish in this room. I'm assuming that things went well. Do tell, Marcus."

—29—

CHAPTER

"COME IN QUICKLY, NICHOLAS. THEY'RE TALKING ABOUT SOME TYPE of gang killing."

Madison pointed at the TV screen as he took a seat beside her on the sofa.

The commentator's voice was played over scenes of police activity. "... and the scene here in Harlem is horrific. The authorities believe it was a gang killing. There are three people dead and from what we have been so far able to determine, there are no witnesses to how it happened.

Those who were interviewed, state they didn't see anything. This is the typical response from the people who live or work in this area. Those that might have seen something, are afraid to talk. Let's now bring on retired Detective Sergeant Mike Mulvany..." Madison pushed down on the mute button.

"Do you think it was the HOs or the other gang members that were killed?"

Lord replied, "The HOs. Seems now the dominant gang in Harlem is the Almighty Black Nation. Colby and I need to pay them another visit, and then hopefully wrap up what still remains to be wrapped up. Then I need to inform Delgado and we're finished with this chapter in our lives."

"Do you really mean it could be over...that we're free to live our life, free of all of this?"

"That's exactly what I mean."

"Oh, Nicholas. I'm one happy woman. I can't believe it."

"Believe it. Now I need to call Colby."

Lord dialed Colby's number and was transferred to his voicemail. He redialed and when the voicemail connection was made again, Lord said, "Check out the local news and call me when you can. Nothing important, just want to chat."

As he was placing the phone down it rang. Without looking at the caller ID Lord answered, "Hello Colby."

The voice replied back, "This ain't no Colby. You know who it is, don't you, Bentley?"

"Yes, I know who it is. Are you still in one piece?"

"Now that's really funny, Bentley. You're in the wrong business. You shoulda been a comedian."

"I am and more, now what can I do for you?"

"It's what I can do for you! Put that bird dog of yours, Colby, on a leash and meet me at my place as soon as you can. Make sure you call before you get here. I'll be waiting."

"Okay. I'm out of town at the moment so I'll need a few hours. My bird dog will call you when we're enroute. Meantime, stay safe. I wouldn't want to hear about anything happening to you before we meet up."

RaJean laughed, then said, "Fat fucking chance. Later, Bentley."

Seconds later the cell rang again. This time Lord looked at the screen. "Hello, Colby."

"Heard it on the radio as I was driving home. Seems the locos did some damage."

"Yep. Seems they've stirred the pot a bit. And by the way, I like how you're picking up Spanish. 'Locos,' crazies, very funny, Colby. Are you studying with a long haired dictionary?" Then Lord laughed.

"Fuck no. I have enough trouble with the English language."

"Okay serious time for a moment. The main man called just before you checked in, and he wants a sit-down ASAP. I'm in Connecticut, so I need an hour to get back to New York and we'll need another fifteen or twenty to get to his place. I'm leaving in a few minutes. I'll let you know when I reach Manhattan."

"I think I'll go back to the condo, Nicholas."

"Why?"

"I don't know, I just thought I'd go back to my place. If you want to hook up later, we can do that. Manhattan is a bit more exciting than watching the grass grow in Connecticut."

Lord chuckled. "I know what you mean about watching the grass grow. Something like watching paint dry," then they both laughed. "Stay here for a few more days while I work things out, or try to. Then I'll go with you to Manhattan, okay?"

"Yes, that's okay. I'll be waiting for you here. When do you think you'll be back?"

"Mid-afternoon. I'll telephone you when I'm leaving New York."

They embraced and kissed.

"I don't want anything to happen that will spoil what you and I have, Nicholas. I'm scared…truly terrified, that something is going to happen that will…" and then Madison stopped.

"Nothing is going to happen, Madison. Maybe it's a few hours, a couple of days or another week or so, then it's over. But right now I've got to get it to the point where I can walk away, and I'm not there yet.

This meeting is a major step in that direction. I'll clue you in when I return. Meantime keep the doors locked," and Lord smiled. "And keep my pistol, the one in the bedroom, with you. Never can tell about these home invasions that are happening with greater frequency in Stamford, New Canaan, Darien and some of the other areas of Connecticut."

Madison nodded her head in a way that conveyed she understood.

Cleotha RaJean, Stefon Walker, Marcus, Baku, Jaden and two lieuten- ants, Kelvin Hill and Urick Edwards, sat on one side of the table. Several gangbangers stood at their rear while others leaned against the various walls.

Colby and Lord sat quietly on opposite sides of the table, waiting for RaJean to start.

When the gangbanger began his voice was below normal.

"We are here, Bentley, to discuss a relationship. For your information the HOs are no more," and RaJean looked at several of his gangbangers. If there was any doubt before regarding who runs Harlem, there's no more doubt. You understand, Bentley?"

Lord didn't answer.

"Did you hear me, Bentley?"

"Of course I heard you, and as far as I'm concerned what you said doesn't require an answer."

RaJean locked eyes with Lord, but didn't reply.

"Look, Mr. RaJean. I don't have all day. You wanted this meeting, so we're meeting. Please get to wherever you want to get to and cut out this back and forth useless word shit. We're both big boys so let's use big boy talk. If you want a relationship with us, this isn't the way to get it."

"Who says we want a relationship? You're the one who proposed it."

Lord looked at Colby. "I think this meeting is over, let's go," and Lord started to get up.

"Whoa there, Bentley. No need for that."

Lord, still standing, looked back at RaJean. "And one more thing before I leave. My name is Lord, Nicholas Lord, and this man is my associate. His name is Colby. He's not a dog on a leash, and I'm not a fucking Bentley. You can get your Murder 8 (Fentanyl) and Dynamite (Heroin and cocaine) from some other source. We're finished here."

As Colby started to stand, several gangbangers moved away from the walls.

RaJean held up his hand, "Whoa there Bent...Mr. Lord. No need for that. Sit-down...please, sit-down, and let's continue."

Still standing, Lord looked at RaJean. "A relationship is built on trust and mutual respect. That's not the way you're coming across. If you think Colby and I are some type of peckerwoods (Racial epithet aimed at whites) you're making one hell of a mistake. You can't get the quality and quantity that we can supply. You underestimate who and what we are, and that, Mr. RaJean, will turn out to be the biggest mistake of your lifetime. Let's go Colby."

"Please wait a minute, Mr. Lord. Seems I've fucked up a bit. Let's start over. I think we've both laid out the groundwork for our relationship, and I'm certain it can be a mutually beneficial one for both of us."

"What do you think, Colby? Walk or talk?"

"Let's talk, Nicholas. We're here and Mr. RaJean seems to have a similar mindset now. So let's talk some more."

"Okay, Mr. RaJean, let's give it another shot," and then Lord sat back down. Peripherally, Lord saw several of the gangbangers move back toward or assume positions against the wall.

"I think we can do business, Mr. Lord. Would you like to have a drink, some champagne, or something else?"

"Colby and I will have whatever you're drinking."

"I'm drinkin' champagne."

"That's perfect."

After the glasses were placed on the table and filled, RaJean said, "To a long and profitable relationship."

Lord repeated the toast, and added,

"And to the good things the money will buy."

"Now let's discuss the specifics, Mr. RaJean. Colby is the one to make contact with. He'll arrange the shipments with Mexico and advise you when and where the delivery will be made. Money covering the shipment will be exchanged at that time. You, the ABN, will be the exclusive supplier for our material in Harlem. You will not purchase material from any other supplier. We expect, in fact, demand, exclusivity. Is there anything I stated that's not understood or you disagree with?"

"Everything is clear except for two things. One, if Colby here, Mr. Colby, is the contact man, what are you?"

"Someone who will make sure everything is as it should be."

RaJean moved his head slightly, then said, "Okay. The second thing is, I'd like to meet the Mexican supplier. Can you or Mr. Colby arrange that?"

"Why do you want to meet the supplier?"

"I always like to know who I'm in bed with."

"You already know. It's Colby, me and the Mexicans."

"Not good enough. I need to eyeball people in order to get a feel."

"I'll see what I can arrange. If there's nothing else, we'll be in contact over the next few days. If there's anything you need us for, contact Colby."

"Just a moment more, Mr Lord. There's someone I'd like you to meet," and RaJean pointed at one of the seated men. Marcus was also in the military."

Lord thought, he knows even that. Got to be careful.

"What branch?"

Marcus answered, "Marines. I was a sniper in Helmand Province, and you?"

"I always admired you guys. Our Army snipers covered our asses pretty good too. What type of rifle did you use?"

"An MK13. These days, I'm using a .308 Winchester with 7.62mm bullets," and then Marcus asked again, "What unit were you with?"

"Fourth Brigade Combat Team, 10th Mountain Division. Afghanistan was a bitch."

"You can say that again."

Both men shook hands and then Lord turned toward the still seated RaJean. "We have everything to gain or everything to lose. Let's work on owning New York."

"I'd like that. Will be waiting to hear from you regarding the Mexicans. Have a good trip back to that high rent district called Connecticut."

"Will do," then Lord with Colby by his side, made their way out of the ABN clubhouse.

— 30 —

CHAPTER

AFTER LORD PARKED HIS CAR IN FRONT OF COLBY'S APARTMENT building, both men remained inside and continued their discussion.

"Like I've said a number of times on the way here, RaJean is one smart dude in certain respects. He does his homework. Knew, for example, that I lived in Connecticut. And now he throws out the military bit. He's baiting us, meaning he wants us to feel that he's in the know about you and me. That's supposed to keep us off balance."

"Agree, Nicholas. What are you going to do about his asking to visit with the Mexicans?"

"I'll run it by Delgado and see if he wants to do it. With the HOs out of commission, the ABN appears to be our best bet?"

"What about the others, like the WHYOs, the Daybreak Boys or the Aces?"

"Good point. I've been thinking about them, but wonder whether they have the muscle, and the network that the ABN has."

"Yeah, doubtful, and I'm thinking, Nicholas, if we don't go with the

ABN after these sit-downs and all, we're inviting some problems, maybe some serious problems."

"You're on the mark, Colby. Let me call Delgado when I get back home and we'll decide a course of action based on what he does or doesn't say."

"Okay Nicholas. I'll wait for your call. As always, it's been a pleasure. See ya!"

As he drove away from Colby's apartment building, Lord dialed Madison's number. "I'm heading toward the West River Drive, be home in about forty-five."

"Be careful. I miss you."

"Same here. Love you."

"Me too. I'll be waiting."

Approximately fifty minutes later, Lord was seated on his sofa with Madison sitting by his side.

"...and that's about it. I need to find out if Delgado is agreeable and then we make the trip."

"So that means you're going away again?"

"Unfortunately, yes. It's just one more of those loose ends that need to be tied. Shouldn't take more than two or three days."

"I'm scared, Nicholas. I'm afraid something bad is going to happen, going to happen to you."

"Hey, Madison, I could get hit by a car as I crossed any street in Manhattan."

"Yes, you could, therefore what?"

"Nothing. I was just trying to make a comparison, but didn't say it the right way. I know, Madison, that as long as I'm involved in this, the greater the chances are of something negative happening. I know that. I'm trying to be as careful as I can and get this situation tied up so we can start living a real life. Unfortunately, it seems that every new day brings on more complications."

"That's just what I mean. It seems you're getting in deeper and getting out becomes more of a problem for you and, obviously, for me too. Better make your telephone call. I'll be in the bedroom."

Lord dialed Delgado's private number.

"¿Cómo estás, Senior Delgado?" (How are you Mr. Delgado)

"Excelente y tú, Nicholas? (Excellent and you Nicholas)

"Bien." (Good)

"Que puedo hacer por ti, Nicholas?" (What can I do for you, Nicholas)

"We've set up a new sales channel. A more powerful one. One with a longer reach. El jefe (The boss) wants to meet with you before we start business."

"Inusual. ¿Lees algo en la solicitud?" (Unusual. Do your read anything into the request)

"No. Seems he wants to see if we are the real deal."

"Doesn't he know that from our involvement with the other channel?"

"Yes, he does, to a degree, but I get the feeling he wants to see how big our operation is. How much muscle we have and whether we're strong enough to mess him up if he doesn't do what he agrees to."

"I have some reservations about this, but it just might be okay. Arrange it, Nicholas, and let me know. We'll keep the visit short, two days maximum, okay? If I get the wrong vibes, and you know what I mean, you just might be returning to New York by yourself."

"Okay, Mr. Delgado. I'll arrange it and call you as soon as it's finalized."

"Ten cuidado, Nicholas," (Be careful) and then the connection ended.

Lord called out, "I'm finished, Madison. Come back please."

"When are you leaving?"

"Haven't made any flight reservations yet. I will in a few moments. Please don't worry. Once this is over, it'll belong to Colby and I'm out." I can't visualize anything that will prevent that."

"You're kidding yourself, aren't you? You know there's always just one more thing, and that one more thing is going to cost us dearly. I can feel it. I can feel it, Nicholas, and I'm scared, really scared."

"All right, I'm not completely at ease myself. What do you think we should do? We can't just cut and run. They'll come after us. Delgado trusts me, and he knows I've delivered. It was me, not Dixx. Dixx was the money. I was the operations, along with Colby and his crew. If I don't get this channel set up, Delgado has to start from scratch here in New York.

He's not going to feel kindly toward the person who caused his headaches, and that person is me. The only loyalty in this business is the one up to the last second. You understand what I mean, don't you, Madison?

I've got to get this to the point where Delgado is okay with the ABNs and that means a one on one between him and the ABN leader. I've got to go to Mexico again. I've got no choice. I can arrange with Colby that several of his crew watch the house or if you feel more comfortable, I can have them stake out your condo. Your choice."

"I think I'll stay here, Nicholas. I'll be okay. You said you'd be back after a couple of days, right?"

"Yes. two days, three max."

"Okay. I'll manage."

"Now I need to make a couple of more calls then we'll do whatever you want."

Madison smiled. I'll be in the bedroom waiting."

Lord called American Airlines and booked two first class tickets for himself and Cleotha RaJean. Then he called Colby, gave him the information and asked him to pass it on to RaJean.

"Make sure he understands I'll meet him at the American Airlines check in counter. The flight leaves at four p.m. He's got to be there a minimum of an hour before. Tell him to get his ass there before three, and you can quote me. Thanks, Colby. We'll talk when I get back Sunday night. Try to keep out of trouble while I'm gone."

"That's not going to be easy, Nicholas, but I'll try. Have a good trip and be careful. Never can tell what's on those Mexican roads."

"That's why I'm flying this time. Talk later."

+ + + + + +

"As the plane taxied toward the gate, Lord said, "Not a bad flight?"

RaJean smiled, "Who you shittin'. If I wanted to fly I would have sprouted wings."

"Maybe you'll get those when you cross over."

"Yeah, maybe, but that ain't going to be for a while."

"You never know. As a close friend of mine once said, every second is a gift."

"Yeah and so is every woman I've been with," and RaJean laughed. "I can't quite make you, Lord, but I'll get the handle shortly."

"What you see, is what you get."

The announcement for first class passengers to disembark came over the intercom.

"That's us. Please grab our bags from the overhead compartment and let's make our way to customs."

Once Lord and RaJean cleared customs, they made their way to the airport lobby where Lord spotted a man holding a sign with his name on it.

"Hola, Enrique. Es bueno verte otra vez." (Hello Enrique. Good to see you again.)

"Aquí igual. ¿Cómo estuvo tu vuelo?" (Same here. How was your flight)

"Aburrido como el infierno." (Boring as hell)

They both laughed. "Este es un asociado, Mr. RaJean." (This is an associate, Mr. RaJean."

"Mr. RaJean, meet Enrique."

Enrique shook hands with RaJean and then pointed toward the garage elevator. As they walked toward the elevator, RaJean asked, "All that babble you and the small guy were jivin'. Anything I should know?"

"Nothing. Just a bunch of long time no see shit. I'll translate when there's something to translate."

"Sounds like you're some kind of poet with that last string of words."

"Could be. I recall you once said I should be a comedian. I'll add poet to my list," then Lord smiled.

"You one crazy ass cracker, Lord."

"That's what makes life so interesting, doesn't it?"

As the car made its turn onto the road that would lead to Delgado's home, RaJean remarked about the mansion-like homes that dotted the hillside. When they reached the entrance to the drug lord's home, RaJean asked, "Just how many people live in this place? Never seen anything this big."

"Impressive, isn't it?"

"That's one way of putting it."

"Gracias Enrique." Then Lord turned toward RaJean. "If you're ready, let's meet the man who owns it."

Lord and RaJean were patted down by two men with AK-47s at the bottom of the steps, then again when they reached the top. After a nod from one of the men, they proceeded through the large door which was held open by the other bodyguard.

Then they followed two men to a double door. After knocking, the men opened one of the doors, then Lord, followed by RaJean, entered the immense room.

The man behind the desk said, "Es muy bueno verte de nuevo, Nicholas." (It's very good to see you again, Nicholas)

"Lo mismo aqui." (The same here)

"Let me introduce an associate, the one I mentioned during our telephone call. This is Cleotha RaJean. Mr. RaJean meet Mr. Ramon Delgado."

Delgado stood up and reached over his desk and shook hands with RaJean.

"Is this your first trip to Mexico, Mr. RaJean?"

"Yes, it is."

"Well, we hope it won't be your last. I understand from Nicholas that you are our new sales channel in New York. Nicholas also tells me that you come with an abundance of experience and connections."

"That's true. I own Harlem, New York. We, the Almighty Black Nation, is Harlem. Nothing will happen there without our involvement."

Delgado looked over at Lord who moved his head several times in a yes motion.

Okay, we can do some business and see how beneficial it is for both of us…a trial period shall we say. Does that work for you, Mr. RaJean?"

"That'll work. But before we go there, I'd like to see how you operate."

"That's exactly what I had in mind. We can go there first, and then we can drop you both off at your hotel. If you'll wait near the steps, I'll be out in a few moments. Any additional questions about what we do can be discussed on site. Now if you excuse me for a few minutes"

Lord and RaJean waited at the bottom of the steps.

———————— ·⟡⟡⟡⟡⟡· ————————

The two SUVs turned onto the first road and stopped next to a pasture containing hundreds of cows. Lord remembered it all from his first trip.

"Just stay cool, Mr. RaJean, and it'll all fall into place. I had the same feelings when I first saw it."

After Lord and RaJean left the car they followed Delgado and five bodyguards into the pasture.

"This is far enough, gentlemen. Please put these on," and Delgado handed Lord and RaJean a respirator and goggles.

"The process is highly toxic. These will prevent serious complications while we are here. We use this pasture as our laboratory to manufacture our Fentanyl. The cooking pots are scattered around the middle of the pasture and the cows cover our activity from the prying eyes of the police and others. We lose a few cows from time to time, but they're replaced by the active birth rate of these animals. As you'll notice, around the perimeter of the property, are a number of armed men. This is another layer of protection during manufacture."

"What percentage of Fentanyl does each of your pills contain?"

"Interesting question, Mr. RaJean. A pill containing over two milligrams would most likely kill a person. We keep the percentage below that, usually one milligram maximum. We like repeat customers," and then Delgado smiled.

"I can understand that, yes," then RaJean smiled back.

"Do you have any further questions, Mr. RaJean?"

"No, what I see and what you've stated covers everything I need to know. I like the way you think, Mr. Delgado...the cows, the pasture and the cooking pots in the middle, who would believe," and then he laughed.

"Yes indeed, who would believe but now you are a believer, aren't you Mr. RaJean?"

"Oh, indeed I am."

"Okay then. If there's nothing more, Enrique will take you both to your hotel and then we'll meet tonight for dinner and socializing, if you're up to it, Mr. RaJean."

"I'm definitely up to whatever it is you want to do. I think we can do it just right, whether it's business or socializing."

"Fine, Enrique will pick you up at your hotel at six, and anything else you need to know about tonight's activity, just ask Nicholas. He's a seasoned veteran, aren't you Nicholas?"

In more ways than one, Mr. Delgado."

— 31 —

CHAPTER

LORD SAT WITH RAJEAN AND DELGADO, AT THE SAME TABLE HE OCCU-pied during the previous visit. For Lord, it seemed like he was in a time warp. Everything seemed to be moving in reverse, instead of forward.

This time, the three ate alone. When they finished their meal, and after the dishes were cleared, Lord excused himself. As he walked away from the table, RaJean turned and faced Delgado.

"I was thinking, Mr. Delgado, that it might be better, certainly easier, if you and I were to communicate directly. Having someone like Lord or Colby in between us, makes the process a bit complicated. With you and I in direct contact, we save a lot of time, and you save some money."

"And when there's a problem, Mr. RaJean, who's going to be able to han-dle it? I'm in Mexico, not in New York. Talking on the phone is dangerous, at both ends. Also it's time consuming to get on a plane and come down here. It's not like being in New York or close enough to it, that a one on one can be arranged, and the problem or problems solved.

Instead of making it easier, Mr. RaJean, I see it as making our relation-ship more complicated. Lord is my man on the scene. He's there to solve our individual and collective problems when and if they occur. Do you understand?"

"Yes, I understand what you said. But without me being able to contact you directly, that puts me and my organization in a somewhat difficult situation if something happens to Lord or Colby. Then what am I supposed to do? I got responsibilities to keep my users supplied and problems with the jakes, sorry, the cops. They're always a problem and you probably got your hands full down here as well.

Do you see what I'm sayin' Mr. Delgado? I sometimes need a decision real quick and I need that decision from the supplier, you. Lord will have to contact you to get an okay in any event, so why not retire him and Colby, and you and me talk the direct talk and do the direct business. No in betweens."

As Lord neared the table, Delgado said, "It won't work. We both need a Lord type between us and for us. It has and always will work better that way. Believe me, you'll grow to like Lord, just as I have."

After Lord sat down, Delgado motioned to the Maitre d', pointed at the table, and then held up three fingers.

Moments later, three women were seated at the table.

Delgado looked at the gangbanger and asked, "Do you know how to dance to our salsa music, Mr. RaJean?"

"To be honest with you Mr. Delgado, I do my best dancin' in bed, but it just so happens that I do have a pair of the two best feet on the planet, so just watch me."

RaJean pointed to the woman seated at his left, and then at the dance floor.

As they made their way in between the tables toward the dance area, Delgado looked at the two other seated women. "This gentleman and I need to discuss something privately. Please give us a few minutes."

They both watched the women leave, then Delgado locked eyes with Lord.

"You know Nicholas we go back a long way. When Dixx made you his contact man with me, I must admit, I had some reservations. However, those reservations were quickly dispelled as you took charge of the operation in New York and we saw the business grow and become very rewarding.

You've been straight up with me, always. When there was a problem and you set out to solve it, you always made sure there wouldn't be any blowback for me down here. That meant a lot to me.

So, I need to be open with you. While you were away from the table, el muchacho negro me dio una cancion y un baile (The black boy gave me a song and dance) about doing business directly, getting you and your man Colby out of the way. As I read that, Nicholas, he wants you gone.

Tendría mucho cuidado. Es alguien en quien ni tú ni yo podemos confiar. Él es una serpiente." (I would be extremely careful. He is someone neither you nor I can trust. He is a snake)

As RaJean and his lady made their way back to the table, Lord and Delgado applauded.

"Very nice indeed, Mr. RaJean."

"I was pretty good if I do say so myself," then he laughed. "If I have time I'll teach both of you a few steps," and then he laughed again.

The two women again joined the table, and the six danced, drank, and talked until Delgado motioned at his watch. "It's that time gentlemen. I must leave with this pretty little thing. The check has been taken care of. Enjoy the rest of your night."

As Delgado rose from his seat, he looked at both Lord and RaJean. "Have a good flight back, and I look forward to a profitable relationship with you, Mr. RaJean."

"And I with you, Mr. Delgado. What I spoke about will happen one way or the other."

A quizzical look on Lord's face prompted RaJean to add, "Mr. Delgado and I discussed a few ways to enlarge our business, and I'll discuss that with you on the plane."

After shaking hands, Delgado, his lady and the bodyguards left, leaving Lord and RaJean and the two women staring at each other.

"Shall we continue, or call it a night?"

"As for me, Lord, I'm taking this little Mexican princess home with me."

"Okay, have fun, and be ready to leave for the airport tomorrow morning at ten sharp."

After RaJean and the woman left, Lord handed the remaining woman a hundred dollar bill. "Thank you for your company. I enjoyed it."

"The woman stared back perplexed and asked, "Hice algo mal?" (Did I do something wrong)

"No. Hiciste todo bien. Soy yo, lo siento." (No. You did everything right. It's me, sorry)

Lord got up from his seat, turned and walked toward the main entrance. Twenty minutes later he was inside his hotel room.

———— ⋅✦✦✦✦⋅ ————

Lord and RaJean sat in the boarding area for the American Airline flight back to New York.

"Delgado didn't ask me about the next shipment. Did he mention anything to you, Mr. RaJean?"

"No, the subject never came up."

"I'm somewhat surprised. Do you have a quantity in mind?"

"I been thinking about it. Not sure whether I want to stay with the pill form or bring in some powder along with the pills. Gotta check with my boys, and then I can let you know."

Lord nodded. "That'll work. You might want to consider some nasal spray to include along with the other two."

"I hadn't thought about that. Just might juice up sales a bit. We can discuss that and quantities once I get back to New York. Now Mr. Lord, if you'll pardon me, I had a long and very strenuous night. My three Bs, my body, my brain and my boonga, are tired. No more business talk. I'm gonna relax, and suggest you do the same."

"What the hell is a boonga?"

RaJean looked at Lord in a strange way and then said, "Are you shitting me, Lord. You don't know what a boonga is?"

"Never heard of it."

"A boonga is a penis, Mr. Lord. Welcome to the world," then RaJean laughed.

"I've got to remember that. Never can tell if I might be on some quiz program," then Lord laughed.

⋅◆◆◆⋅⋅

After clearing customs, Lord and the gangbanger walked to the airport lobby.

"There's several of my men. Be seeing you, Lord."

Lord watched as RaJean and his men gave each other high fives, then he took the shuttle bus to the long term parking lot. Once there he telephoned Madison and a little over an hour later, he was inside his Stamford, Connecticut home.

After a few kisses, Madison and Lord settled down at the kitchen table.

"The coffee is freshly brewed, Nicholas, and I hate to drink alone."

Madison smiled as she poured two cups and then moved one across the table with her fingers until it was in front of where he was sitting.

"Just what I need."

"So how was your trip?"

"An eye opener."

"Do you want to explain?"

"It seems the gangbanger made a move on me and Colby. The short version is that he approached Delgado to establish a direct channel. Meaning cutting Colby and yours truly out of the loop."

"Wouldn't that be just what you want? You're getting out, so does it really matter if the gangbanger wants to go direct? As far as Colby goes, I know you feel some obligation, but what can you do for him?"

"I'll answer that in a moment. It was Delgado that informed me of what the gangbanger proposed. He urged caution on my part. That's something he didn't have to add, since I don't trust the gangbanger as far as I could throw him."

"Now that the gangbanger made a direct approach to Delgado and Delgado didn't react one way or the other, where does that put you? WAIT!

— 195 —

I can answer that question myself. It places you in harm's way, don't you agree, Nicholas?"

"Very definitely. I need to talk with Colby. Do you mind if I invite him to come here?"

"What am I supposed to do while he's here? Hide in the closet?"

"That's funny. Didn't think about that, but what's the problem with him seeing you here? Dixx is history, and we're the present."

Madison shrugged her shoulders.

"If you'd rather go back to New York, I can meet Colby there and we can stay at your place."

"No, I don't want to go to New York. What you told me about Delgado and the gangbanger frightens me. I'd rather you ask Colby to come here."

"Okay I'll call him and set it up."

———— ✦✦✦✦✦ ————

Stefon Walker, Marcus and Baku sat across from RaJean in the ABN clubhouse.

"...and that's pretty much the story. Ain't gonna be no direct business as long as Lord and his dog are around."

"Even after they're gone, MJ, what makes you think that the spick will go with us?"

"What's he gonna do, Stefon? He ain't got another outlet to use now that the HOs are fucked up. As far as I can tell, this Mexican Uptown with his fancy digs (Slang for home) and trimmings, ain't never been outta Mexico, so what does he know about what we do or how we do it? He relies on Lord and the bird dog."

"What do you have in mind, MJ?"

"We smoke (Kill) Bentley and his dog."

Everyone remained quiet as the seconds passed. Then Stefon spoke up. "You're the number one, MJ, and what you say goes, but I'm just wondering, with all the heat from the HO episode, shouldn't we be cooling it until it all settles down? Why create another situation?"

RaJean held up his hand so that no one else spoke.

"I don't think the jakes (Cops) are gonna be able to tie the two happenings together. I'm thinking we smoke Bentley in Connecticut. I know his address from our man in the 25th P. (25th police precinct) I understand there are lots of woods in Connecticut and Bentley lives in a high rent district neighborhood.

Plenty of trees around everywhere for cover. Why don't you, Marcus and Baku, do some huddling, like in planning and we'll talk later. Now me and Stefon have some personal shit to discuss."

<hr />

Colby arrived at Lord's home during the late afternoon. After they were seated in the living room, Lord asked Colby if he wanted anything to drink.

After Lord told him he wouldn't be drinking alone, Colby agreed to a vodka.

Lord went to the wet bar and then came back with a tray holding three Waterford glasses of Stolichnaya vodka, over ice, each with a slice of lemon peel.

As Lord set the glasses down, Colby asked, "Trying to save yourself the trouble of getting a refill?"

"Nope, it's for someone who will be joining us momentarily."

Several moments later, Madison walked into the room.

Colby stared at the elegantly attired woman, looked over at Lord, and then back at Madison.

"Surprised, Colby?"

"Not really. Nice to see you again, Madison."

"Likewise. Have I kept you boys from anything?"

"Nope. We're just about to start on the first one," and then Colby lifted his glass. "To the best of times, and the time to enjoy it."

"Not a bad toast, Colby. I'll drink to that," and then Madison took a sip from her glass.

"I haven't seen you since Mr. Dixx..." and then Colby started to apologize.

"No need for that Colby. That was then, and this is now. I've enjoyed this brief catch-up, and I'll leave you both alone to do whatever it is you're going to do. See you both later."

After Madison left the room, Lord began. "I think we've got some serious problems with RaJean. Problems with him means problems with the ABN. The son of a bitch tried an end run around us with Delgado. He told Delgado that you and I weren't necessary and that they, RaJean and Delgado, could handle everything directly. There's more, but that's it in a nutshell.

Delgado wants things as is, but I got a strong feeling that RaJean isn't going to go with that. The bottom line is that we're both targets. If RaJean gets us smoked, Delgado doesn't have any other choice. He doesn't know any other outlet here that could be put in place quickly if the ABN closes him out. So the picture is pretty clear. We take him out before he takes us."

"Too bad it's come to this, Mr. Lord."

"Colby, no more Mr. Lord shit. You can use, Nicholas. We're in this together, sink or swim. As far as my last name goes, there is one thing you do have to remember. What the Lord giveth, the Lord also can taketh," and then he smiled as he lifted his glass.

Colby smiled back.

"Sorry to interrupt boys, but it's getting close to dinner time. How about some Chinese food? If you two are willing, I'll phone in the order, then pick it up so you can continue your conversation."

When both men answered yes, Madison handed them a menu.

"Take a look and decide. It's all good."

— 32 —

CHAPTER

MJ NODDED HIS HEAD IN A WAY THAT CONVEYED A YES.

"Okay, MJ, if there's nothing else to discuss, Jaden and I are going to leave in a few minutes. We should be back sometime tonight."

RaJean nodded again. "Get it done," then he stood up and left the room.

"You ready, Jaden?"

"I'm ready."

"Okay. I'll meet you out back after I get my gear."

Marcus carried the .308 Winchester rifle with a mounted scope, along with a small bag, to the black Chrysler sedan parked at the back entrance to the ABN clubhouse.

Jaden opened one of the rear doors and pressed a button embedded in the door panel. The rear seat back slowly moved into a horizontal position so that it and the floor of the trunk were now at the same level.

"Marcus, it's ready."

Marcus entered the vehicle through the rear door, crawled slowly through the opening where the back seat was, and then into the trunk. The blankets were already spread out on the trunk's floor.

Marcus placed the rifle by his right side, then lifted one of the three firing ports cut into the car's trunk lid. After looking through the port, he let the cover fall back into place. He did the same with the other two, then removed a magazine from the bag and proceeded to arm the rifle and screw on the silencer. When he finished he called out, "Jaden, ready when you are."

Jaden closed the rear door, got in the driver's seat, and started the car.

When they entered the Stamford, Connecticut cul-de-sac, Jaden positioned the car so that the trunk faced the front of Lord's house. After looking at his watch, he called out Marcus' name.

When he answered, Jaden said, "it's just about six-fifty."

"Noted. I'm nixing the woods. Won't work. The house windows and doors offer the better option. Keep the car where it is. I'll watch through one of the portals. Only one shot, maybe two at the most, and then we're out of here like quick. When I'm ready, I'll tell you, then start the car and stay in place, until I say go."

Both men watched as a Mercedes convertible pulled into the driveway. A woman, carrying several brown bags, walked to the front door and knocked.

Marcus called out, "If I have a clean shot I'll take it. Be ready to move outta here. Start the car up."

The door was opened by a man Marcus assumed was Lord, but the way the woman was positioned, he doubted he could make a clean kill.

"I don't have a clean shot, Jaden. Shut it down, We'll wait."

Jaden turned off the car's engine, and let out some air escape from the right side of his mouth.

───── ✦✦✦✦ ─────

After Madison set up the dining room table, she removed the various food items from their plastic containers and placed them on porcelain plates. Then a bottle of cold Rolling Rock beer was placed to the right side of each of the three plates.

"Gentlemen, if you're ready, so am I. Please hurry before it gets cold or before I eat it all."

Colby and Lord laughed as they took their seats.

After they finished their meal, and a second round of drinks, Colby looked at his watch. "Wow, how time flies when you're eating, talking, and drinking."

"Seems to always be that way," and then Madison smiled.

"I think I've overstayed my welcome. It's almost nine and I have at least an hour driving time to get back to Manhattan. It's been nice to see you again, Madison, and I really mean that. I was wondering what happened to you after Mr. Dixx…" and then Colby stopped.

He looked over at Lord. "I understand what you've stated, Nicholas. I know, you're right. The sooner the better. Let me know how I can help once you've refined your plan. Meantime I'll let things go along as is, and I won't contact RaJean. If he calls me, I'll stall him and then let you know he's made contact with me.

I know the way out. Stay put and enjoy what's left of that excellent food. Thanks again, Madison, for your very kind hospitality," and then Colby walked to the front door.

As he was opening the door, Madison called out, "What no goodbye hug, Colby?"

The door remained in the halfway open position, as Colby turned back toward Madison.

The 7.62mm bullet struck Colby's right shoulder driving him back into the foyer area and then into the tiled floor.

Running past the screaming woman, Lord shoved the door closed, then dropped quickly to the floor.

"Get down, Madison, and crawl away from here. Get back to the dining room and stay under the table. I'll check on Colby."

"Colby, look at me. You've got a shoulder wound. Hang tight. I'm calling 911. You'll be okay. Just manage the pain."

Lord took out his cell phone and dialed. When the 911 operator answered, he related what had just happened.

"Sending an ambulance and the police immediately. Please stay on the line with me until they arrive."

Marcus watched as the bullet impacted the man at the front door. Then after the command from Marcus, Jaden drove away from the cul-de-sac. Once he was merged into light traffic, Jaden eased up on the accelerator as he continued driving toward the I-95 south, which would take them back to New York City.

As they parked the sedan at the rear of the ABN clubhouse, word of their return was passed to RaJean.

As Jaden and Marcus walked through the back door, RaJean was standing several steps away.

"How did it go?"

"Got him. Saw him drop, but not sure it was Lord. If it wasn't Lord, it was someone connected to him. Either way, MJ, the message was clear."

"I'm not so sure of that. If it wasn't Lord that you off'd, (Killed) then we're gonna have a problem that's gonna be more difficult to solve."

The police detectives took the report from Lord and Madison while the EMS people (Emergency Medical Service) transferred Colby to Stamford Hospital.

A general search of the area came up with nothing.

One of the police detectives handed Lord his card and said that he'd be in touch in the morning. When they left, Lord said, "I think I need a drink."

"Yeah, I think we both do."

"Quite an end to an evening, wouldn't you say, Madison?"

"That's putting it mildly. What is going on, Nicholas?"

"I'm not entirely sure, but I've got a few ideas. I need to go and visit with Colby. Why don't you stay here? I won't be long."

"Are you crazy? After what happened tonight, I'm not staying here alone. I'll go with you."

They finished their drinks quickly, then Lord and Madison drove to Stamford Hospital.

They waited for more than an hour, before a physician finally approached them.

"He is out of surgery. Your friend had significant bone fracture, tissue destruction, and experienced hypovolemic shock. This is a condition characterized by an inadequate delivery of oxygen due to blood loss. It will take time, but we expect him to make a full recovery. May I suggest you both go home now. You can return tomorrow when he'll be a bit more receptive to visitors."

The doctor gave them both his three thousand dollar smile, a wave and then left.

✦✦✦✦✦✦

After Lord and Madison were back home, they decided on separate bedrooms.

Sleep was evasive for Lord and despite the early hour, he decided to begin his day. He went to the kitchen, removed a small metal coffee pot and brewed some coffee. After pouring a cup, he walked to the microwave and placed the cup inside. Then set the timer for forty-five seconds and pushed the start button. After the microwave message flashed that the coffee was ready, he carried the steaming cup to the kitchen table and sat down.

As he sipped the coffee he reflected on the trip to Mexico with RaJean and last night's shooting. It was simple enough to reach a quick conclusion.

Lord knew what he would put into play and when. It was relatively simple and would achieve the results he wanted while providing the anonymity he needed.

He pushed the coffee cup aside and went back to the bedroom. Sleep came quickly.

When he awoke it was to the sound of Madison's voice.

"Welcome to a new day, Nicholas. I made fresh coffee. Want a cup?"

"Sure. Be with you in a minute."

"You were up before, weren't you?"

"Yes. Couldn't sleep. Needed to clarify a few things."

"And did you?"

"Yes. I know what I need to do, and plan on doing it today. By the way, what time is it?"

"A little after six a.m."

"The middle of the night."

"Heck no. I hate to drink alone and need you."

"I thought that drinking alone only applied to alcohol."

"Nope, as you just found out."

"Are we going to visit Colby this morning?"

"Definitely, but after I make a very important phone call."

Lord showered and dressed, then removed a burner phone from one of his bureau drawers and walked to his den. As he sat at his desk he googled the telephone number of the twenty-fifth police precinct in Harlem.

When the desk sergeant identified himself, Lord asked for the detective bureau.

"This is Detective Ramsey, how can I help you?"

"I can help you, Detective Ramsey. Listen careful because I'm going to say this only once. The killing several weeks ago involving members of the Harlem Originals street gang was done by members of the Almighty Black Nation. Check out their King Shorty named Cleotha RaJean, who you folks already know all too well.

The shooters were ABN gangbangers named Baku and Marcus. Marcus is a former marine sniper. Saw action in Afghanistan. Uses a .308 Winchester rifle and a gray van with rifle ports cut into the rear doors. The bullets the coroner types removed from the HO's bodies will match up with the Winchester rifle. Also, if you scratch the surface a bit, you'll find the ABN were responsible for burning a block of your New York real estate. Better get your asses moving, and have a great day, Detective Ramsey."

After hanging up, Lord started walking toward the door leading to the garage. Just before he opened the door, he called out to Madison, "Need to get something done in the garage. Be back in a few minutes."

Lord lifted the lid of his tool box and took out a hammer. Then he reached into his pocket and pulled out the burner phone.

After removing the memory and SIM cards from the burner phone, he placed cards on the concrete floor, then whacked the cards a number of times until the cards broke into small pieces.

Then he used the hammer again to smash the burner phone. Sweeping up the various pieces of phone and cards into a dustpan, Lord then emptied them into several, small polyethylene bags. The bags would be deposited in separate trash cans.

When Lord returned to the kitchen, Madison pointed to the coffee pot."

"No thanks, I'm coffeed out."

"Okay then, I'll get dressed and we'll go to the hospital."

"You've read my mind."

As Lord waited for Madison, he thought about the incident with Colby, the phone call he made to the twenty-fifth precinct, the ANB, Delgado and the mess that now seemed to be swallowing him up. Maybe Madison had it right from the beginning.

Just cut and run to someplace else. Start over, but where, and how? Someone, or a lot of someones, would come after them. Payback is always important to these types, then he laughed as he thought about the words that crossed his mind, 'these types'. Wasn't he one of these types?

His train of thought was broken as Madison called out, "I'm ready."

They drove to one of the hospital's parking lots, and then walked to the entrance. Just shy of the door was a trash receptacle. Lord removed one of the polyethylene bags from his pocket and placed it in the can.

As they walked the corridor toward the elevator bank, Lord deposited another polyethylene bag in a trash can.

When they reached the nurses' desk on the second floor, Lord asked one of the nurses if they could visit Colby in room 211.

They were informed that the doctor left instructions that the patient wasn't allowed visitors today, and that they should check with the hospital tomorrow.

Lord asked for specifics, but the nurse only replied that she knew nothing more and was only following instructions.

They followed the same route back to the parking lot. Once they were in the car, Lord asked, "Do you want to go back home or someplace else?"

"Like where, South America?"

"I was thinking of someplace closer, like a diner where we can chill out a bit. I guess things aren't good with Colby and that pretty much sums up why we couldn't see him."

Madison shook her head in agreement. "Okay, let's chill out as you suggested. Know a good restaurant?"

"I know an okay one," and then Lord started the car and drove toward the exit.

Twenty-five minutes later they were seated in the Parkside Diner, staring at each other.

"Let's order something, Nicholas. We just can't sit here."

"I'm ready. Eggs or do you want something more interesting?"

"Scrambled eggs will be fine, Some home fries, dry toast, jelly and a chocolate milkshake."

When the waitress came over Nicholas ordered for both of them, including the chocolate milkshake.

As they waited, Madison said, "It's getting complicated. We're getting deeper into something I don't understand, but I can sense it's going to kill us."

"Those are strong words, Madison."

"I said what I felt. Have you forgotten about last night, about Colby and everything else that seems to be choking the oxygen out of us? We have money. My money, the money Dixx left me. It can take us somewhere. Why are we still here when everything seems to be falling apart?

I wanted to believe you, that you could get away from all of this, and we could start a new life...that we didn't have to leave here, that we could stay in place and just live, but we can't, can we, Nicholas?"

Lord was about to reply when the waitress approached with their order.

After the waitress left, Nicholas said, "I understand, I do, but I can assure you, they'll come after us. They could be the ABN gangbangers, Delgado's group, what's left of the Harlem Originals, or who knows what. Once we start running, we can never stop. We need to make a stand, and I think that stand should be where we are."

"That's not what I wanted to hear. Maybe we should just go our separate ways."

"Is that really what you want, Madison? Words, once said, are not easily retracted. If you want out and you've reached that decision after evaluating everything carefully, then that's the way it will be. I don't want that to happen, but I can understand where you're coming from and the trepidation you're feeling."

"I don't feel hungry any more, Nicholas. Can we leave, please?"

Silence prevailed during the twelve minute drive back to Lord's house.

Once they were inside, Madison went directly to the bedroom she was using. Minutes later she reappeared, suitcase in hand and a dejected look on her face.

"It's that bad, Madison?"

"Yes. This is not what I want, Nicholas, but as I've told you more than once, I'm scared, very scared. I can't live this life. I had other hopes and dreams, but it seems this is the only life you can offer me. I'm going back to my condo and then make some decisions. Good night Nicholas, or is it goodbye?"

33

CHAPTER

AROUND TEN A.M. THE NEXT MORNING, LORD SAT IN THE WAITING
room on the second floor of Stamford Hospital toying with his cell phone
and debating whether he should try Madison's number again. All of his previous calls went to voicemail, and none of them were returned.

Just as he was about to redial again, he heard his name called and looked
up. A physician, he hadn't seen before, was standing near the entrance to the
waiting room and motioned with his hand for Lord to move in his direction.

Once they were standing together, the physician introduced himself,
then said, "There's been a significant improvement since yesterday. The
fever has subsided, and Mr. Colby's body is reacting well to the medicine
we've administered. If you will assure me that your visit will be brief, I can
let you have five or so minutes."

"Yes, I'll make it quick."

Then please follow me, Mr. Lord."

Lord trailed the doctor by a step as they walked toward room 211.

Once inside the room, the physician again repeated his instructions about making the visit brief. Then he and the nurse left, leaving Lord alone with Colby.

"You look like shit, Colby."

"And I feel worse than that. Who was the fucker that did this?"

"I'm assuming someone from the ABN. If it makes you feel any better, I was the target, not you. I've got a few wheels in motion to even the score. Won't know how it turns out for a day or two.

Meantime, get your ass back into one piece. I don't have many friends left, and I consider you a friend, Colby. No one does what they did to a friend, and lives. The doc said I've got to keep this visit brief, so before he shows up and kicks me out of here, do you need anything? Can I bring you anything?"

"I'm okay, Nicholas. Just got to realize I'm fucked up and it's going to take time to piece me together."

Colby tried to laugh, but instead winced in pain.

The doctor knocked lightly on the doorframe.

Lord acknowledged with a headshake, then turned back toward Colby. "I'll come back tomorrow. If there's anything you want, tell one of the nurses to call me. You know my number. Now be a good little boy and do what the pretty nurses tell you to do."

Lord waved his hand as he turned and left the room.

‹ ✦✦✦✦✦ ›

As he drove home, Lord considered several of his options. None of them seemed to solve his dilemma.

Somewhere deep within the caverns of his mind, a voice resonated, *You're stuck between a rock and a hard place. Find the solution or you'll be crushed.*

Lord slammed on his brakes as he turned the steering wheel hard right. The Bentley skid sideways, miraculously missing the rear of the Honda Civic as it careened through the red light and raced across the intersection.

Lord watched as the car disappeared into the night, then placed the Bentley in reverse and moved back from the intersection. As he waited for the light to change, he thought, when it rains, it pours, and somehow he found the will to smile. Then he intoned just above a whisper, "It can only get worse."

After Lord closed the garage door, he walked through the laundry room and into his den. He went to the wet bar, poured some vodka into a glass then carried it back to the kitchen. After he placed several ice cubes in the glass, he went to the kitchen table and sat down.

He looked across the table and stared at the chair Madison usually occupied. After a number of moments, Lord lifted his glass and said. "To what could have been," then he took a long swallow and placed the glass down.

⁕⁕⁕⁕⁕⁕⁕

Earlier that morning, at approximately five twenty-five a.m., a twenty-four member SWAT team consisting of a ground team, snipers, tactical medics and K-9 handlers, approached the front and rear of the ABN clubhouse.

The ground team would breach the front entrance while a second team, a containment team, would seal off the rear, preventing anyone from escaping.

After an extended firefight, the SWAT team, with the help of additional police reinforcements, brought the situation under control.

The city medical personnel removed the dead and wounded from the scene. Other ABN members were arrested and transported to Rikers Island in New York's East River and processed.

The police discovered both the gray van and Chrysler sedan, with the rifle portals, parked behind the ABN clubhouse. Both vehicles were removed to a police lot for further examination.

Law enforcement personnel started departing the area as segments were cordoned off. After twenty minutes, only a small police presence remained in place.

⁕⁕⁕⁕⁕⁕⁕

Lord moved from the kitchen to the living room, the drink still in his hand. He sat down on the sofa and reached for the remote control, then watched as the fifty-two inch screen came to life.

As he depressed the volume button to lower the level, Lord focused on the words of the reporter.

"...and the successful raid this morning by New York's finest, resulted in the capture and the death of members of the notorious Almighty Black Nation criminal gang. This gang has been implicated in the sale and distribution of fentanyl, heroin, methamphetamine, and a host of other illicit drugs throughout Harlem. They have..." and then Lord pressed down hard on the off button.

As he finished his drink, Lord wondered if RaJean was one of those killed. Then he thought, no such luck.

He leaned his head back and closed his eyes. Then his mind formulated a picture of Madison. He wondered, could her feelings for him be turned off just like that? Wasn't he trying to disengage, trying to break away and hand it all over to Colby? It just didn't come together as quickly as he thought it would. So now what?

He'd check on Colby later this afternoon. Meantime, he will just bide his time until the right moment and the right decision would develop, hopefully simultaneously.

✦✦✦✦✦✦

Cleotha RaJean, along with a number of other ABN gang members were booked on a variety of charges. RaJean's third in command, Stefon Walker, and eleven other ABN members, were killed during the standoff.

During a search of the ABN clubhouse, the police discovered an underground chamber containing drugs, gold coins and bullion, an estimated one hundred and fifty thousand dollars in cash, and an assortment of weapons.

The lead Detective examining the underground chamber was the one Lord called with the burner phone.

As his team packed the drugs, paper money, gold coins and bullion in marked boxes, Ramsey and two other detectives looked through the assortment of weapons for a .308 Winchester rifle. They quickly found the weapon, and placed it in a sealed plastic cover and tagged it.

Two days later, ballistics experts identified the rifle as the one used in the killing of several Harlem Original gangbangers.

Lord walked up to the nurses desk and after a brief exchange, continued toward Colby's room.

Colby was sitting up, and smiling.

"Nice to see you're getting your old self back. Nice smile. Did you have a liaison with one of the night nurses?"

Colby laughed. "I wish. I'm not there yet."

"I don't know if you caught the latest on TV about the ABN raid. Seems RaJean and a number of his bangers survived and were booked on a variety of charges. During the search of the clubhouse, the jakes discovered an underground room loaded with money, drugs and weapons.

I'm assuming one of those weapons was used to smoke the HOs and probably the same shooter used the weapon to do you. Their ballistic people should be able to tie it all together."

"I've got some good news, Nicholas. They're going to release me tomorrow, but they want me back for the next week to check progress or lack thereof. Can I stay at your house?"

"Yes."

"I don't want to be a burden in any way. I owe you enough from that Mexican episode, where you saved my worthless ass. Besides, I don't want to burden Madison in any way."

"You won't be burdening her. She left and I'm assuming she went to her New York condo. So it's just you and me who will play house."

Colby laughed again, and Lord joined in.

It was five days later when the attending physician discharged Colby along with instructions to consult with his primary care doctor through his transition back.

Lord, driving Colby's car, returned to Manhattan. Lord parked the vehicle in the building's garage, then accompanied Colby to his apartment.

"I really appreciate all you've done for me, Nicholas. I won't forget it. Per our discussion, I'll contact the WHYOs and set up a meeting. I'm also tired of working with these black dudes. The white boys will be a welcomed change. Be callin' ya. Thanks again, and say hello to Madison for me."

Lord waited for the Uber pickup at the corner of the block where Colby lived.

When it arrived, Lord gave the driver Madison's address.

After the Uber parked, Lord leaned toward the driver and said, "I won't be long, ten or fifteen minutes at the most." Then Lord got out and walked toward the condo complex.

Stopping a few steps away from the front entrance, Lord read the posted sign at the right side of the door, 'CONDO FOR SALE'.

Lord entered the foyer and saw another sign next to the name board that read, 'Two bedroom condo, fourth floor, for sale. Telephone 'Morgan Hill, Hill Realty,' and then the phone number was indicated.

For the hell of it, Lord pressed the buzzer to Madison's condo although he knew that it wouldn't be answered. After several seconds, he returned to the Uber.

"Okay. Let's go to Connecticut,"

Lord leaned his head back, closed his eyes, and visualized the 'For Sale' sign again, but this time there were only three words on the sign, 'Goodbye, I'm gone.'

Lord jolted up and shouted, "No!"

The driver hit the brakes as he called out, "What's wrong?"

"Nothing, I'm okay. Just had a bad dream. I'm okay. Sorry. Keep driving. I'll try to stay awake. It was a long night."

The Uber driver shook his head, as he continued toward the Henry Hudson Parkway and Connecticut.

— 34 —

CHAPTER

FOUR DAYS AFTER COLBY RETURNED HOME, A MEETING WAS ARranged with the WHYOs street gang.

Colby, during one of their several telephone conversations informed Lord that he had made contact with Joko Rapolo and that Rapolo would attend the sit-down.

Lord stayed at Colby's home the night before the meeting and discussed in detail the upcoming sit-down with Colby and Rapolo. They agreed that Lord would start off the discussion, then Colby would take over the lead.

The next morning they drove in Colby's car to an address in the Bronx, New York.

Seated at a table were four men facing Colby, Lord and Rapolo.

After the introductions, Lord began.

"I don't want to waste your time or ours, so I'll make it short and to the point. Some of what I'm about to say you already know, but I'll say it again. We represent a major Mexican manufacturer of Smack, Blow and Murder 8 (Heroin, Cocaine and Fentanyl) along with a number of other drugs that may be of interest to you.

The channel we previously used, and you know who they are, or were, didn't measure up. We're now looking for another channel that can handle large quantities of what we have to sell, and has the muscle to ensure that our products will dominate the market. Colby here, speaks highly of your group and you, Mr. Craig, and…"

Lord continued speaking for several additional minutes, then turned it over to Colby who answered the questions from the gang boss, William, 'Ice Pick Willie,' Craig and his lieutenants.

After the meeting was concluded, the seven people talked individually and collectively as they drank whiskey, vodka and beer and listened to hip hop music blaring through several wall speakers.

Just shy of three hours later, Colby, Lord and Rapolo left and returned to Colby's house.

Sitting in Colby's modest living room, Rapolo remarked that he thought the meeting went okay. Colby nodded in agreement.

Lord smiled, and then said, "They've sized us up, individually and as a team. They have to make sure what happened to the HOs and the ABNs won't happen to them. If I was 'Ice Pick Willie' I'd like to know some facts regarding why the HOs were smoked and then how did the jakes (Police) decide to raid the ABN clubhouse. If I were Craig, I'd like some real answers before I'd climb in bed with just anyone."

Colby spoke up. "We aren't just anyone, Nicholas. We are a major supplier of quality drugs and the WHYOs know that. They're savvy to the shit that goes down in Harlem. There's always some gangbanging group that is trying to take over another banger's turf. Rumbles between gangs happen all the time."

Rapolo was about to speak when Lord held up his hand.

"Hold it a moment, Joko. You're not far off, Colby, but I still say, they're not going to bed with us until they feel comfortable with the arrangement, and I didn't get that feeling. Did you see the way Craig kept eying your arm? While he didn't ask about it, he's still damn curious."

Rapolo spoke up. "I think Mr. Lord has it more or less right. I didn't leave with the feeling that we crossed the finish line, but I think we're close. While we're the same skin color and that helps in the negotiation, I think they want to know that we're strong enough to handle whatever shit comes down the pike, and I don't think we got that across."

"In a way we did." Then Lord locked eyes with both men to assure himself that he had their attention. "The fact that we are able to bring drugs across the southern border and get them into New York, without a problem, shows we're strong enough. Let's see what happens in a day or two. If Colby doesn't hear from Craig, then he makes contact, and we ask for another sit-down. If Craig tells us to fuck off, we'll try the Aces or the Daybreak Boys.

I'll contact Delgado and bring him up to speed. Are you both all okay with what I've said?"

Both men nodded yes.

"Okay then. I'll be in touch after I speak with Delgado. I'll be waiting to hear from you, Colby, about the sit-down and anything else Craig might say that tells us which direction they're leaning. Now, if we're finished, I need to arrange an Uber to get me back to Connecticut."

✦✦✦✦✦✦

When Lord arrived home he dialed Delgado. After the twenty minute conversation ended, he decided to try Madison's number again.

When it went to voicemail, Lord left the message he had numerous times before. "Please call back. Whatever it is, we can work it out. I love you."

He didn't expect a return call, but nothing was lost by trying again.

Staring at the phone, Lord's thoughts moved from Madison to his conversation with Delgado and the need to bring Colby up to date.

When Colby answered, he updated Lord on the WHYOs, stating that nothing was received back from their meeting.

Lord shifted the conversation to Delgado. "He's not a happy camper. He was upset, to put it mildly. Better we discuss this together and not over the phone. Contact Rapolo and we'll meet at your house. Does that work?"

"It works, but that means you have to drive here again."

"Doesn't matter. All I have right now is time. Should be there in an hour, eleven at the latest."

After Lord hung up he just stared at the phone. He thought about how his last comment was on the mark. *Seems all I have right now is time, maybe too much of that.* Then Lord turned, grabbed a jacket that was casually tossed over the back of the sofa, and walked toward the door that would lead him to the garage.

———————— ·♦♦♦♦♦· ————————

As the three men sat together, the mood was somber.

Lord broke the silence. "There's no reason to keep beating ourselves up. We laid it out as simply as we could. They're big boys, playing big boy games. They damn well know that the HOs and ABN wouldn't go to bed with us unless they were okay with the arrangement, and that means the quality of what we sell, the price, and what they can make on the street."

Joko then said, "They're more interested in the why question. When the ABN went to war and took out the HOs, why would they fuck around with the HO's main supplier rather than just step in and run all of Harlem or the major part of it?"

"That's not exactly the way it went down, Joko. We and the ABN had an agreement of sorts, and we were close to getting them supplied with the first shipment. Before anything could be finalized, the jakes raided their clubhouse."

Joko stared at Colby for several moments, and then looked back at Lord.

"What Colby says is the way it was, Joko. Maybe not an iron clad agreement, but one in principle. After the jakes raided the place, the ABN infrastructure, and their leadership, plus a number of their gangbangers are now at Rikers Island, jailed on a variety of charges, from drugs, to firearm violation. They're in deep shit, and we're adrift with no sales channel."

Joko and Colby nodded their heads.

"So now what do we do?"

Colby answered Joko. "The way I see it, we have two options, maybe three. The first is to sit tight. The second is to call Craig back and ask for another talking session. The third is to find another sales channel like the Daybreak Boys or the Aces."

Lord was about to say something when Colby's cell rang. After looking at the screen, he said, "Craig."

"Hello."

"Yes, we were expecting your call. That'll work. What time?"

"Can we make it earlier, say in an hour?"

"Yes, he'll be there. He's been called a lot of names, but the one you just used is probably a first as far as I know." Colby chuckled and then said, "Later."

Lord leaned forward in his chair. "Okay you've sparked my curiosity. How did he refer to me?"

"He called you 'fine vines,' like in the clothing you wear. And indeed, Mr. Lord, if I do say so myself, you do wear some very elegant fine vines," and then Colby laughed with Lord and Rapolo joining in.

"I think we all needed a good laugh and that gangbanger provided us with one. We've got another sit-down in an hour, noon to be exact, so we should go over a few things regarding the direction we want this sit-down to go. I'll start off, and then either Nicholas or Joko can continue."

Lord liked the way Colby was taking charge. He would re-emphasize, during the sit-down, that Colby was the go to man. This would erase any doubt for Craig or for any other attending WHYO.

⋅⋅◆◆◆◆⋅⋅

This time the meeting was attended by a few more of the WHYO's leadership. Craig pointed to several of the new ones.

"That man holding up the wall is Pat 'the Cat' Clark. The one off to his right a bit, with the scarf around his neck, is 'Chee-Chee' Miller, and the other one standing next to him is Taro Moore. We have been thinking about what was discussed during our last meeting, and we've got a few questions."

"Fire away,' and then Colby said, "Forget how I phrased that. Just ask, and I'll answer."

Colby smiled, and then waited for the gangbanger's questions.

Craig eyed Colby's arm. "Seems your wing lost some of its feathers."

"Yep. it did. Some ABN gangbangers thought he could go directly to our source and cut us out. It didn't happen that way. I took a bullet in the arm and he's now at Rikers Island, hopefully a boy toy for a few of the sex starved inmates. At least one can hope," then Colby chuckled.

"Okay, got that. Who runs the show, you or Mr. 'Fancy Vines' over there?"

"You'll deal primarily with me. Mr. Lord, over there," and Colby enunciated the words 'over there,' "is our main connection with the Mexican supplier. There's no way anyone, no matter how much territory they control or how much product they move, will get in between Mr. Lord and the supplier. Relationships are respected south of the border, and Mr. Lord and the head honcho go back a long way. Remember, 'What the Lord giveth, the Lord taketh'. Got that?"

Craig moved his head in an up and down motion, then looked over at Lord and grinned.

After locking eyes with Craig, Lord said, "The word Colby used to describe the person in charge of our Mexican operation, 'honcho, head honcho,' comes from the Japanese word, 'han' which means squad, and from the word 'cho' which is defined as head or chief. I just thought you might like to know the etymology," then Lord smiled again.

"Oh, one more thing. The word, etymology, means the study of the origin of words. In addition to the fine vines I wear, I'm educated and savvy about a whole lot of shit."

Craig smiled back. "And why the fuck would I be interested in knowing any of that shit?"

"For two reasons. One, you can never tell when you'll be on a quiz program, and the other is to impress some female chicken you hope to take to bed."

Lord laughed and despite himself, Craig joined in. Soon the others were laughing as well.

"Ya know something Vines, I'm gettin' a warm feeling all over my body about you, Colby there, and Jocko over there,"

Rapolo spoke up. "It's Joko, Mr. Craig."

"Joko, Jacko or Jocko, what the fuck is the difference? Just answer to all of them."

Then Craig began laughing and soon the others were smiling and laughing.

"Okay, business time. If we join your party, it's an exclusive arrangement. You don't supply no one else. Agreed?"

Colby nodded yes.

"We want to start off small, see how it goes. If there's going to be a fuck up I don't want to get my ass burned big time, so we start small, okay?"

"How small is small?"

"Let's start off with say twenty thousand China White pills. What's your price, Mr. Colby?"

"Do you want to answer, Nicholas?"

"Give him your best price, Colby."

"For twenty thousand China White pills with one milligram of fentanyl each, it's going to run you one hundred thousand large. When you sell the pills on the street for between ten to twenty dollars per pill, that's one hundred to three hundred thousand profit. Not a bad way to start a business. Take your time. Think it over. Maybe you want to increase the quantity at such a good price," then Colby smiled.

"We'll do just that. We'll think about it. You'll be hearing from me, Colby. Appreciate you, Vines and Jacko coming here for this talk. And one more thing, Colby. Don't lose any more feathers on that wing."

"Thanks for the concern. I'll definitely keep that in mind and I look forward to hearing from you."

35

CHAPTER

JOKO STARTED OFF THE CONVERSATION AS THE THREE SAT IN COLBY'S living room.

"I think it went just dandy. We broke through, and it seems they're okay with us since they're talking quantity and price. That isn't something they'd do unless they plan to work with us. I'm thinking we should get a call in a few hours, not a few days."

Lord pointed to Joko. "You're on target. They will work with us."

Colby nodded in agreement.

Lord asked Colby, "Do you want to bring Delgado up to speed or wait until Craig confirms?"

"I think we better wait until he confirms. If we call Delgado now and the deal falls through, we look like shit with the Mexicans."

"How do you feel, Joko?"

"Likewise. Let's wait until we have confirmation from the WHYOs. But if it's longer than twenty-four hours with nothing happening, I think we should make contact with Delgado. Silence isn't necessarily golden in this business, especially with a supplier who wants to move product."

"Nice thinking, Joko. Are you okay with that, Colby?"

"Okay by me. We wait twenty-four hours and then one way or the other we contact Delgado. Are you going to make the call, Nicholas, or do you want me to?"

"You're going to make it. You are the number one and Joko is your number two. By the way, it was a nice move juicing up the price to one hundred thousand. A definite improvement over the price we sold the HOs."

Colby smiled, then said, "Before either of you go, let's have a drink," then he looked at his watch.

"It's three thirty-five, certainly time for a shot or two. What will you boys be drinking?"

"Vodka for me," and then Joko parroted Lord, and requested the same.

As the three were working on their second round of drinks, Colby's cell rang.

"Hello Mr. Craig. What a surprise," then Colby looked at Lord and Joko and smiled.

"Yes, that's exactly what was discussed and I'll be contacting the other party immediately after we hang up. I'll come back to you, at the latest, tomorrow at this time regarding when and where.

And as an added bonus we're going to have the merchandise imprinted with a blue W. Your customers will get to know about it and will ask for the product with the W… and we'll make sure, Mr. Craig, that they can get it easier than mothers can purchase baby formula," and then Colby laughed.

Lord and Joko smiled as they listened to the one-sided conversation.

Lord thought Colby handled that well enough. I would have phrased it differently, but I'm not the number one anymore. Should be okay and it makes it easier for me to leave.

"Well done Colby. You'll need to clue in Delgado. I'll make a call to him as well and inform him that you're running things in New York. Now if there's nothing else gentlemen, I think I'll head back to Connecticut. After you contact Delgado, call me and we'll talk."

As Lord drove along the Hutchinson River Parkway toward Connecticut, a number of thoughts flashed across his mind.

Thoughts of how lucrative this business had been. How, because of it, he lived a lifestyle few could imagine. Thoughts of whether it would be possible to completely cut the tie to Delgado, Colby and now the WHYOs? Thoughts about whether he was making the right decision, and thoughts about what he was going to do to maintain this style of living that he'd become so accustomed to?

No matter how Lord tried, he couldn't justify what he was contemplating. When he thought of Madison and how his entire life changed when she left, he wondered whether he was crazy for thinking about severing ties to the only life he knew. A life that rewarded him handsomely, and although it had its dangers, didn't he handle everything that came his way? He was savvy, smart, and cruel when he needed to be. Didn't he prove that more times than he cared to remember?

As Lord crossed over the boundary line separating New York from Connecticut, he turned up the volume and tried to concentrate on the song that was blaring from the Bang & Olufsen speakers.

Fifteen minutes later, Lord left the Merritt Parkway at Exit 35 and drove another twelve minutes until he reached his driveway. Just as he was about to turn in, he saw the Mercedes-Benz convertible.

After parking behind the car, Lord remained seated for several minutes before finally opening the driver's side door.

As he walked slowly toward his front door, it opened with Madison standing slightly to the rear of the doorframe.

"Is it Christmas?"

"Why? Do you deserve a present?"

"Absolutely. and the one I'm staring at, is the one present I want."

Madison flung her arms around Lord and kissed him. When they uncoupled, she took a hold of his hand and pulled him gently through the doorway. Once inside Madison pointed toward the living room.

After they were both seated, Lord said, "I tried to reach you a number of times. Each time I left a message, but you never returned my calls. I couldn't understand…" and then Lord stopped speaking.

"I needed to get away, far away. Away to someplace where I could think things out. I knew if I called you back before I was ready, I wouldn't be in the place I needed to be.

If I couldn't get to that place, there was nothing for either of us. I believe I have reached that place, Nicholas, and I've come back to see if we can rekindle what we once had. I need to ask you some questions, Nicholas, okay?"

Lord nodded.

"You said you were leaving the Mexicans and this life. Are you leaving?"

"Yes. I've told Colby as much a few hours ago. We've established a new sales channel with the WHYOs and they know Colby is the number one, and the man to go to. Colby will telephone Delgado and brief him on the WHYOs etc. I told him that I'd be calling Delgado as well when I got back to Connecticut."

"Do it Nicholas, Call him now. Do whatever you have to do and let's start our life together."

"I'll make the call to Delgado from the den."

Twenty-two minutes later, Lord walked back to the living room.

"How did it go?"

"Delgado wasn't a happy camper, but he's more or less okay with the arrangement. Colby called him about an hour before, and they went over the trial shipment and background of the WHYOs. I gave Delgado some additional background on Colby. He'd rather have me, but I think he's okay with Colby. What choice does he have?"

"I'm really happy, Nicholas…" then Madison stopped as Lord cell rang.

Lord motioned for Madison to stay, as he answered the call.

"Hello Colby. Yes I just finished with Delgado moments ago. Yes, he seems okay with everything the way you laid it out. I gave him some additional background on you and your crew, and he's looking forward to working with you. Just make sure you watch your back and keep cool. You'll do fine.

Yeah, we can always catch up over a beer. Take care," then Lord ended the call.

"I want to assure you, Madison, that I'll always take care of you, and the children we'll have. There may be times when we're looking over our shoulder. I'm not trying to frighten you. It's just something that goes with the territory I'm leaving."

"I'm okay with everything, or I think I will be. I trust you and love you, Nicholas, and I will do whatever I can to be the best wife possible."

"Let's get married, Madison. The sooner the better."

"I'm okay with that. Do you want to do a Las Vegas wedding?"

"Not a bad idea."

Madison smiled and then kissed him passionately.

"Let's have a drink, Nicholas, and toast our new life."

As Lord followed Madison toward the wet bar, he wondered what the future would really hold for them. Could he cut ties with his former life and start a new one with Madison, or would his past follow them wherever they went?

Yes, he thought, whatever will come at us, I'll handle it as I always have. And yes, Madison, we will have a good life together, guaranteed!

HARRIS L. KLIGMAN

BORN AND EDUCATED IN THE "CITY OF BROTHERLY LOVE," THE AUTHOR left Philadelphia, Pennsylvania in his early twenties. For over thirty-five years, he interacted with various military governments and business entities who dominated the spheres of influence throughout the Far East, Africa, and South America.

A linguist, a devotee to the Martial Arts (holder of a Black Belt in Hapkido earned while living in South Korea), a retired United States Army Intelligence Officer, and cross trained as an Infantry Officer, the author brings his varied experiences to these writings.

Made in the USA
Middletown, DE
25 April 2023

29076832R00136